Table of Contents

Chapter One –
Friday Night Lights

The town of Lincoln, Ohio lived by the metronome of Friday nights in the fall. Long before the first whistle blew, the whole town seemed to lean toward the stadium. Main Street emptied early. Storefronts dimmed. Families packed into trucks and minivans, decked in blue and gold. Even the old men at the barbershop closed up early, promising haircuts could wait but kickoff could not.

From the highway, the glow of the lights was visible for miles, rising like a beacon in the night sky. By the time the band began its warm-up notes, the bleachers were already alive, buzzing with chatter, cowbells, and the scent of popcorn drifting on the cool September air.

And at the center of it all was Aidan McAllister.

Seventeen years old. Senior year. Starting quarterback. His helmet bobbed in rhythm with each step as he jogged through the narrow tunnel and out onto the turf, the noise of the crowd hitting him like a wave. Signs with his number — **#4** — waved from nearly every section. Kids perched on the railings with painted faces, reaching for high-fives. Aidan slapped a few hands as he jogged by, the grin on his face more natural than forced. He had grown up here. These lights had always been his compass.

The stadium roared louder when Marcus Johnson, Aidan's best friend since grade school and the team's star wide receiver, appeared at his side. Marcus was taller, leaner, with a smile that could charm teachers into granting extensions. He slapped Aidan's shoulder pads. "Ready to put on a show?"

Aidan smirked. "Always."

They sprinted onto the field together, the rest of the Lions piling out of the tunnel behind them. The sound of the band's fight song clashed with the roar of the crowd until it became a single pulse — steady, alive, and electric.

Coach Dempsey, a stocky man with a shaved head and a whistle permanently looped around his neck, gathered the team at midfield. "All right, listen up," he barked, his voice cutting clean through the chaos. "First game of the season. You set the tone tonight. Defense, hit hard, hit smart. Offense—" His eyes locked on Aidan. "—run the field like you own it. Show them what Lincoln football means."

Aidan's chest swelled. This was what he lived for.

The coin toss came and went. The Lions took the ball first.

On the sideline, Karen and John McAllister sat shoulder to shoulder. Karen's hands gripped the thermos in her lap so tightly her knuckles turned white. She had been coming to games since Aidan was eight years old, and she still jumped at every hit. John, though no less invested, was calmer — outwardly, at least. He wore his old college letterman jacket, the sleeves faded, the stitching loose, but he sat tall, proud, watching his son like he was watching a dream play out.

The whistle shrieked. The game began.

The first play was a simple handoff, easing into rhythm. The line crashed forward, helmets clanging, and the crowd let out a collective groan when the back was stopped short. Second down.

Aidan jogged back to the huddle, calm, eyes scanning the defense. He knew this drill. He had studied the Franklin Falcons' defense on tape all week, breaking it down late into the night while Marcus snored on the couch beside him. He knew they bit hard on play-action.

"Fake right, slant left," he called in the huddle, his voice steady.

The team broke. He crouched under center, called the cadence, and felt the ball snap into his hands. He pivoted right, selling the fake. The defense lunged toward the runner, just as he knew they would. Aidan straightened, snapped his arm, and fired the ball across the middle. Marcus was there, hands sure as glue, cutting between two defenders.

The crowd erupted. First down.

From there, Aidan found the rhythm he loved most. Play after play, the field opened before him. Short completions to steady the pace. A draw play for surprise yardage. A deep out to Marcus that drew gasps as it spiraled fifty yards through the air, dropping perfectly into his stride.

By halftime, the Lions led 14–3, and the stadium buzzed with the unshakable confidence that their quarterback was untouchable.

On the sideline, cheerleaders waved pom-poms, the band blasted their medleys, and kids chanted, "FOUR! FOUR! FOUR!"

Aidan tugged off his helmet, sweat dripping down his temple. His chest heaved, but his grin stayed fixed. He glanced up at the stands, where his mom gave him a nervous smile and his dad pumped a fist in the air. For a second, the weight of the town's expectation pressed down. But then Marcus clapped his back.

"Light work," Marcus said with a laugh.

Aidan smirked. "Let's finish it."

The second half was even better. Aidan scrambled out of sacks like smoke, juking defenders who dove and missed. He threw two more touchdowns, both to Marcus, who seemed to glide past defenders as if they were stuck in mud. On one play, the pocket collapsed around him, three defenders converging, but Aidan ducked low, sprinted right, and dove headfirst over the pylon for a rushing touchdown that sent the crowd into chaos.

By the time the final whistle blew, the scoreboard read **Lincoln 28 – Franklin 10.**

The band struck up the fight song once more, and the students stormed the fence line, screaming, chanting, pressing against each other for a glimpse of their hero. Aidan raised his helmet high, the number 4 gleaming under the lights.

As he jogged off the field, Marcus alongside him, he looked up once more at the stands. Karen had tears streaming down her cheeks, though her smile was radiant. John clapped so hard his palms stung. For them, for this town, for himself — it was the perfect night.

The locker room buzzed with energy afterward. Boys shouted, laughed, slammed lockers, and retold plays as though they hadn't just happened minutes earlier. Coach Dempsey stood in the doorway, arms folded, a rare smile pulling at his lips.

"Good start," he said gruffly. "But one win means nothing. You've got Riverton next week, and they'll be meaner than Franklin. Don't get soft."

The players groaned, but Aidan just nodded. He loved it — the grind, the pressure, the knowledge that every week was another chance to prove himself.

That night, long after the crowds had gone home, after the lights dimmed and the field lay empty, Aidan sat on the hood of Marcus's beat-up truck with his helmet at his side. The air was cool, the sky clear, the stars faint against the memory of stadium lights.

Marcus cracked open a soda and handed it to him. "You know this is it, right? Our year."

Aidan nodded, staring out at the dark field. "Our year."

But in the back of his mind, he felt something else. Not doubt —
never doubt — but a sense that time was moving faster than he could
catch it. He pushed it aside, lifting the soda in a mock toast.

"To state," he said.

Marcus clinked his can against Aidan's. "To state."

The night swallowed their voices, carrying them across the empty
field, into the silence that always followed the roar.

Chapter Two – Lincoln's Pride

Saturday mornings in Lincoln had a rhythm of their own. By eight o'clock the streets were already lined with cars, not for shopping or errands, but for breakfast. The Cloverleaf Diner, a squat brick building with a faded sign and chrome-trimmed windows, was the unofficial gathering place for anyone who had spent Friday night under the stadium lights. Which was, in truth, just about everyone.

Inside, the smell of bacon and coffee hit like a warm embrace. The bell above the door jingled constantly as families shuffled in, voices rising in a steady hum. Booths filled with people wearing blue-and-gold jackets, kids in miniature jerseys, and grandparents with game programs still folded under their arms. The place buzzed not just with conversation but with pride.

Everywhere Aidan turned, he heard himself.

"Did you see that pass in the second quarter? Kid's got a cannon."

"He's the best quarterback we've ever had. Mark my words — he's going to college ball."

"Nah, pro. He's got that something you can't coach."

Sliding into a corner booth with Marcus, Aidan tried not to let the words stick too deeply. He wanted to act casual, just another teenager ordering pancakes, but the eyes on him made the back of his neck burn.

Marcus grinned, catching his discomfort. "Whole town's counting on you, you know."

"Counting on *us,*" Aidan corrected, grabbing the menu.

Marcus smirked. "Yeah, but you're the one they chant about. I don't hear the student section yelling 'Number Twelve' every time I catch a ball."

Aidan rolled his eyes, but he knew Marcus was right. The quarterback carried the glory and the blame. When the team won, he was a hero. When they lost, he'd wear it like a scar.

A waitress named Lila, who had worked at the diner since before either boy was born, appeared with her pad. "The usual?" she asked, smiling.

"Yes, ma'am," Aidan said. "Double stack with bacon."

"And for you, Marcus?"

"Pancakes, eggs, sausage. Everything you've got."

She chuckled, jotting it down. "Y'all played like men last night. Whole town's still talking about it."

"Thank you," Aidan said politely, though he ducked his head, wishing she wouldn't announce it so loud.

Lila leaned closer, lowering her voice. "My grandson was in the stands. Says you're his hero."

Aidan forced a smile. "Tell him to keep working hard. That's all it takes."

When she walked away, Marcus kicked him under the table. "Hero, huh?"

"Shut up," Aidan muttered, but his grin betrayed him.

The food came fast, plates steaming, syrup glistening in the morning light. For a while they ate in silence, the kind of easy silence that came from years of friendship. They had been playing together since Pop Warner, running routes in backyards until the streetlights came on. Marcus had always been the one who could make Aidan laugh when the weight of expectations pressed too hard.

"Think Coach will ease up this week?" Marcus asked around a mouthful of sausage.

Aidan snorted. "Not a chance. Riverton's coming."

Marcus groaned. "They've got monsters on the line this year. I saw their roster. Left tackle's six-four, two-forty."

"We'll be fine," Aidan said confidently, though in truth, he already felt the anticipation curling in his stomach. Riverton games were always brutal, and this year, with scouts in the stands, every play mattered.

As they ate, the diner grew louder. A group of old men at the counter argued about stats from the night before, thumping their coffee mugs on the counter for emphasis. A cluster of middle schoolers wearing replica Lions jerseys pointed toward Aidan's booth, whispering excitedly until one of them finally built up the courage to approach.

"Um… excuse me?" the boy stammered, clutching a football against his chest. "Could you… maybe sign this?"

Aidan blinked, then smiled. "Sure thing." He scrawled his name across the worn leather, adding a quick "Go Lions!" before handing it back. The boy beamed and ran back to his friends, who erupted in cheers.

Marcus leaned back, arms crossed. "See what I mean? Hero."

"More like circus act," Aidan said, but there was warmth in his tone.

When the check came, Lila waved them off. "On the house. Consider it thanks for giving this town something to believe in."

Outside, the morning sun was already hot, gleaming off parked cars. Aidan paused on the diner steps, looking back through the glass at the families still talking, still smiling, their lives briefly brighter because of a football game.

For the first time, he let himself feel it fully — the weight of expectation. It wasn't just about him or the team. It was about every kid who painted his number on their cheek, every parent who hoped Lincoln might finally bring home a state trophy, every neighbor who leaned on the Lions to carry the town through long winters.

It was exhilarating. It was terrifying.

Marcus nudged him. "Don't think too hard, QB. Just keep throwing touchdowns."

Aidan laughed, climbing into the passenger seat of Marcus's beat-up truck. "Yeah," he said, more to himself than Marcus. "Just keep throwing."

As they pulled away, the stadium lights from the night before still flickered in his mind. For a brief, shining moment, it felt like nothing could touch him.

Chapter Three –
The Hit

Home on Saturday afternoon smelled like cut grass and detergent. Karen had the washing machine going and every open window let in a line of September air that lifted the curtains like slow breathing. In the garage, John had the folding table pulled out and covered it with last night's game film—printed stills, scribbled notes, a yellow legal pad with arrows so emphatic they tore the page.

"Footwork on the third drive," he said, tapping a photo with a thick finger. "You were drifting right even though protection was solid. Step, plant, throw. Don't make Marcus work for a ball you can put on his chin."

Aidan leaned on the table, a bottle of water sweating cold on his palm. "We scored on that drive."

"Doesn't mean it was clean," John said, but there was a smile tucked in the corner of his mouth. He loved this—the ritual of it, the way a Saturday could be given over to football in a thousand tiny, satisfying corrections.

They watched a clip together on John's tablet. The screen showed the third-and-nine early in the second quarter when the pocket collapsed and Aidan spun out, buying an impossible second before firing to the tight end. The crowd's roar bled through the poor mic.

John paused it. "You felt that backside end?"

"Helmet breathed on my ear."

"Good. Feel it sooner and hit the checkdown if they're bailing on the deep route. Save your body."

"Noted," Aidan said, and meant it, at least for now. He loved the film room rhythm with his dad—rewind, pause, needle of criticism, thread of praise. It felt like they were co-authoring something, stitching a map he could run on Friday nights.

From the kitchen, Karen called, "You two done tearing each other apart?"

"Constructively," John called back.

She appeared in the doorway wiping her hands on a dish towel, hair pulled into a loose bun, a pen still tucked behind her ear. "I made sandwiches."

John pointed the pen at the still frame of Aidan mid-throw. "Two steps and the ball's out, not three."

"John," Karen said, a shade of a warning.

John raised both hands in surrender. "I'm done. For thirty minutes." He winked at Aidan. "Eat. Then we rip apart Riverton's tape."

Karen rolled her eyes and returned to the kitchen. Aidan watched her go, the way her shoulders were always a notch higher during football season, like she couldn't set them down. He peeled off his sweaty T-shirt and wiped his face, then joined her inside.

The kitchen table was a spread of ordinary Saturday: turkey sandwiches, chips, carrot sticks because Karen refused to let a meal pass without something that crunched. The back door stayed open and the neighborhood hummed—lawn mowers, a dog barking, somebody practicing trumpet three houses over.

Karen set a sandwich in front of him and another where John would sit. "You were great last night," she said. It came out gentle, not cheering, a quiet statement of fact. "That throw to Marcus in the corner…" She shook her head, half astonished even though she'd watched him throw a thousand passes. "You make it look easy."

Aidan took a bite, then another. His hunger always hit the day after. "It's easier when he's out there. He makes me look better than I am."

"Humility looks good on you," she said. Her voice softened. "You sleeping okay?"

"Yeah." He reached for his water. "I'm fine."

Karen watched the way he flexed his right hand before picking up the glass, a habit he'd developed when he started lifting heavier last spring. "You know," she said, easing into a different lane, "the college essay doesn't have to be done this second, but if you start jotting ideas—"

He groaned. "Mom."

"Two paragraphs," she bargained. "Not even a full page. You could write about leadership. Or—better—write about something small. The bus rides. Taping your wrists. The sound before the snap. Admissions folks read a lot of speeches about destiny. They remember the details."

He grinned despite himself. "You just gave me the essay in three sentences."

"I'm very good at my job," she said, playing it light. Then, softer: "I just don't want everything you are to shrink to one game. Even if you think it's the biggest game."

"Right now it is," he said, not unkindly. "But I'll write the two paragraphs. Promise."

John clomped in, smelling like cut grass and motor oil, a grin picking up where their film session had left off. He stole a carrot stick and popped it into his mouth. "Riverton's left tackle has bricks for feet," he said. "We can crash the edge."

"Chew first," Karen said.

He kissed her on the cheek and sat. For a couple minutes they ate without talking, the way families do when the day has drawn its own map. Aidan watched his parents in the quiet intervals—his dad's hands, scarred from years of work; his mom's pen knocked askew on the counter, proof that she never entirely stopped thinking about her students. He wondered, briefly, if they had ever felt as sure of anything as he felt about football. Then the thought slipped away and the sandwich reasserted itself.

After lunch, Karen shooed them out. "Go do your film. I'm grading until my eyes give out."

In the living room, John hooked the tablet up to the TV. Riverton's defense marched across the screen—thick-bodied and mean, a different kind of problem than last night's finesse. John froze the frame and drew routes with his finger as if the pixels would obey. "They'll roll cover two and dare you to throw the hole shot. Take it if it's there. Don't force it if the boundary corner's cheating. One bad look can become six the other way."

Aidan nodded and said the things quarterbacks say—"I'll look the safety off," "We'll win first down," "We'll run it if they live in nickel"—but a part of him was watching his dad more than the film. The way John sat forward, muscles coiled, as if he could will himself back into a game that ended twenty years ago. The way his voice always softened after a critique, like an apology folded into the lesson.

"Hey," Aidan said when a play ended. "You ever miss it? Playing?"

"Every day," John said without hesitation. "Not the hits. Not the cold tubs. The huddle." He glanced at his son. "You never forget the way ten other people look at you and wait for what you're going to do."

Aidan held his gaze. "What if I mess up?"

"You will," John said. "The trick is messing up in the right direction." He smiled, then clicked to the next clip. "Also: throw it away on third-and-forget-it if the lane's not there."

They spent an hour, then two. When the light shifted long across the carpet, John finally clicked the TV off and stretched until his back popped. "We've done enough damage for one day." He tossed Aidan a ball. "Five minutes in the backyard. Loosen your shoulder."

The yard was a rectangle of grass bordered by a slouched fence. Aidan lined up by the maple tree and John by the shed. They threw without talking at first, just the soft hiss of the ball and the thump of leather in hands. Ten yards. Fifteen. Twenty. Aidan's arm warmed and then sang. He threw a deep out that flattened into the exact window he'd pictured. John whistled. "That one plays on Sundays."

Aidan laughed and felt, as he always did mid-throw, the joy of something pure and exact. A couple more reps and his right side tugged, just a thread of tightness under the ribs. He rolled his shoulder and threw again, not wanting to give the sensation a name. It passed the way little things pass when you refuse them a seat.

From the kitchen window, Karen watched them. She loved this view—the two of them turned into a single line the ball traced again and again. She watched long enough to feel comforted and then, traitorously, long enough to feel the pinprick worry that always came when Aidan winced and pretended he hadn't.

At dusk, they dragged themselves inside. Karen had spaghetti on the stove and a loaf of bread cooling on the counter. They ate in the cozy way families do at the end of a day fully used. Talk meandered—Mr. Tanner's math test, the principal's new parking policy, a neighbor's yappy dog. Football threaded through it all, but didn't dominate. Aidan liked nights when the game could be just one piece of the house.

After dinner, he carried plates to the sink. Karen flicked on the radio to a station that always seemed to play songs from her college years, and for a moment the kitchen felt like time travel—steam, water, a mother humming, a father drying dishes with a towel worn thin. Aidan could almost imagine being ten again, small enough to be scooped into this warmth without thinking about Riverton's blitz packages.

When the dishes were done, he retreated to his room with a notebook. Two paragraphs, he'd promised. He sat at his desk under the too-bright lamp, flipped to a clean page, and stared. He tried a grand opening—*Football taught me leadership*—then scratched it out, hearing his mom's imagined groan. He tried again: *On the bus, the windows fog and the world turns into a tunnel of light. I tape my wrists the same way every time—left first, two turns, right second, three—and when the trainer pulls the tape tight, it feels like my bones remember what to do.* He paused, surprised by the way the small things unspooled once he started.

He wrote for ten minutes, then fifteen, until the page held a set of moments the size of a life: the weight of the helmet, the hush in a huddle, the way the field smelled after rain. He stopped before it got pretty, left it plain like his mother liked, and dated the top corner. When he stood, a pinch under his rib cage made him catch his breath. He pressed his palm there, counted to five, and let it go. He was fine. He would be fine. Tomorrow would be film and jogging and maybe catching a movie with Marcus if Coach didn't call an early practice.

Downstairs, the house settled. John watched a late ballgame with the sound low. Karen spread essays across the coffee table and drew soft, thoughtful lines with her red pen. Aidan drifted into the living room and dropped onto the couch between them, long legs taking up too much space the way they always had since last summer's growth spurt.

Karen leaned into him. "Two paragraphs?"

"Three," he said.

She smiled, proud but careful not to overpraise. "Let me see tomorrow."

"Maybe," he said, which was son for yes.

John ruffled his hair. "Riverton's going to blitz on second down. Sleep like they won't."

"I always do," Aidan said.

When the news came on, the local sports segment replayed last night's highlights. There he was on the TV—number 4 under lights, the ball leaving his hand, Marcus toe-tapping in the corner of the end zone. The camera caught his grin on the jog off the field, the way he glanced up into the stands like he was trying to memorize something beyond the scoreboard. He watched himself and felt oddly distant, like the person on the screen was a version of him whose edges had been smoothed by pixels.

He turned the volume down another notch. The living room dimmed to the glow of the screen and the small lamp by the couch. Karen's head tilted onto his shoulder; John's feet found the coffee table with the entitlement of long marriage. For a while they were only breath and warmth, a family of three inside a room that loved them back.

Before bed, Aidan stepped onto the back porch. The night had cooled, the yard quiet, the maple leaves whispering something even quieter. He looked up at a sky that was still remembering the lights and felt a clean thread of gratitude that surprised him. For the game. For this house. For the way his dad said "step, plant, throw" like a prayer. For the way his mom believed in writing down the small gears of a thing you love so that, if it ever slips from your hands, you'll still know how it worked.

He pressed his palm to the railing and made himself a promise he didn't speak aloud: to give all of it everything he had, every play, every day, until there was nothing left to give.

Inside, he clicked off his lamp and lay back, bones tired the good way. A tug ran under his ribs as if a knot had tied itself while he wasn't looking. He breathed through it the way Coach taught them to breathe on fourth and long. It eased. He turned onto his side and chased sleep like a defender he could outrun if he just kept his feet.

Down the hall, Karen paused in his doorway and watched him for a beat, the way mothers do when the day is finished and the boy is not a boy anymore but not yet anything else. She tucked the blanket a little closer to his shoulder, then withdrew, humming a fragment of a lullaby she hadn't sung in years.

The house went still. In the quiet, the season waited, patient as a coming storm.

Chapter Four –
Rivals (Expanded)

Riverton arrived with the confidence of a team that liked to hit first and harder. Their buses pulled up two hours before kickoff and a tide of red-and-black poured onto Lincoln's track: thick-bodied linemen in shirtsleeves despite the chill, coaches who barked even when nobody had spoken, a quarterback in mirrored visor who jogged without looking at anything except the far end zone. They carried themselves like they'd already stolen something and dared you to take it back.

By six o'clock, the bleachers were a single restless animal. The student section thumped drums; the band clipped through scales; cowbells clanged without rhythm. Painted bed sheets stretched across the railings—**Bury Riverton**; **Protect Our House**—and paper signs with a hand-drawn **4** bobbed in pockets of blue and gold. Down below, Aidan tied and retied the strap of his helmet like a ritual. He'd watched Riverton's tape all week. They were heavier than Franklin, slower laterally, but mean in a straight line. They sat in Cover 2 on early downs, disguising the safeties, and bailed into a robber look on third and long. They brought pressure off the boundary if you let them believe you were greedy.

"First series is ours," Coach Dempsey said in the pregame huddle, voice low, eyes hot. "Ten plays, set the tone, make them feel Lincoln. O-line, punch and climb. Receivers, get hands inside. Quarterback—

" His gaze caught and held Aidan's. "Paint the picture and drop the brush. They'll try to knock it out of your hand."

"Yes sir," Aidan said, and meant the yes like a promise.

Marcus bumped his shoulder pad, mouthguard jutting like a crooked smile. "You draw the picture; I'll sign it."

"Trips right, I'm thinking smash early," Aidan said. "Hole shot if the corner squats."

Marcus shrugged, as if the idea of threading a ball between a corner's ear and a safety's knee were a thing to consider and not lunacy. "Throw it before I'm open. I'll be there."

Across the track, John and Karen climbed toward their usual seats. John balanced two hot chocolates and a roped-off chunk of nerves. "They'll test him early," he said, mostly to himself. "They want to see if he'll take the bait."

Karen said nothing. She folded the blanket across her lap and watched her son on the sideline. He looked so much like himself in pads— loose shouldered, easy jawed—that she could almost forget the part of football that took as much as it gave.

The coin toss clinked in the air and fell for Lincoln. The crowd stood before the offense even stepped onto the field. Aidan jogged to the huddle, breath steady, voice steady, the world reduced to eleven faces, the white hash marks, and the little bits of moss that sometimes grew in the seams of the turf.

"Trips right, sixty-two Smash, on one," he said. "Eyes up; good tempo."

They broke. He walked to the line and let his eyes sweep. Both safeties ten yards deep, even feet. Boundary corner heavy on his heels, clouding the flat. Nickel murmuring to the backer. The left end rolled his shoulders like a bouncer. Aidan's hands went under center, the laces a ghost he still felt on his palm.

"Blue! Blue! Set—hut!"

The snap thunked. He turned, flashed a fake to the back, and snapped up to find the corner dropping too soon. There was the widow's-walk space between him and the safety, a place good quarterbacks could land a ball if they trusted the geometry more than their fear. Aidan hit the back of his drop and ripped it. The ball traced a wire over the corner's fingers and under the safety's chase, skimming for a heartbeat and then falling soft into Marcus's hands by the sideline. Twenty-two yards. First down. The stadium shed a layer of tension and exhaled as if this moment had been scripted.

"Keep them honest," Aidan said in the huddle, trying not to grin. "Same look, run it."

They ran inside zone; the line rolled their hips; three yards became five when the back kept his legs churning. Second and five. They went quick to the line. Riverton overadjusted, barking, late getting their nickel set. Aidan hard-counted and the left end jumped.

"Take the free five," the umpire sang, moving the ball.

Two plays later, on a second-and-eight just past midfield, Riverton sent pressure off the boundary. Aidan felt it before he saw it, his peripheral vision reading the twitch of a backer's toes. He didn't wait for the route to declare. He flipped his hips and popped a hot to the slot on a little jerk route. Sixteen yards, almost by accident. The crowd's noise rose in amazement, not quite a roar, more like the sound people make when a card trick resolves and they've been willing participants all along.

"Hey," Marcus said as they huddled again, breath fogging. "Don't get bored. They'll give you the grass."

"I'm never bored," Aidan said. "I'm impatient."

They pounded and nudged and made choices an inch at a time until the red zone shrank around them to geometry and guts. On second and goal from the nine, Coach sent in a play they loved and Riverton hadn't scouted: a switch release that looked like a rub but wasn't. Aidan sold the fade to the boundary and then watched the nickel trip over his own ankles when Marcus snapped back inside. The window was small. He threw it anyway. Six. The first touchdown floated down like a feather and the band hit the fight song so fast the trumpet section tripped over the first bar.

Karen put her hands over her mouth. John eased the hot chocolates onto the concrete under his feet and let out a breath he felt in his ribs. "He saw it early," he said to nobody in particular, but the older man two rows up nodded like he'd been waiting for the right person to recognize it.

Riverton did what good teams do: they answered. Their back was a square-hipped boy who ran like a freight car. When they got the ball, they punched. Their line down-blocked and folded Lincoln's front into itself. Six, eight, eleven. The safety missed in the alley and the back spun through. By the time the quarter ended, the score was tied and the game felt like a heavy door both teams had their shoulders against, one inch open, nobody willing to give.

"Win first down," Coach said between quarters, eyes bright as if the cold made him sharper. "We don't need a hero, we need the right read. One yard turns into four turns into a drive. Stay on the grass."

Aidan listened and nodded and tried not to look at the heat packs the trainers were stuffing into linemen's gloves. He thought about his father talking film at the kitchen table, about the line in his notebook he'd written the night before: *The world becomes small before the snap. That's good. Small means I can see all of it.* He breathed in through his nose, out through his mouth, counted cadence in his head, and went back to work.

Midway through the second quarter Riverton tested his patience. They disguised a robber and sucked him toward a seam that wasn't there, daring him to force one into the gut of the field. He looked it off, checked it down, got four. The crowd groaned because four didn't look like fireworks. Aidan raised a hand and gestured them closer with his palm. Stay with me. Second and six. They ran power and got two. Third and four. He tagged the Y on a stick route and hit him on the outside shoulder where only his man could touch it. Move the chains. The groan turned tentative, then grateful.

Two plays later, Riverton decided they didn't want grateful. They brought six. The first man sounded like a low drum when he collided with the back. The second found Aidan's chest. He took the hit and folded over the ball, feet in the air for a moment before gravity reeled him back in. When he stood, the world under his sternum vibrated for a beat, like a struck tuning fork. He rolled his shoulders and forced his vision to sharpen. He didn't look at the sideline. He called the next play.

From high in the bleachers, Karen's hands clenched and unclenched around the edge of the blanket. "He's okay," John said, because saying it sometimes made it so. "He's fine."

Riverton got a field goal before half. Lincoln got one back. Ten-ten, and the field had the look of a long negotiation.

In the locker room, steam and breath turned the air thick. Helmets sat upside down like waiting mouths. Coach Dempsey didn't waste time. "They want you to blink," he said. "They want one throw you shouldn't make, one ball on the ground, one block you whiff. Don't give it to them. This is patience with teeth." He jabbed the whiteboard with a pen. "We're going to drag 'em across the field. Mesh, mesh, mesh. Make those backers run laterally until they hate their own legs. Then we pop the wheel."

Marcus grinned, wolfish. "Amen."

They started the third quarter with two shallow crossers that made Riverton's linebackers chase ghosts. Aidan let the ball go on time and watched four become seven become ten as receivers knifed through traffic. He added a draw on second-and-long after a wide fade just to make the ends think. When Riverton finally got their cleats under

25

them, Coach gave the signal: the wheel tagged to the mesh. Aidan winked at the back in the huddle. "Don't get pretty. Run past him."

The snap came clean. The crosser and the sit route tangled the hook defenders. The nickel bumped and then drifted, eyes wrong. The back ghosted past him into the right flat and then up the sideline as if he'd been erased and redrawn. The safety was late because the look told him to be late. Aidan put the ball in the only spot that existed, a foot off the back's outside shoulder, and the stadium's scream climbed from hope to certainty in the arc of that ball. Touchdown.

Riverton answered with rage. Two plays into their next series, their guard trapped and their back knifed for nineteen. Aidan stood on the sideline bouncing on the balls of his feet, not because he was cold but because he hated standing still when a game tilted. He repeated the situation in his head—up seven, eight minutes left in the third, don't do more than you have to—and tried to fold the knowledge into his blood. Riverton bled the clock and kicked. 17–13.

The fourth quarter arrived like someone had grabbed the stadium lights and turned the dimmer up. Breath plumed in thicker clouds. Each hit sounded flatter, more final. Lincoln had the ball near midfield, second and nine, when the thing Riverton had been waiting on all night finally opened: the hitch-and-go they kept showing and not throwing. Aidan had sold it three times; the corner had sat three times. Now the corner couldn't help himself.

"Now," Marcus said in the huddle, barely moving his lips.

"Now," Aidan agreed, but he kept his voice level, because sometimes a defense could hear your heartbeat if you let it.

They aligned tight to the numbers. The corner crept. Aidan took the snap and stared left at the safety so long his own coaches might have worried. He snapped back. Marcus took three hard steps, slammed his foot, and gave the tiniest lean that said *hitch* to a man who wanted to hear it. The corner bit, knifing downhill. Marcus re-accelerated, shoulders stacked, space opening like a secret door. Aidan threw it from the top of his drop, before the space even fully existed, and trusted his friend to be there.

The ball fell over the corner's outstretched hand and under the safety's desperate angle. Marcus never even broke stride. Fifty-three yards later, he eased into the end zone and placed the ball on the painted L like a note.

The stadium turned feral. The band lost the melody and found a better one. Karen's fingers went from her mouth to her cheeks to John's wrist as if checking his pulse would confirm the reality of what she'd just seen. John just laughed quiet and shook his head. "They finally took it," he said. "They finally took it."

Riverton, to their credit, refused the role of foil. They hammered to midfield, benefited from a borderline late hit that had Coach Dempsey chewing a referee's ear so hard his toothpick snapped, and then found a tight end up the seam when Lincoln's safety looked into the backfield on a playaction he'd seen too many times. 24–20. The clock said four minutes. The stadium said forever.

On the bench, Aidan bent to retie his right cleat even though it didn't need tying. He stared at the laces, let the chatter of the sideline fade, and found the square of stillness he'd been taught to find on fourth and long. He stood, helmet in hand, and felt the weight of it settle the way a good sentence settles on a page. "One more drive," he said to Marcus, to the line, to himself. "That's all."

They started with something plain: quick outs, a stick, an inside zone that got three and a half instead of two because the guard stayed on his double a heartbeat longer. The clock ran. The crowd's noise braided into something like prayer. Second and six on the Riverton forty-two. Aidan looked to the sideline. Coach rolled his hand for tempo. Keep them on their heels.

He called a concept he loved against Cover 2: smash on the boundary with a backside dig that had a little more bite than it should. The presnap told him the corner was tired of being patient; his feet were too square. The safety's split was wrong by a yard. It was enough. Aidan hit the back of his drop, planted, and threw the hole shot like he had on the first play of the game, only this time he felt everything in it—the hours of film with his father, the sweat hung to dry in the garage, the sting in his ribs that visited and receded like a superstition. The ball kissed the sideline over the corner's helmet and out of the safety's hope. Marcus toe-tapped, dragged rubber into crumbs, and the official's hands flashed up.

Two plays later they were at the ten. Coach sent in a runner; Aidan shook his head and sent him back. Dempsey looked ready to explode, then saw Aidan's face and swallowed his words. He'd promised trust as long as the kid didn't lie to his body. Aidan's body was humming like a struck chord, but he could still hear the note.

"Zone read, keep if the end crashes," he said in the huddle, voice calm. "Hat on a hat. We're walking out of here with their pride."

The end crashed as if ordered. Aidan pulled the ball, tucked it under his elbow, and scraped behind his tackle. A linebacker filled like a thunderclap. Aidan lowered his shoulder to meet him not because it was smart but because sometimes it mattered to show a man you couldn't be moved. They collided two yards shy of the goal line and the world bucked. Aidan's feet skated; a hand found his hip and shoved; another met his back and lifted. He stretched the ball as he went down. The nose scraped white paint.

The ref's arms shot sideways, then up.

Touchdown.

This time, Aidan didn't pop to his feet. He lay there for a beat, the lights fracturing in his vision, a quick sting sewing itself under his ribs. He let the field cool against his cheek like a compress and listened to the roar crest and curl and come back for him. Then he rolled, accepted Marcus's hand, and stood. He nodded once at the sideline—*I'm good*—and trotted off, even if he had to tell his legs *we are trotting now* to make them believe it.

Karen's knees gave. She found the bench with the back of her calves and sat before she fell. John didn't sit. He stayed on his feet and clapped and clapped until his palms stung, and when he stopped, he wiped his eyes with the back of one wrist as if sweat had found him in the bleachers.

Lincoln's defense made the last stop not with a sack or an interception but with the small bravery of eleven men tackling exactly where they were supposed to. A third-and-three became a pile that didn't move. Fourth-and-one became a silent Riverton huddle full of eyes that had lost their argument. The clock expired like a door clicking shut.

In the handshake line, Riverton's coach leaned toward Aidan and said something only he could hear. Later, he would not remember the exact words, only the tone—grudging respect wrapped in a warning: *We'll see you again.* Aidan nodded and kept moving.

In the locker room, he let the roar wash over him with his helmet in his lap and his head tilted back against cool metal. Tape peeled from his wrists in pale curls. The ache under his sternum settled to a manageable hum. Marcus slid down beside him until their shoulders touched.

"Hole shot was rude," Marcus said, grinning.

"You liked it."

"I loved it."

Aidan sniffed a laugh and looked around. Helmets hung like moons. Steam rose in veils. Coach Dempsey stood in the doorway, arms folded, a rare softness in his jaw.

"Enjoy this one," the coach said when the noise dipped enough to hear him. "Because it wasn't luck. You made choices, you trusted each other, and you did the hard thing at the right speed. Monday we go back to work. Tonight, you earned the lights."

They whooped again because boys must, and when it was quiet enough to hear his own breath, Aidan found, for a moment, the exact feeling he chased every week. Not glory. Not even victory. The precise rightness of having done what the game required, no more, no less.

Later, when the stadium was empty and the parking lot thinned to a few stubborn cars, Aidan stepped out into the night air. Karen met him halfway and wrapped him in both arms, the way she had since he was small, as if she could keep him from dissolving into the dark. John clapped him once on the back and let his hand linger there.

"You saw it," John said, eyes proud and wet. "You saw the whole thing."

Aidan shrugged, embarrassed and pleased. "We saw it."

They walked to the truck together, cleats clacking like a metronome against the concrete. Somewhere behind them, the grounds crew killed a bank of lights. The field dimmed, but a glow stayed with him, the kind that lifts from a night you owned and follows you home like a secret you don't have to tell to keep.

Chapter Five – School Days

Monday morning came too soon. Aidan's alarm blared at six-thirty, and for a moment he lay still, staring at the ceiling fan spinning lazily above his head. His ribs ached dully, a reminder of the hit he'd taken Friday night. He pressed a hand there, winced slightly, then swung his legs over the side of the bed. No excuses. School and practice waited, and so did the expectations of an entire town.

By the time he pulled into the Lincoln High parking lot, the lot was already buzzing. Clusters of students leaned against cars, backpacks slung low, voices carrying. As soon as Aidan stepped out of his old Chevy, he felt it: eyes on him, whispers trailing.

"There's QB1."

"He's the reason we're going all the way."

"Did you see that scramble Friday? Dude's untouchable."

Aidan adjusted the strap of his bag and forced a casual smile, nodding at a couple of sophomores who looked starstruck just to be acknowledged.

Inside, the hallways pulsed with Monday energy — lockers slamming, sneakers squeaking, the smell of pencil shavings and cafeteria breakfast lingering in the air. The trophy case at the front entrance gleamed with polished footballs, plaques, and newspaper clippings from seasons past. Front and center, taped to the glass, was a photo of Aidan launching a pass under the Friday night lights. Beneath it, someone had scrawled in Sharpie: **STATE OR BUST.**

"Yo, QB1!" a sophomore shouted, slapping Aidan on the back. "Take us to state!"

"Working on it," Aidan said with an easy grin, though inside he felt a flicker of pressure. Every word of praise came with invisible weight.

He found Marcus at his locker, spinning the dial lazily. Marcus smirked. "Look who finally showed up. Thought you'd be too busy signing autographs at the diner."

"Shut up," Aidan muttered, grinning.

"Seriously, though," Marcus lowered his voice, "you good? You looked… off for a second after that hit."

"I'm fine," Aidan said automatically.

"You always say that."

"Because it's true." Aidan snapped his locker shut, forcing finality into the sound.

The first period was English, Mrs. Reynolds's class. She was the kind of teacher who loved books so much she spoke about them like old friends. Today she was dissecting *The Great Gatsby*, talking about ambition and the weight of dreams.

"Dreams can be heavy," she said, her gaze drifting over the class. "Sometimes they carry us, but sometimes they crush us."

Aidan felt her eyes linger on him just a second longer than on anyone else. He dropped his gaze to the open page, where Gatsby reached for the green light, and swallowed against the strange knot in his chest.

Between classes, more whispers.

"Did you hear? His ribs are broken."

"No way. He was running fine."

32

"My brother said his dad told Coach it's worse than that."

The rumor mill ran faster than any offense Aidan had ever faced. He clenched his jaw, kept walking.

By lunchtime, he was tired of the stares, tired of pretending not to notice when conversations hushed as he passed. He grabbed a tray, slid into the seat across from Marcus, and stabbed at his pizza.

"Relax," Marcus said. "They're just kids."

"They're our classmates," Aidan said. "They look at me like I'm not even in school anymore. Like I'm—" He stopped. Like I'm already something else. Like I'm already halfway gone.

"Like you're famous," Marcus offered. "Which you kinda are."

Aidan forced a laugh, but it sounded hollow.

Halfway through lunch, Emily Hart walked by. She was quiet, reserved, the kind of girl who sat near the window in class and always had a notebook open. She wasn't part of the football crowd, but she offered Aidan a small smile as she passed, one that felt different — not hero worship, not expectation. Just… human. Aidan found himself smiling back.

The afternoon dragged. In math, Mr. Tanner actually smiled when Aidan answered a question right, as if being QB1 made him immune to algebra's traps. In history, Coach Dempsey subbed in, rolling the TV cart to show a grainy documentary on World War II but occasionally muttering about Riverton's defensive schemes under his breath. The team laughed, but Aidan listened, filing away every note.

After the final bell, the halls emptied. Aidan lingered, collecting his books slowly. He felt both larger and smaller than he'd ever felt before — too big for the classrooms, too small for the burden everyone seemed to place on his shoulders.

When he stepped outside, the cool air hit him, clearing his head. Marcus jogged up beside him. "Practice?"

"Yeah," Aidan said. "Always."

As they walked toward the locker room, Aidan glanced back at the school, its windows reflecting the fading afternoon light. For a second, he wondered what it would feel like to just be another student, invisible, free. Then he pushed the thought aside. He wasn't invisible. He was Aidan McAllister, quarterback, number 4. And like it or not, Lincoln needed him.

Chapter Six –
The Hit

Friday night returned with all its rituals — the hum of lights warming, the brass of the band tuning, the buzz of students spilling into the bleachers with faces painted blue and gold. For Aidan, it was just another game night, though the dull throb in his ribs lingered like an echo he refused to name.

The opponent was Franklin High, a team known for their speed and for one linebacker in particular — Dylan Carter, a senior who hit like a freight train. Coaches had warned about him all week. In the locker room, Coach Dempsey reminded them again.

"Eyes up on fifty-two," Dempsey said, jabbing a finger at the whiteboard where Carter's number was circled. "He'll be gunning for the ball. Protect the quarterback. Protect the play."

The team roared agreement. Aidan buckled his chinstrap tighter, jaw set. Protect the play. That was all that mattered.

The first quarter went well. Aidan threw sharp, quick passes, spreading the ball to Marcus and the slot receivers, keeping Franklin's defense guessing. The crowd roared with every completion, the rhythm of the game swelling with each snap.

But by the second quarter, Franklin adjusted. They pressed the receivers, collapsed the pocket, and hit hard every chance they got. By the third drive, Aidan was picking himself off the turf more often than he wanted to admit.

On second-and-long, with the score tied 7–7, the call came in for a rollout pass. Aidan jogged to the huddle, hiding the ache in his ribs.

"All right," he said, voice steady. "Trips left, boot right, ninety-two flood. Marcus, watch the corner. It's there if we sell it."

They broke. Aidan crouched under center, scanning the defense. The safeties cheated up. The linebackers shifted. He could see it — the corner bite was coming.

The snap hit his hands. He pivoted right, selling the fake handoff, tucking the ball into his gut before pulling it free. He sprinted toward the sideline, eyes scanning, Marcus cutting hard across the field. The crowd rose with the play, sensing the moment.

Then it happened.

From his blindside, Dylan Carter blitzed. Aidan never saw him. The hit landed under his ribs with brutal precision, a helmet and shoulder slamming into bone and muscle with the force of a car crash.

The air exploded from his lungs. His vision jolted white. The ball flew loose, bouncing wildly before a lineman pounced on it.

The stadium gasped as one.

Aidan crumpled on the turf, clutching his side, the pain radiating sharp and hot. The roar of the game faded, replaced by ringing in his ears.

Marcus was the first to reach him. "Aidan! Talk to me, man!" He dropped to his knees, hands shaking as he touched Aidan's shoulder.

Trainers sprinted across the field, whistles shrieking. Coach Dempsey followed, his face pale under the lights. The stadium went silent, an entire town holding its breath.

Karen clutched John's arm in the stands, her knuckles white. "Oh my God," she whispered. "John—"

"He's tough," John said hoarsely, though his throat tightened. "He'll get up."

But Aidan didn't get up. Not this time.

Trainers knelt beside him, voices low. "Where's the pain, son?"

"My ribs," he gasped, his voice thin. "Feels… wrong."

They stabilized him, sliding a board under his back. The crowd watched, unmoving, as he was strapped in, his helmet still on, his eyes glassy under the visor.

As they lifted him, Aidan forced his arm up. His fist clenched weakly, raised just enough to signal to the crowd: *I'm okay. Keep cheering.*

The roar that followed was half relief, half fear. Applause and sobs mingled, the band striking up a shaky fight song to cover the tension.

Marcus walked alongside the stretcher until a trainer stopped him. His helmet dangled from his hand, his eyes wet.

In the stands, Karen was already crying. John held her close, his jaw locked, his gaze never leaving his son.

The ambulance lights flickered against the stadium walls as the doors closed. Inside, Aidan stared at the ceiling, his breath shallow, every bump in the road rattling through his ribs. He thought of the play, the throw that never left his hand, the win slipping away.

And in the hollow quiet of the ride, a thought he had pushed away all season pressed in with sudden, undeniable force: *Something's wrong. More than football wrong.*

Chapter Seven – The Hospital

The hospital smelled of antiseptic and lemon polish, a sharp scent that clung to Aidan's throat. The fluorescent lights buzzed faintly overhead, too bright, washing every shadow from the hallway until it looked more like a laboratory than a place of healing.

They wheeled him through double doors, trainers jogging alongside until a nurse guided them out with a firm wave. "Family only."

Karen gripped his hand the entire time, her fingers trembling despite her effort to appear calm. John walked on the other side, his construction-rough hands clenched into fists that couldn't fix this problem no matter how badly he wanted to.

Aidan lay still on the gurney, ribs throbbing with each breath. The ceiling tiles slipped by in endless squares. His helmet was gone now, and without it he felt exposed, like the boy he still was beneath all the gear.

They parked him in a curtained bay. A nurse clipped sensors to his chest, a monitor beeped into rhythm, and a tech wheeled in a portable X-ray. "Just a precaution," she said, her tone brisk, professional.

The films came quick. So did the whispers. He caught fragments through the curtain — "shadow on the rib margin… unusual density… we'll need further imaging."

John stiffened. "What does that mean?"

No one answered right away.

Then Dr. Patel arrived. Mid-forties, kind eyes behind wire-rim glasses, his face carried the weight of someone used to delivering news families didn't want to hear. He pulled a chair close, sat at Aidan's bedside, and spoke softly.

"The good news," he began, "is that the hit didn't cause major fractures. Your ribs are bruised, but they'll heal. What concerns us… is what we found in the scans."

Karen's hand tightened around Aidan's. "What do you mean?"

Patel folded his hands. "There's a mass near your ribcage. It's not from the injury. It's been there for some time. We need to run more tests — an MRI, a biopsy — to know exactly what it is."

The word mass echoed in Aidan's head like a whistle in an empty stadium.

"A tumor?" John asked flatly.

Patel nodded slowly. "That's a possibility."

Silence settled heavy in the room. Karen's eyes welled instantly, tears slipping free. John shook his head, jaw tight. "He's seventeen. He runs three miles every morning. He's the healthiest kid you'll meet."

Patel's voice was calm, steady. "Sometimes these things happen without symptoms until we stumble upon them. The impact from the game likely made it visible sooner than it otherwise would have been."

Aidan lay frozen, staring at the monitor above him, the green line rising and falling, indifferent to the storm below. A tumor. The word felt foreign, impossible. He was an athlete. Strong. Invincible under the lights. Not this.

Patel leaned closer. "We'll need to admit you tonight for further testing. I'll do everything I can to get answers quickly."

Karen broke down, covering her face with both hands. John sat beside her, pulling her close, though his own eyes shimmered with unshed tears.

Aidan turned his head away, blinking up at the ceiling. He hated the pity, hated the silence. "So... what does that mean for football?" His voice was thin, but the question felt like the only one he could control.

Patel hesitated. "Right now, your health is the priority. We need to determine exactly what this is before—"

"So I can't play," Aidan said, finishing the thought.

No one answered. The monitor beeped steadily, a metronome to the unraveling of his world.

Chapter Eight –
Breaking the News

They kept him for hours anyway. More blood, another round of X-rays, an ultrasound that pressed cold against his side and made him flinch. Nurses came and went with soft-soled steps and the kind of voices people learn when they've seen hard nights. By ten o'clock, Dr. Patel returned with a clipboard and an apology in his eyes.

"We're booking an MRI first thing in the morning," he said. "I wanted to admit you, Aidan, but there aren't beds. And—" he glanced at Karen "—you'll probably all rest better at home. No food after midnight. Be back here by six."

He handed over a folder thick with papers: instructions, consent forms, a stapled FAQ with words that felt like they belonged to other people's lives. Karen held the packet the way someone holds a newborn, carefully and close. John took the discharge form and signed where he was told, his pen strokes too hard.

When they wheeled Aidan to the exit, he noticed the hospital's night sounds—elevators pinging, carts rattling, the low murmur of a TV somewhere behind a curtain. The automatic doors sighed open and the September air pooled against his face, warmer than the corridors, full of distant crickets and a faint sweetness from cut grass. He felt suddenly, absurdly, like he should be carrying his helmet.

The ride home started with the quiet thump of tires over the painted crosswalk, then nothing but the engine and Karen's muffled breaths.

John kept both hands at ten and two. The dashboard clock said 10:22. The radio was off, but Aidan could still hear a ghost of a fight song in his head, like his brain refused to admit the lights were out.

He sat in the back because moving hurt less when he could stretch across the seat. The town slid by—closed storefronts, the dark blank slate of the barber's mirror, a banner on Main Street that hadn't been taken down since last season: **LINCOLN LIONS: ALL HEART.** Past the diner, where the neon sign hummed to no one, and up the hill where the stadium crouched like a sleeping thing. The lights were off, the grandstand a black shape against the sky, but Aidan could still see it lit in his mind: the field green as an answer, the white lines sure.

Karen spoke first. "We don't have to tell anyone tonight."

"We should tell Coach," John said, voice low. "At least that he's out tomorrow."

"I'm not out," Aidan said, too quickly. Pain flared under his ribs, sharp enough to steal his breath. He swallowed and tried again, softer. "We don't even know what it is."

Karen turned in her seat, her silhouette a question mark in the dashboard glow. "We know enough to be careful."

The car hummed over the bridge. Water slid black beneath them. Aidan stared out at the faint lights scattered along the far bank and thought of his name shouted across a field, of the ball's perfect spin leaving his hand. He typed without looking down, his thumbs moving on muscle memory.

To: Marcus

Still alive. Ribs mad. Got weird scan. MRI in the morning. Don't say anything yet.

The dots appeared, disappeared, then stuck.

Marcus: *You scared the hell out of us. I'm coming over.*

Aidan: *No. Not tonight. 6 a.m. hospital. Coach will kill you if you're late to film.*

Marcus: *Screw Coach. You good?*

Aidan stared at the screen, at the blank white space where truth and comfort fought. He typed the thing he'd been telling everyone since Pop Warner, the first language he learned.

Aidan: *I'm fine.*

Three dots. A long pause.

Marcus: *You don't have to be.*

Aidan put the phone face down on his knee. His throat burned. He blinked until the stadium on the hill blurred and sharpened and blurred again.

At home, Karen went straight to the kitchen, where she poured water, spilled a little, wiped the counter with deliberate care. John carried the folder to the table and flipped to the page that said WHAT IS SARCOMA? in bold, then closed it because the words arranged themselves into a shape he refused to recognize. Aidan eased down onto the couch, elbows on knees, careful with the way he breathed.

"We'll call Coach in the morning," Karen said. "We'll… we'll figure out who else to tell after the MRI."

"I'll call him now," John said. "I don't want him hearing anything from anyone else."

He stepped onto the back porch to make the call. Through the screen door, Aidan heard the low murmur of Dempsey's voice, the yeses and okays, the coach-tone that tried to put order to anything if you just made a plan and executed. When John came back in, his face looked older.

"He'll meet us at the hospital," John said. "He said—" he stopped, searching for the right translation "—he said whatever happens, he's in our corner."

Karen nodded, eyes on the table. She smoothed the edge of the consent form with her thumb until the corner bent, then straightened again. "I'm going to put together a bag. Toothbrush, sweats. If they keep you after."

Aidan watched his mom move through the house he'd always known—past the shelf with his third-grade clay bowl, past the framed team photo where he was all knees and elbows, the jersey comically big. He followed her with his eyes until she turned the corner, then leaned back and pulled the phone close again.

He typed *sarcoma* into a search bar and regretted it immediately. The results were all words like *aggressive* and *rare* and *prognosis*. He scrolled anyway, as if there were a secret page that would say **FALSE ALARM: YOU'RE SEVENTEEN AND INVINCIBLE.** There wasn't. He clicked out, then back, then closed the phone and pressed it flat on the cushion beside him like he could smother the future.

His notifications lit—group chat pings, a teammate's meme about the hit, a photo someone had posted from the stands with #QB1 and a flame emoji. He should post something simple, he thought. *I'm good. Love you, Lincoln.* He opened the app, drafted the words, and stared at them until they looked like camouflage. He deleted the post and set the phone face down again.

The house settled into the kind of hush that made every appliance sound like it had a heartbeat. Karen came back with a duffel and set it by the door. She crossed the room and sat beside Aidan, close enough that their shoulders touched. For a minute she didn't say anything. She just breathed with him, counting quietly, in through the nose, out through the mouth, the way she'd taught him as a kid when nightmares came.

"Am I going to die?" he asked, not looking at her.

Her breath hitched, but her voice stayed steady. "We don't know anything yet. And I refuse to have that conversation in our living room because of a scan we don't understand."

He nodded, a short, sharp movement. "Okay."

She rested her head lightly against his shoulder. "You can be mad."

"I don't know what I am." He swallowed. "I keep thinking about… next Friday. About the first drive. That's stupid."

"It's not stupid," she said. "It's yours."

Footsteps creaked on the porch. John came back in and leaned on the doorway like he'd arrived at a line and wasn't sure which side to stand on. "You should try to sleep," he said. "Morning's going to come too fast."

Aidan stood carefully. The room tilted, then righted. At the base of the stairs he stopped and turned back. "If… if it's what he thinks." He didn't finish the sentence. He didn't have to. "I can't—" he gestured toward the hallway wall where old team photos marched in a cheerful parade "—I can't just stop, Mom. Not like that. Not before—" He looked at his dad. "Not before we see what this team can do."

Karen's eyes closed for a second, the longest blink in the world. When she opened them, the softness had edges. "We'll talk after the MRI," she said. "We'll talk with the doctor. With Coach. Not tonight."

Aidan nodded because it was the only word that fit.

Upstairs, his room was both exactly the same and somehow strange, like a movie set of his life. Practice jersey draped over the chair. Cleats by the door. A play sheet tucked under a book on the nightstand. He peeled off his T-shirt and caught his reflection: bruised along the ribs, a faint yellow shadow already pooling, the sharp angles of a boy who had grown faster than the world around him.

He lay down and found a position that hurt least, one hand over the tender place like he could hold the ache still. The ceiling fan sliced the dark into slower pieces. He tried to pray but could only manage a list: Mom, Dad, Coach, Marcus, the line, the safety who always bit on the post, the field under lights, the smell of cut grass, the feeling right before the snap when the world got small enough to understand. He whispered, "Please," without a noun to anchor it to.

Through the wall, his parents' voices braided into a quiet argument. Karen's cadence: careful, punctuated, as if she were grading reality. John's: rougher, a low saw that hit knots and kept going.

"We can't let him go back out there," Karen said.

"We don't know anything yet," John answered.

"You heard the doctor."

"I heard a lot of maybes."

"A helmet to the ribs and—John, what if—" Her voice thinned. She stopped, breathed, tried again. "What if playing makes it worse?"

Down the hall, Aidan squeezed his eyes shut until stars flared. He didn't want to be the subject of sentences that started with *what if*. He wanted film to watch, plays to script, fixes he could practice in the backyard until they lived in his bones.

The floorboard outside his room sighed. The door opened just enough for Karen to stick her head in, the hall light a halo behind her. "Do you need anything?" she asked, already halfway in.

"I'm okay."

She crossed the carpet and sat on the edge of his bed like she had when fever measured his nights by thermometers. She smoothed his hair and didn't comment on the way he'd let it grow too long. "When you were little," she said softly, "you'd fall asleep with a football under your chin. I used to move it because I was afraid you'd bruise your nose." She laughed once, a small sound. "You'd wake up and find it in the morning and look at me like I'd betrayed you."

Aidan smiled in the dark. "I remember."

She kissed his temple and stood. "Set your alarm for five. If you can't sleep, just rest." At the door she paused. "I love you."

"Love you, too," he said, and listened to the hallway swallow her steps.

He tried. He closed his eyes and counted his breaths and went downstairs in his mind and picked up the folder and willed the words to rearrange. He failed. He rolled onto his side and the ache sharpened, then dulled, the way a distant train gets louder and then is gone.

At 1:13 a.m., the phone buzzed. *You up?* Marcus.

Aidan: *Yeah.*

Marcus: *I told my mom I'm sleeping at Jake's. I'm outside your window.*

Aidan pushed himself upright, hissed, shuffled to the glass, and peeled the curtain back. There was Marcus, a shadow on the lawn, arms crossed, hoodie up. Aidan cracked the window. "You're an idiot."

"Top ten." Marcus's voice floated up. "Come down?"

Aidan thought of his mother's face when she found the empty bed; thought of the MRI at six; thought of being seventeen and of the only friend who never made him feel like a statue on a pedestal. "Give me two."

They sat on the back steps, sweatshirts over bare feet, the duffel by the door like a quiet chaperone. The yard smelled like leaves thinking about turning. Somewhere a dog objected to a raccoon. They didn't say anything for a while.

"Scared?" Marcus asked eventually.

"Yeah."

"Me too." Marcus nudged him with his knee. "You don't have to be anything for me. Not QB1. Not brave."

"I don't know how to be anything else."

"You do," Marcus said. "You're the guy who makes jokes when Coach pretends he doesn't laugh. You bring extra tape because you know I always forget. You find my hands when I think I've lost them."

Aidan stared at the dark rectangle of the yard. "If it's bad—"

"If it's bad, we deal," Marcus said, too quickly, like a coach ending film on a mistake. He softened. "If it's bad, we don't let you be alone in it."

Aidan breathed. The word *alone* loosened something he didn't know was tied. "I can't stop playing yet."

"I know," Marcus said. "I knew that before you did." He stood, stretched. "Text me when you head out. I'll meet you there."

"You don't have to."

"I do," Marcus said, and grinned in the dark, and slipped away like a wideout into a seam.

Inside, the house had shifted to that deep, middle-of-the-night silence that felt almost physical. Aidan brushed his teeth slowly, careful not to jostle the tender spot. In the mirror, his face looked both older and smaller—eyes rimmed with a tired he couldn't explain, jaw set like he was bracing for a blitz. He set two alarms. He lay down and watched the red digits assemble minutes and carry them away.

At 4:57, he gave up on pretending and got dressed. Sweatpants. Hoodie. The old slides he wore to weight room sessions. He packed the play sheet out of reflex, then took it out of the bag, then put it back in, because who knew how hard habit was wired.

Downstairs, John was already at the table with coffee and the look of a man who had been up all night but would deny it. Karen moved quietly, her hair braided back, her face bare of makeup. The three of them stood for a moment around the duffel like it required a blessing.

"You ready?" John asked.

"No," Aidan said. "But yeah."

Karen touched his cheek. "We're with you."

He nodded. He picked up the bag. They stepped into the predawn. The air held that particular cold that made everything sharper, even the faint outline of the stadium against the paling sky. As they got into the car, Aidan looked up the hill and made himself a promise he would not speak: *Don't take the game from me yet. Let me finish what I started.*

On the way to the hospital, the radio stayed off. At a stoplight, his phone buzzed.

Marcus: *At the entrance. Coach is here. We got you.*

Aidan tucked the phone into his pocket and watched the light change. The street ahead unfurled—one block, then another, then the turn. He could not see beyond that, not really. But the car moved anyway, and he moved with it, and the morning opened.

Chapter Nine – The Tests

The hospital at dawn was a different creature than it had been the night before. The lobby was quiet, the vending machines humming like sentries. Aidan walked between his parents, the duffel slung over one shoulder, trying not to notice the stares of the early patients who still recognized him even here. He kept his hood up, head down.

"McAllister?" a nurse called from the check-in desk.

They followed her through winding halls that smelled faintly of disinfectant and coffee. The MRI suite was tucked deep inside the building, past signs pointing to cardiology and oncology. Aidan caught the last one and flinched. Oncology. He wasn't ready for that word.

The room was cold, the machine a massive white tunnel that looked more like something from science fiction than medicine. The tech explained the process in a calm, practiced voice. "You'll lie flat, stay very still. It's loud, so we'll give you headphones. About forty-five minutes. Just try to relax."

"Forty-five minutes?" Aidan asked. "What if I sneeze?"

"You won't," the tech said kindly, as if willing it to be true.

They slid him in. The ceiling disappeared, replaced by the narrowing tunnel. The headphones crackled with faint music, but mostly it was the machine itself: clunks and whirs, a mechanical heartbeat. Aidan closed his eyes. He tried to picture the field, the feel of turf under his cleats, Marcus's hands raised downfield, the ball spinning from his grip. But the sounds drilled through the memory, replacing the crowd's roar with machinery.

His ribs ached under the straps. His mind churned: *What if it spreads? What if I never play again? What if they're already planning my funeral in whispers?*

He clenched his fists, then forced them open. He counted. One, two, three—like play clock counts in his head. When forty-five minutes finally ended, the tray slid out and the world widened again.

Karen was there instantly, stroking his hair. "You did great," she whispered. John nodded, but his eyes darted toward the tech, looking for answers in a face trained not to give them.

They were sent upstairs to wait. The waiting room was painted in pastel blues, meant to be calming, but the chairs were too stiff, the magazines months old. A toddler played with blocks on the floor while her exhausted mother scrolled her phone. Aidan sat hunched, hoodie pulled low, while Karen filled out more paperwork and John paced near the coffee machine.

When Dr. Patel finally appeared, he carried a folder under one arm, his expression careful. He invited them into a small consultation room with a round table and no windows. Aidan hated the room instantly.

Patel laid out the films, black and white scans with ghostly ribs framing a dark shape. He pointed with a capped pen. "This is the mass we saw. The MRI confirms it's solid, not fluid. Its features are consistent with what we call sarcoma."

The word dropped heavy. Karen pressed her hands together, knuckles whitening. John's jaw flexed. Aidan stared at the blur on the film that was supposed to be his body and couldn't reconcile the fact that the enemy was already inside.

"What's next?" John asked. His voice had that brittle edge, like steel ground too thin.

"A biopsy," Patel said. "We need a tissue sample. That will tell us the exact type. From there, we can build a treatment plan."

"Treatment," Aidan echoed, the word tasting like metal.

Patel nodded. "Chemotherapy, possibly radiation. Depending on size and spread, surgery could be an option."

Karen broke then, tears streaming, though she tried to muffle them with her sleeve. "He's seventeen."

Patel's voice softened. "And because he's young and strong, that works in his favor. But this is serious. We need to act quickly."

Aidan barely heard the rest. The words chemotherapy, radiation, surgery bled together, like being told a new playbook in a foreign language. He heard *young and strong* and clung to it, though it sounded flimsy. He was supposed to be invincible, the one who got up after every hit. And yet here he was, sitting still while people talked about saving his life like it was already in jeopardy.

When the meeting ended, Karen wrapped both arms around him as if she could shield him from the folder still sitting on the table. John put a hand on his shoulder, firm, grounding.

On the way out, teammates' texts buzzed his phone — memes, gifs, jokes about Friday's hit. They didn't know. No one knew yet. Aidan typed nothing back.

In the car, the silence was thicker than before. John finally asked, "You all right, kid?"

Aidan looked out the window at the stadium on the hill, its bleachers empty under the morning sun. His ribs still throbbed, but the ache was nothing compared to the new weight in his chest.

"No," he said honestly. Then, after a beat: "But I have to be."

Chapter Ten –
The Bargain

The McAllister kitchen table had always been neutral ground. It was where report cards got dissected, where summer plans were argued, where laughter softened the edges of long days. But that night it felt like a courtroom, every plate of reheated lasagna a prop in a trial no one wanted to hold.

The biopsy was scheduled for Wednesday. Dr. Patel had used phrases like *aggressive, no delay, time is precious.* Karen had nodded furiously, her pen scribbled notes until the ink bled. John had listened with his arms crossed, eyes distant. Aidan had just stared at the black dot on the linoleum floor and thought: *The season doesn't pause. Riverton comes Friday whether I'm there or not.*

Now, at the table, Karen pushed her plate away untouched. "We start immediately after the biopsy. Patel said—"

"After the season," Aidan interrupted. His voice was quiet, but it cut like glass.

Karen's head snapped up. "Aidan, did you hear him? This isn't—this isn't about sprained ribs or bruises. This is cancer. You don't get to schedule it around football."

"I do," Aidan said, firmer now. He looked at her, then at his father. "I need to finish. If I stop now, if I don't play… it'll feel like I never started."

Karen's eyes brimmed. "Honey—"

"No." He slammed his palm on the table, wincing instantly at the pain it sent shooting through his side, but he didn't back down. "You raised me on this game. Both of you. Friday nights, trophies on the wall, Dad breaking down film until midnight. You can't take it away now. Not when it matters most."

"You're asking us to risk your life for football" She whispered.

"I'm asking you to let me live before I have to fight to." He said before pausing and looking away as if he seen something then continued. "You know those stadium lights? The crowd roaring? THAT'S my LIFE." He finished.

John exhaled slowly, rubbing his temples. "Son, I know what you're saying. I do. But you heard the doctor. Every week you wait—"

"Every week I don't wait, I live," Aidan shot back. His throat tightened, but the words came anyway. "What if this is all I get? What if this is my only season? Do you really want me to spend it in a hospital bed instead of on the field? No Dad. This is my year. My shot. I've worked too hard for this since Pop Warner. Scouts are coming. Colleges are watching. His voice grew desperate. "I can't just… sit out.""

The question hung heavily. Karen covered her face with her hands. John sat frozen, torn between his wife's fear and his son's fire.

The silence broke when the phone rang. Coach Dempsey. John answered, put it on speaker.

"John? Karen? How's he doing?"

Karen swallowed hard. "He wants to play Friday. He needs Doctors, not football."

On the other end, silence. Then Coach's gravelly voice: "Put me on with him."

Aidan took the phone. "Coach."

"You're asking me," Dempsey said, "to stamp approval on a risk I can't justify. If you were mine—my own son—I'd sit you. Hell, I'd lock your pads in a closet."

"I'm asking you not to take the game from me before it takes itself," Aidan said. His voice cracked, but the words came steadily.

Dempsey sighed long and hard. "You want me to live with this on my conscience."

"I'll live with it on mine," Aidan said. "Just give me the chance."

The coach was quiet for a long time. Finally: "Your parents' consent. That's my line. They say yes, I say yes. But the second your body says sit—you sit. No heroics. You hear me?"

"Yes, sir."

Karen's sob broke through. "Coach—"

"Kare," Dempsey said gently, "I know. I know. But I've seen a lot of boys. Some are good. Some are great. Aidan... he's carrying something bigger than himself. If this is what he needs—"

The call ended, but the bargain stayed, echoing in the small kitchen.

Karen leaned forward, her voice barely a whisper. "If you play, you could—" She stopped, unable to finish.

"I know," Aidan said. His chest heaved. "But if I don't play, I already have."

John reached across the table, his hand trembling as it closed over his son's. For the first time, he didn't argue.

The bargain was struck.

Chapter Eleven –
Coach's Office

Coach Dempsey's office was smaller than anyone imagined from the bleachers. A battered desk, two mismatched chairs, a corkboard dense with depth charts and laminated call sheets, a whiteboard ghosted with the remains of past weeks' protections. On the back wall: a framed photo of a younger Dempsey in a college jersey, mud to his knees, and beside it a Polaroid collage of boys he'd coached—smiles under eye black, arms thrown over shoulders, moments caught before real life pulled them apart.

Aidan stood in the doorway, helmet under his arm though he'd come straight from school. Some habits traveled with you. He knocked on the open frame.

"Get in here," Dempsey said without looking up. He was turning a toothpick between his teeth the way some men turned a coin in their pocket. When he finally glanced up and saw Aidan's eyes—red-rimmed from a night that wasn't sleep—his face softened. "Close it."

Aidan sat. The chair complained like it had opinions.

"Your old man called me," Dempsey said. "Told me the plan."

Aidan nodded. "The bargain. I know what I'm asking."

"What you're asking," Dempsey said, setting the toothpick on a stack of film notes, "is permission to walk a cliff edge and call it a sidewalk."

"Coach—"

"Let me be plain." He leaned forward, forearms on the desk. "There are two things I answer to: your mother's eyes, and the truth of what your body can do. You lie to either one, I'll sit you so fast you won't remember where your helmet is."

"I won't lie," Aidan said. The words were out before he could file them. He felt them anyway. "I can't."

Dempsey studied him like he was studying a new defense. "You sure as hell can. You're a quarterback. You lie every play—show one thing, deliver another. This is different. We need rules."

He stood and dragged the whiteboard closer. "Rule one: Trainers run point. You check in with Ms. Rivera twice a day. Morning, after school. She says you sit, you sit. That includes practice."

"Twice a day," Aidan repeated.

"Rule two: No contact in practice. You wear red. We whistle you dead if a defender breathes on you wrong."

"I need reps," Aidan protested.

"You'll get a thousand mental reps. Footwork on air. Routes on air. Protection calls at the line with no ball if that's what it takes. You don't need your ribs tenderized to know where the safety's lying."

Aidan bit back a retort and nodded.

"Rule three: Film." Dempsey pointed to the clock. "We start at six every morning. You and me. We get ahead so Friday can go slower."

"Six," Aidan said. He'd been up at five his whole life when football mattered. It was almost a relief to hear a number.

"Rule four: A word," Dempsey said. "You need out, you say it. Not a tough-guy hand wave, not a stare in my direction hoping I read your mind. A word that means you're done for that series, that quarter, that night."

Aidan's instinct was to deflect with a joke. He didn't. "What word?"

Dempsey looked at him for a long moment, then uncapped a marker. He wrote in block letters: **TRUTH.**

"You say it," he said, tapping the board, "and there's no argument. I don't ask why. I don't make you justify. You give me truth, I give you respect."

Aidan swallowed. "Truth," he said, quietly first, then again like he wanted to test the fit. "Truth."

"Last one," Dempsey said. "Rule five: Captains know. Nobody else. You don't need a parade of pity. You need a huddle that holds. We tell them enough to protect you. Not enough to make you a saint."

"Marcus will hate not telling the others," Aidan said.

"Marcus will do what you ask him to do," Dempsey said, but there was a smile in it. "And he'll do it loud."

The door clicked softly and Ms. Rivera stepped in without knocking—a habit earned by a thousand sprained ankles. She set a clipboard on the desk. "Vitals, symptom log, daily weight," she said briskly. "I'm not a witch doctor. I can't see inside your chest. But I can watch trends. You drop five pounds this week or your pulse lives in the red, I pull you and I don't argue."

"I'll drink whatever you hand me," Aidan said, half-meaning it. The Gatorade jugs, the salt tabs, the bland toast—he'd eat the playbook if they told him it had electrolytes.

Rivera's eyes were gentle and precise. "Your mom gave me permission to call her if you skip a check-in," she added.

Aidan grimaced. "Of course she did."

"Good mothers do," Rivera said. She softened. "I'm in your corner, kid. But the corner isn't the ring."

When she was gone, the room shrank again, back to the three of them: Aidan, the coach, the board with the word that felt like a dare.

"Walk me through Riverton's first series last week," Dempsey said suddenly. "Start in trips, motion across. What do they want?"

"Force you to declare," Aidan said, the familiar gear slipping back into place. "They bump the backer, try to widen the alley so the trap has room."

"How do you beat it?"

"Tempo. Get to the line before they can stem. Hard count, take the free five if they're antsy. If they sit, tag the stick. Take grass."

Dempsey flicked his eyes to the corner of the ceiling where a faint water stain made the paint pucker. It was a tell for him: thinking, measuring. "Third-and-seven, boundary corner with lazy feet, safety at eleven, weight on his heels?"

"Hole shot," Aidan said, and couldn't help the half-smile. "Throw it before it exists."

"There you are," Dempsey said, almost to himself.

A knock. The door opened a sliver and Marcus stuck his head in, eyes switching from Aidan to Coach. "We doing secrets in here?"

"Get in," Dempsey said. "Close it."

Marcus slid into the second chair without being asked and stole the toothpick, twirling it. "I know enough to know you're both about to tell me to keep my mouth shut."

"That about covers it," Dempsey said. He told him the shape of things—biopsy, treatment words still knitting themselves into a plan, the bargain. He didn't dramatize. He didn't minimize. He drew the line and asked if Marcus could hold it.

Marcus's gaze went to Aidan, not the coach. "You sure?" he asked. "Because if you hand me this, I keep it."

"I'm sure," Aidan said. "I need you to run the room. Keep noise off me. And I need you to be my eyes if mine get stupid."

"Your eyes get stupid, your mouth says 'truth,'" Marcus said, catching sight of the board. He repeated it under his breath. "Truth." He nodded once. "Okay."

Dempsey stood and the meeting, which had felt like a secret, became official. He called the other captains—left tackle Will, middle linebacker Cruz—into the office and shut the door again. He told them less. Enough to draw their bodies around Aidan's like a quiet scheme. "He's playing," Dempsey said, voice even. "We protect him. No hits in practice. No macho nonsense. Anyone who thinks they're proving something by testing him will discover how much running a man can do after sundown."

Cruz lifted a hand. "What about Friday?"

"We play our brand," Dempsey said. "No theatrics. If I sit him, you nod and move the huddle forward. Got it?"

Will cleared his throat. "Coach, you want me to slide protection more his way?"

"I want you to slide protection wherever the math tells you," Dempsey said. "We're not rewriting ball. We're tightening the bolts."

They broke with a quiet "Yes, sir," and the word **truth** hanging in the air like a thread they all pretended not to see.

When the door shut, it was just Aidan again. The afternoon sun found the edge of the blinds and laid a bright bar across the desk between them.

"Your mom will hate me for this," Dempsey said, not quite smiling.

"She'll hate me more," Aidan said. Then: "She'll love us anyway."

"That's what scares me," Dempsey said softly. He stood and picked up a box from the file cabinet. From it he pulled a faded red practice jersey—the non-contact color—and tossed it across the desk. "Wear it. If anyone forgets, this will remind them."

Aidan turned the fabric in his hands. It was lighter than the game blue, the mesh rougher. He could smell ten years of boys who had worn it when the body needed mercy. "I don't want pity," he said.

"You're not getting pity," Dempsey said. "You're getting a plan."

He set the red jersey aside and reached for the marker again, drawing up the first ten on the whiteboard the way they did every week. "Openers," he said. "We'll lean on tempo. You don't have to force a single thing. They'll hand you yards because they don't believe you'll take them." He scribbled: *Trips rt 62 Smash, Duo Check, Mesh Tag Wheel, Zone Keep Only if End Crashes*—and underlined the last twice.

They stood shoulder to shoulder, two sets of eyes tracking the lines, and it felt for a moment like the world had narrowed to the simple, solvable space between chalk and grass.

"You ever wish you were just a teacher?" Aidan asked, surprising himself.

Dempsey grunted. "I am."

Aidan shook his head. "Like… not this. Not… everything riding on the thing you love."

Dempsey capped the marker. "I was a decent guard once. Thought the game owed me something. My junior year a kid broke my ankle by falling on it wrong—wasn't even a hit worth telling. Took my shot. I thought I'd die from smallness after that. I didn't. Turns out the thing I loved wasn't my feet, it was huddles." He looked at Aidan. "You don't get to choose every part of your story, kid. But you get to choose what you do with the parts you get."

A knock. Ms. Rivera again, holding a small plastic cup. "Baseline," she said. "Hydration."

Aidan took it and tossed it back, grimaced. "This tastes like a lake."

"Win Friday and it'll taste like champagne," she said dryly. "Vitals in the training room. Don't run from me."

"I won't," he said, and meant it, at least as much as he could mean anything that wasn't the feel of laces.

When she left, Dempsey picked up the toothpick like it might anchor him. "You tell Emily?" he asked, casual as a checkdown.

Aidan blinked. "Emily?"

"Quiet girl. Window seat. Writes in the margins. The one you look at without knowing you're looking."

Heat climbed Aidan's neck. "We don't... I barely know her."

Dempsey shrugged. "Then tell the people you do. Your line. Your dad. Your mother most of all." He looked back at the word on the board. "Tell yourself."

They were quiet for a while. The hallway offered the familiar chorus—weights clanking, a whistle somewhere too insistent. The world was proceeding like always even though theirs had tilted.

"Go check in with Rivera," Dempsey said at last. "Then go home. Sleep like a thief. Tomorrow we start at six."

Aidan rose. His knees felt older than they should, but his mind—it clicked. Rules, routines, film, the red jersey folded over his forearm like a flag of truce. He reached for the door, then paused and turned back. "Coach?"

Dempsey lifted his eyebrows.

"If I say it—truth—" Aidan began, tasting the word. "And you sit me... will you hate me?"

Dempsey didn't answer right away. He ringed the toothpick between finger and thumb, then set it down carefully on the desk, as if the gesture itself needed doing right. "I will be proud of you," he said simply. "And then I'll probably go yell at a referee so nobody sees me feeling anything else."

Aidan breathed out. He nodded, once, like the end of a cadence. "See you at six."

In the hallway, the air felt different. Not lighter, exactly. Sharper. He walked past the photos of boys who had come and gone and wondered how many bargains had been struck in rooms like that, how many truths spoken and how many swallowed. Ms. Rivera caught him with a cuff and a stethoscope and a look that said *I'm not letting you disappear.* He let her do the work. He let himself be measured.

On his way out, he found Marcus in the weight room, spotting a sophomore who was all elbows and eagerness. Marcus racked the bar and jogged over, eyes asking without asking.

"We have rules," Aidan said.

"Good ones?"

"The only ones," Aidan said. "Truth."

Marcus nodded. "Then we'll run them."

They bumped fists—a quiet seal—and stepped out into the late-afternoon light. The field beyond the glass doors lay bright and ordinary, hash marks white as paper. Practice would start soon. The red jersey felt heavier than its mesh should allow.

For a moment, Aidan stood and let the sun warm the bruise beneath his ribs. The ache answered, present and honest. He didn't look away from it. He didn't rename it. He tucked the jersey under his arm like a play he was sure of and walked toward the locker room, toward the huddle, toward the week that would ask things of him and, for now, still let him answer.

Chapter Twelve –
Red Jersey

Tuesday's practice field looked the same as always under the late September sun—green turf, white lines, the echo of whistles cutting the air. But for Aidan, everything had changed.

He pulled the red mesh practice jersey over his pads, the fabric thin and scratchy against his neck. It felt wrong instantly. He was used to the bold navy of the offense, the jersey that matched the rest of the huddle, the color that said *we're in this together.* Red was exile. Red meant *hands off.*

When he jogged out of the locker room, the chatter in the huddle fell for half a second. Teammates tried not to stare, but they did. Even the freshmen wide-eyed at the sight: their captain marked different, fragile in a color reserved for quarterbacks who needed saving.

Coach Dempsey blew his whistle, sharp enough to cut the air. "Don't get sentimental. He's running the offense. Red just means you don't touch him. Understand?"

"Yes, sir," the team answered in a chorus.

Aidan set his jaw and jogged to the line. He refused to let the jersey define him. He clapped his hands. "Trips right, zone left. Let's go."

The play ran smooth. The line fired off, the back tucked behind the guard, four yards. Aidan carried out the fake, ribs protesting the twist, but he didn't flinch. He jogged back to the huddle, forcing energy into his voice.

"Good pad level, Will. Let's do it again."

They ran mesh, stick, smash—the rhythm of practice. Each time Aidan barked the cadence, he felt normal again. Each time he let the ball fly and watched Marcus snatch it with sure hands, the noise in his head quieted.

But then came the moments he couldn't ignore. The line collapsed a beat late, a defender surged through, and instinct told Aidan to roll, to fight for space. Instead, Coach's whistle shrieked.

"Dead! Dead! That's a sack!"

Aidan stopped, teeth clenched. He hated it. Hated standing still when he could have escaped. Hated watching defenders grin like they'd won when in a real game he would have slipped away.

Coach caught his eyes. "Rules, Four. You live by them."

Aidan nodded curtly. "Yes, sir."

At water break, Marcus jogged beside him. "You're glaring holes through your facemask. Relax."

"Feels like I'm in a cage."

Marcus tilted his head. "Cages keep things safe. Sometimes even lions."

Aidan smirked despite himself. "That was terrible."

"Yeah, well, so's that jersey." Marcus bumped his shoulder gently. "Doesn't change who you are."

Ms. Rivera approached with her clipboard, pen poised. "Heart rate?"

"Fine."

She arched an eyebrow. "Numbers, McAllister."

He sighed, tapping the sensor on his wrist. She jotted it down. "Weight's holding," she murmured. "Keep hydrating." Her eyes softened. "You look tired."

"I'm always tired in September."

"Not like this." She didn't push further, just scribbled and walked away.

By the second hour of practice, the team began to adjust. They stopped flinching at the sight of red. They ran harder, cleaner, because if Aidan wasn't going to carry hits, they needed to. Cruz, the middle linebacker, barked at his unit louder than ever, making sure they disguised coverage sharp, forcing Aidan to see the whole field without the crash of pads to test him.

At one point, Will—the left tackle—grabbed a sophomore by the facemask after he drifted too close. "You ever touch him, I'll bury you in gassers 'til Christmas. Got it?"

"Y-yes, sir," the kid stammered, backing away.

Aidan saw it all. Saw how they bent the rules of practice around him. Saw how the huddle held a little tighter when he called plays. It burned, but it also built something else—an awareness that this team was already protecting him, not because of pity, but because they believed in him enough to share the risk.

After sprints, the team collapsed on the sideline, helmets tipped back, chests heaving. Dempsey stood in the middle, whistle dangling, voice like gravel.

"Riverton doesn't care about your colors," he said. "They'll come for our quarterback like wolves. You answer with discipline, with trust, with execution. You do not answer with pity. You answer with football. Understand?"

"Yes, sir!"

He turned to Aidan. "How's it feel?"

Aidan locked eyes with him. He thought of the ache under his ribs, the fatigue seeping earlier than usual, the whispers still chasing him in the hallways. He thought of the word written on the board in Dempsey's office.

"Feels like football," he said.

Coach nodded once. "That's all it needs to feel like."

Practice ended with a team huddle, arms over shoulders, helmets touching. Cruz's voice led the chant, but Aidan's rang loudest. When they broke, he lingered on the field, helmet in hand, the red jersey glowing like a warning in the evening sun.

Karen was waiting at the edge of the bleachers, arms folded, watching every move. He jogged over, sweat dripping, smile forced.

"How was it?" she asked, voice careful.

"I threw well. No picks. Timing's sharp."

"I meant you," she said.

He hesitated, then lied gently. "I'm fine."

She searched his face, then pulled him into a hug anyway, her arms firm against the pads. "Don't forget, I'm allowed to love you more than the game."

"I know," he whispered.

That night, Aidan lay in bed with the red jersey crumpled on the chair beside him. He hated it. He needed it. He thought about truth, about bargains, about what it meant to live one more Friday like it was the last. Sleep came late, tangled with dreams of lights and whistles and the echo of his mother's voice saying his name across a field he could never quite reach.

Chapter Thirteen – The Locker Room

By Thursday the week had sharpened to a point. The hallways buzzed with Riverton talk—scores from last year, rumors about their linebacker who benched a truck, a student section theme that involved enough baby powder to choke a marching band. Posters bloomed across the walls: **BLUE OUT. PROTECT OUR HOUSE.** Aidan moved through it all like a man walking under water. He laughed when he was supposed to, signed a kid's spiral notebook at lunch, nodded at teachers who wished him luck as if luck were a thing you could put in your pocket and take to the huddle.

After last bell, the team funneled down the corridor toward the locker room, cleat bags slapping against shins, the air thickening with that pre-practice cocktail of rubber, detergent, and nerves. The old stereo in the corner coughed to life and argued with itself—linemen lobbying for country, receivers for trap, specialists for something that sounded like wind chimes over a drumline. Eventually Cruz, the middle linebacker, rolled his eyes and put on a playlist nobody loved and everyone could live with. Aidan let the noise sit at the edge of his hearing and focused on his hands.

He taped his wrists the way he always had—left first, two turns; right, three. He pressed the seam with his thumb, made sure it lay flat. He reached for the black Sharpie that lived in the bottom of his locker and hesitated. Then, with a small breath, he wrote a word along the inside of the white tape where he could read it if he flexed his hand just so: **truth**. The letters bled slightly into the weave. He closed his fingers over them and felt steadier, the way a good cadence steadies a nervous huddle.

"Coach wants you in the training room," Ms. Rivera called across the clatter without looking up from her clipboard. She had perfected the art of sounding like a drill sergeant and a favorite aunt at the same time.

Aidan hopped down from the bench and wove through the maze of shoulder pads and open lockers. In the training room the light was cooler, sharper. Rivera's cuff climbed his arm. "Pulse?"

"Sixty-eight," he said, catching a glimpse of the number on his watch.

"Mm." She watched the needle. "Down a half a pound from Tuesday. Could be nothing. Could be sweat. Drink more than you want." She wrapped the cuff tighter. "Any dizziness?"

"No."

"Shortness of breath?"

"Only when Coach makes us run gassers for your amusement."

A smile tugged at her mouth. "You boys always think I enjoy it." She peeled the cuff away and scribbled. "You playing tomorrow?"

"I'm dressing."

"That wasn't the question."

He looked at her, feeling the tape on his wrist against his palm. "I'm playing."

"Then you'll need this." She handed him a small zip bag—salt tabs, a honey packet, two acetaminophen, a strip of kinesio tape. "Before warm-ups. Halfway through the second quarter. If you puke, I'm telling your mother it's because you didn't listen to me."

"Fair."

Rivera's voice softened. "You know, I can't stand the sight of that red jersey on you." Before he could bristle, she added, "Because it reminds me to see the boy and not just the quarterback."

Aidan swallowed around something that wasn't pain. "Thanks."

Back at his locker, Marcus perched upside down on the bench like a bat, feet on the backrest, head hanging. He looked at Aidan's wrist. "You write me a love note?"

"Only word I can't afford to forget."

Marcus righted himself in a spring. "Then we won't let you." He tried to steal the Sharpie; Aidan snapped it shut, reflexes intact, and the ridiculous normalcy of that tiny contest calmed them both.

Coach Dempsey's whistle cut the room in half. "Walk-through in five. Helmets and shells. Red means red."

They filed out to the field with the sun hanging low, the sky doing that Ohio thing where it tried on October for an hour and then remembered September again. Walk-throughs felt like church—quiet, precise, the body practicing belief. They rehearsed openers. They aligned, shifted, re-aligned, breathing as one organism, learning where the stress would fall. Aidan worked the cadence like a metronome, the ball leaving his hand in a clean heartbeat. When the defense flashed a look Riverton liked, Cruz barked them into the right check and Dempsey's toothpick twitched, his tell for satisfaction he refused to say out loud.

On the last script rep, a sophomore edge rusher forgot and spun too close to Aidan on a play fake. Before Coach could cook him alive, Will—left tackle, future union negotiator by temperament—snagged the kid by his jersey and walked him back five steps. "We do not graze the red," he said, voice flat, as if reading a law. The kid's eyes went wide; he nodded in the way boys do when they've been embarrassed into understanding. Aidan wanted to hate the bubble wrapped around him, and couldn't. It was protection, yes, but also a kind of love.

They broke down the last play and trooped back inside. The locker room's temperature rose with the steam of thirty boys. Someone banged a helmet against a locker in a rhythm that eventually became a chant. Cruz dropped to a knee in the narrow aisle and the circle closed around him, arms slung over shoulders, foreheads slick. His prayer was short, more gratitude than plea: thank you for breath, for light, for a field and a chance to do our work. He ended the way they always ended, with the call-and-response that belonged to this group and no other: "Who are we?"

"Brothers."

"Who do we protect?"

"The man to my left and right."

"Who are we?"

"Lincoln."

The echo lingered in the metal.

When the knot broke, Dempsey didn't climb onto a bench or raise his voice. He stood in the doorway with his hands in his pockets and the word *Friday* written in tiny letters at the corner of his mouth. "Riverton has teeth," he said simply. "They'll try to make you panic. Panic lives in the feet first. Play with your eyes and your feet. If your eyes are right and your feet are quiet, your hands will do the rest."

He looked at Aidan, just for a second. "We don't need heroes. We need the right thing, at the right speed, again and again. Make boring look beautiful. That's how you break a team that only understands loud."

There was a murmur of something—agreement, excitement—that felt like wind gathering.

"Captains," Dempsey said. "Room two."

Aidan, Marcus, Will, and Cruz followed him into the coaches' film closet that doubled as a strategy room. It smelled like dry-erase markers and optimism. Dempsey closed the door with a thumb and drew a quick box on the board. "Keys," he said, tapping each corner: "Win first down. Stay out of third and stupid. No free yards. Be patient." He underlined the last word twice. "They will give you throws because they don't believe you'll take them. Take the grass. When they get mad, we go over the top."

Cruz nodded like he was filing the rhythm into his bones. Will cracked his knuckles. Marcus bounced once and then stood perfectly still. Aidan watched the marker squeak along the board and felt the old joy rise—a play solving itself, a plan you could hold.

Dempsey uncapped a red pen and, under the keys, drew a short line in block letters: **TRUTH = RESPECT.** He capped the pen and said, "You say it, I sit you. No questions. You'll hate me for exactly one minute. Then we'll move the huddle forward."

Aidan looked at the word he'd already written on his wrist and nodded.

They stepped back into the main room and the noise swallowed them. The boy energy—stupid jokes, towel snaps, the way someone always tried to balance a water bottle on a helmet—worked at the edges of Aidan's focus like a balm. He dressed down, slid his practice jersey off and hung it carefully. When he reached for the game blue, he paused. In the corner of his locker, tucked under his spare gloves, was a folded index card.

He glanced around—Marcus was in a glove debate with a sophomore; Cruz and Will were head-butting each other's shoulder pads like rutting elk; Rivera was pretending not to see any of it. Aidan unfolded the card.

I don't know anything about football. But I know something about pages. Some are blank because you're scared to write the wrong sentence. Some are blank because you're saving space for something worth it. — E.

Under the initial was a tiny sketch of a field line, a little hash mark and a dot like a ball sitting where it belonged. He didn't have to guess the sender. Emily Hart printed her letters like she pressed them into the paper. He read it again. The thing inside his ribs that wasn't medical throbbed once, different than pain.

He slid the card into his wallet and told himself it would be good luck if he never called it that out loud.

"Yo," Marcus said at his shoulder, pretending he hadn't noticed anything even as his curiosity flared. "You good?"

"Yeah."

"Liar." Marcus thumped his helmet against Aidan's lightly. "Tomorrow, if the corner sits, I'm gone."

"I'll throw it before you're open."

"You always do." Marcus grinned. "And I always am."

As the room emptied by trickles, boys peeling off toward cars and dinners and Thursday-night rituals, Aidan stayed. He liked the way a locker room sounded when the roar had drained out—the tap of water from a shower somebody didn't twist tight, the distant thud of a ball being punished by a punter who refused to leave, the hum of the soda machine trying to be useful. He sat on the bench and laced his shoes with a concentration he usually reserved for two-minute drills.

John texted: *Pasta is on. Film after?*

Karen: *You okay?*

Coach (surprisingly): *Sleep. 6 a.m.*

He typed back to his parents—*on my way*—and left Dempsey at "read." He slipped the wallet, with Emily's card tucked inside, into his backpack and swung the strap over his shoulder. He stood for a breath and touched the top edge of his helmet where the paint had chipped into a little white crescent. He pressed his thumb there until it warmed.

On his way out he passed the whiteboard where somebody had scrawled a cartoon of their offensive line with capes, and below it Will had written **NO FREE RUSHERS** in letters big enough a blind man could read them. Under that someone had added, smaller, **NO FREE DOUBT**. Aidan didn't know who had written that one. It felt like a dare more than a rule.

He pushed the door open and the evening met him—a thin ribbon of gold along the tops of the bleachers, the field beyond empty and clean. The red jersey was gone from his body but it hung in his mind, not as a shame now, but as a bright thread in the pattern of a week that had taught him how to play under a new gravity. He flexed his left hand and the tape creased, the word on the inside forming against his skin.

Truth.

Tomorrow there would be whistles and a band and a line of boys in red and black who wanted to knock the breath out of him. Tomorrow there would be a coach who held him to his own promise, a friend who ran until space appeared, a town that wanted a story and would settle for a win. Tonight there was home, and film with his father, and his mother's pasta steaming on the table. There was a card in his wallet with a field line and a dot.

He walked toward the parking lot, shoulders squaring on instinct, like he was already under the lights.

Chapter Fourteen – Friday Night Lights Again

By Friday morning, the air in Lincoln was different. You could feel it in the hallways before first bell, in the way students walked faster, voices lifted, as if the town itself had more voltage. Riverton week was never quiet, but this time it thrummed. Every locker door, every bulletin board, every shirt in the crowd was blue or gold.

The pep rally took over the gym. The cheerleaders led chants, the band blasted the fight song until the bleachers vibrated, and Coach Dempsey gave the kind of speech he usually hated—loud, broad strokes, easy applause lines. He preferred film rooms and chalk talks, but today wasn't about details. It was about reminding the school what tonight meant.

"Lincoln doesn't back down!" he thundered into the mic, and the crowd roared.

Aidan stood with his teammates on the floor, arms folded, helmet tucked under his arm. When the chant started—*State or bust! State or bust!*—the sound rattled his ribs. He smiled, but behind it his thoughts were quiet, a steady drumbeat: *Don't let them see the crack. Don't let them see you wince.*

After lunch, classes blurred. Teachers gave up on lessons, letting the day dissolve into blue-and-gold chaos. In English, Mrs. Reynolds caught Aidan's eye and offered a soft smile instead of Gatsby questions. In history, Coach had them watch highlight reels under the guise of "studying strategy."

By the final bell, the halls emptied faster than ever. Everyone was heading to the stadium early.

At home, Karen laid spaghetti and garlic bread on the table—game-day tradition. She moved around the kitchen with a nervous precision, hands busy to keep her mind from wandering. John sat across from Aidan, fork twirling but hardly eating, too locked in.

"You've got them if you stay patient," John said, as if the game were another math problem. "Riverton will blitz to prove a point. Let them. Grass is yours."

Aidan nodded. "I know." He pushed food around his plate, appetite gone but not wanting to show it. Karen finally stopped and looked at him, really looked.

"You don't have to be perfect tonight," she said.

He met her eyes. "I do."

She flinched, as if he'd struck her, then nodded, tears threatening. "Then be perfect safe."

He kissed her cheek before heading upstairs. In his room, he sat on the edge of the bed with his jersey folded beside him. He stared at the number stitched across it—**4**—and traced it with his fingers. His ribs throbbed, his body reminding him of last week's hit. He thought about the MRI films, the dark blur on the scan, Dr. Patel's careful voice. Then he shoved the thought down and pulled the jersey on. Tonight, he was not a patient. Tonight, he was QB1.

The team bus ride to the stadium was quiet, each boy wrapped in headphones or muttered prayers. Marcus sat beside him, tapping his thigh in rhythm. When the bus turned the corner and the stadium lights came into view—twin beacons blazing against the dusk—the team collectively inhaled. It was time.

Lincoln's stadium was already overflowing. Cars lined the streets, the stands a mosaic of blue and gold, banners waving. The band's drums pounded like a heartbeat. Smoke machines puffed at the tunnel entrance, ready for their run-out. The announcer's voice boomed across the loudspeakers: "Your Lincoln Lions!"

The team burst from the tunnel in a wave, helmets raised, pads colliding. Aidan led them, chest high, legs pumping. The roar was physical, a wall of sound that pressed against him and lifted him at the same time.

He jogged to the sideline, scanning the stands. He saw Karen in her blanket, John on his feet, Emily near the student section with her notebook clutched against her chest. Their faces blurred into one, into many, into the reason he had bargained for this moment.

Warmups felt mechanical—stretches, passing lines, cadence calls. His throws were sharp, spiraling clean through the evening air. Marcus caught each one with a snap, eyes burning with promise.

"Looks good," Marcus said.

"Feels good," Aidan lied.

The captains met at midfield for the coin toss. Riverton's players looked bigger up close, their linebacker Carter glaring like a man already plotting the next collision. Aidan stared back, unflinching. The coin flipped, caught the light, fell. Lincoln won. The crowd erupted again.

Back on the sideline, Coach Dempsey gripped Aidan's facemask briefly, pulling him close. "First drive, take what they give. Patience. Truth if you need it."

Aidan nodded, heart hammering, the word pressed against his wrist where he'd written it again under fresh tape.

The whistle blew. The band surged. The ball teed up, waiting.

As the kicker jogged forward, the world shrank. The roar became a tunnel. The lights turned the field into a stage. Aidan inhaled, exhaled, and told himself the same thing he had since Pop Warner, since backyards and streetlights and Saturday mornings at the diner.

It's just football.

The ball sailed through the air, spiraling down into the waiting arms of Lincoln's return man. The game began.

And Aidan knew: every snap, every breath tonight would count more than it ever had.

Chapter Fifteen – The First Half

The ball hung in the lights like a coin no one had called. It dropped into Jamal's arms at the five, and he slashed to the twenty-eight before Riverton's wedge collapsed him in a thud of pads. The roar crested, settled. Aidan trotted onto the field with the huddle forming around him, breath steaming in the early chill, the paint smell of fresh lines in his nose.

He didn't feel the red jersey now. This was blue—game blue—and the bargain that had delivered him here rode quiet along his ribs. He rubbed his thumb once across the inside of his taped wrist, felt the ridge of the letters he'd written there, then leaned in.

"Trips right. Sixty-two Smash on one," he said, the calm of a practiced voice hiding the drum in his chest. "Eyes up. Tempo."

They broke. Riverton showed two high, corners with patient feet, the nickel muttering across the line. Aidan counted the box, watched the safety's weight, and took the snap. Three steps, plant, ball out: the out route chewed six yards clean. Will, at left tackle, clapped once behind the play, a sound like punctuation.

Second and four. Duo check to inside zone. The back danced, found a crease, burrowed for three. Third and a yard. The stadium leaned forward. Aidan slid to the line and hard-counted; the boundary end twitched and then jumped, cursing at himself as the official walked the ball forward. Free first down. "Stay patient," Aidan told himself, and the whole town, and anyone else listening.

Riverton decided patience was an insult. On the next snap they brought five, the nickel scraping in late. Aidan felt the pressure before he saw it—how the air changes when a man decides to arrive—and popped the hot to Marcus on the jerk. Marcus caught, pivoted inside, took a hit that rattled teeth, and still fell forward for eight.

"Grass is ours," Marcus said in the huddle, not quite grinning.

"Then mow it," Aidan said.

They did: stick, draw, a quick glance to the boundary when the corner's cushion got lazy. The drive wasn't pretty; it was a hand saw—steady, true, chewing. At the twenty-two, Riverton finally won a down with a slant that knifed through. Second and twelve. Aidan didn't chase it. He tagged a slant-flat and took five. Third and seven. He checked to mesh, watched the linebackers bump too deep, and feathered it to the sit route at the sticks. Move the chains.

The red zone tightened like a throat. On second and goal, the call came for a switch release they'd loved all week. Aidan sold the fade, glanced the safety with his eyes, and then ripped the dig that opened like a trapdoor. The ball kissed the receiver's chest at the two, and a Riverton safety arrived with bad intentions, separating man from ball. It skittered away, incomplete, the stadium groaning as one.

Third and goal. Dempsey's voice on the sideline: "No heroics. Take points if they make you." Aidan nodded, even though the coach wasn't looking at him. He checked to a fade if the corner's feet got flat; they didn't. He threw the underneath, took four when eight wouldn't come, and let the field goal team jog on. The kick split the uprights, neat as a seam. Three-nothing, Lincoln.

On the sideline, Aidan's heart thudded not from sprinting but from the narrowness of everything. Ms. Rivera materialized with her clipboard like a magician who only did one trick. "Rate?" she asked.

"Eighty-two," he said after a glance.

She frowned but only said, "Salt," and pressed a capsule into his palm. He swallowed, grimaced at the chemical tang, and lifted his gaze to the field where Riverton's offense slid on.

Cruz set the defense like a metronome. Riverton tried to bully; Lincoln answered by filling with all eleven. First down run—stuffed by a scraping safety and a corner who wasn't too proud to tackle. Second down—play-action, Cruz turned and ran with the tight end like he'd been born backpedaling. Third and long—Cruz green-dogged when the back stayed in and flushed the quarterback into a throw that hit the track more than the receiver. The stadium roared like it had done the tackling.

Riverton punted, the ball tumbling end-over-end. Marcus waved poison and let it bounce into the end zone. Aidan jogged back out.

"More grass," he said. "Make boring look beautiful."

Boring lasted exactly one snap. Riverton walked the boundary corner up, jaw set. Aidan's hands twitched under center—he could make the hole shot exist if he wanted to, if he threw it from the top of his drop and trusted the geometry and Marcus's feet. The urge burned; the voice of Dempsey's rule—*patience*—rose to meet it. He took the checkdown instead. Three yards. A scattered boo from the student section turned into a shrug as second down became third-and-manageable and then another first when the tight end sat in the only window that mattered.

A drive later, patience paid rent. Riverton rolled to one high, buzzing the hook, daring the slot to get cute. Aidan tagged the back on a wheel against a linebacker who had been right twice and decided to be right again. He wasn't. The back ghosted past him into daylight. Aidan lofted the ball like a secret only they knew, and it fell over the back's outside shoulder as if the air had practiced the catch. Twenty-three yards, tackled at midfield.

Now the crowd sang. Now the band found a key the drums liked. Aidan let it lift him but not move him. He looked to the sideline. Dempsey rolled his hand for tempo, then drew a finger across his throat—no substitutions, keep them in the wrong people. Aidan clapped them to the line and rattled off cadence. Inside zone for four, stick for five, a quarterback sneak that looked like a shrug and felt like theft. The clock bled. The quarter tilted.

On the first snap of the second, Riverton sent Dylan Carter—the linebacker with a face like a door—on a delayed blitz. Will got enough, the back got a shoulder, and still the man was there, helmet under Aidan's ribs in a way that woke echoes from last week. The world whitened at the edges. The ball hung in his hands like a decision. He tucked it, took the hit, and folded around the leather to keep it off the grass. When he stood, the field seemed a half-step to the left.

He almost said it. The word pressed against the inside of his wrist like heat. *Truth.*

Instead he looked to the sideline, fixed his eyes on Dempsey, and nodded once—*I'm here.* Rivera hovered but didn't breach the white. Will thumped Aidan's shoulder pads twice, apology and promise in the same touch. "My bad," he said, voice tight. "Next time I'll bury him in the band."

Aidan found Marcus's eyes. "Now?"

"Not yet," Marcus said, reading the coverage like a tarot. "They're still proud."

So they bled them. They called mesh; Marcus snagged it and turned three into seven because his feet could always make an argument the math couldn't. They ran draw into a box they had no business running into and stole four anyway. Third and short; a hard count got a flinch but not a flag. They ran the sneak again, and Aidan felt the line's trust in the way their backs bent, their hands finding anchor points on him like they could will him the yard. First down. The stadium's noise was less roar than relief, a thousand people exhaling.

At the twenty, Aidan finally took a shot. Riverton showed single high, the safety flat-footed at eleven, the corner with just enough greed in his stance to write the story. The call came in: hitch-and-go to the boundary.

"Throw it before I'm open," Marcus said, mouth barely moving in the huddle.

"Always," Aidan said.

The snap. Three hard steps. Marcus sold the hitch with a hitch of his own, the corner diving like a kid after a quarter tossed into a pool. Marcus re-accelerated, shoulders stacked. Aidan threw from the top of his drop, trusting space that did not yet exist, and watched the ball arc past the corner's outstretched hand and under the safety's late angle. It hit Marcus in stride at the goal line.

The place detonated.

Except there was a flag, top of the screen, the yellow a sin in the corner of Aidan's vision. A tug on Will's jersey that no one in blue agreed had happened. The play came back. The roar turned into something ragged, then angry, then determined.

"Shake it," Dempsey barked from the sideline. "Next play."

Next play was a screen that looked like a gift and played like an apology—seven yards. The next after that a slant caught in traffic. Third and three. They took the flat and got the spot by a link in the chain. The drive ended three plays later as the red zone clamped again and the safety, perhaps embarrassed by the hitch-and-go, arrived too early on a dig and dared the umpire to throw. He didn't. Field goal. Six-nothing.

Riverton took the ball like an insult. They banged the line twice for four, then found a tight end on a little leak for fifteen when Lincoln's backers got caught peeking. The clock ticked into the belly of the quarter. Cruz thumped his chest and the defense reset. Third and long after a toss swept into the sideline, and the Riverton quarterback, perhaps sick of patience, tried to fit one into a window that was not a window. The ball tipped—once, twice—off hands that belonged to no one for a terrifying heartbeat, and then fell cruelly to turf. Punt. The stadium used the moment to find its lungs again.

Two minutes, change remaining in the half. Two-minute drill—it had always been Aidan's favorite math problem. He gathered them.

"Clock and sideline," he said. "No hero balls. We take what's there and make them hate it."

First play: out route, toe-tap, stop clock. Second: draw into a light box, lay down in bounds after eight, hustle to the line. Third: middle read; the linebacker's hips told a lie; Aidan threw where the truth would be. Marcus snagged it and got out. The ball crossed midfield with a minute and a blink left.

Dempsey rolled his hand—tempo, tempo—and then touched his own wrist where a watch would be if he wore one. "One shot," his mouth said without sound.

Riverton showed quarters. The hole shot begged again like a dare from a friend who loves trouble. Aidan checked to a sail concept instead, dragging the flat defender down and lofting the corner behind his ear. Seventeen yards. Tick, tick. The student section stomped bleachers into a heartbeat.

Twenty-seven seconds. One timeout. Aidan glanced at the band; the trumpets had their mouths on metal and their eyes on him. He smiled inside his helmet because the absurdity of that—their faith, his body, a season—that was the only joke he had time for.

He called something they almost never called: a quarterback draw out of empty with a built-in slide at seven yards if the world looked wrong. The world did not look wrong. The middle opened like a book.

He cut once, felt a hand scrape across his rib pads like a match that didn't catch, and slid at eight, popping up quick to sell to the officials that he was fine, he was fine, he was fine. Timeout.

Twelve seconds. Ball at the twenty. The sideline shouted a dozen possibilities. Dempsey's voice cut them. "Two shots or one smart one," he said, which was as close as he would ever get to poetry.

Aidan chose one smart one. He tagged a concept to steal the back pylon if the safety bit. The safety did not bite; the corner played inside leverage like it was a religion. Aidan held and held and, at the last possible beat, threw the ball into the first row. Booing from the impatient parts of the stadium; a nod from Dempsey; a look from Rivera that said *thank you for not being an idiot.*

Nine seconds. Field goal team. The kick came true. Nine-nothing, and the halftime horn still in its mouth.

Except Riverton, who hated even numbers, returned the kickoff like a kicked hive. A wedge, a crease, a missed tackle, and Jamal had to angle him out at the forty-eight with two seconds remaining. Riverton tried the Hail Mary anyway. The ball arced high, the crowd held its breath, and Cruz, who would have head-butted a brick if it made the right sound, rose among hands and helmets and batted it to ground like he was clearing a dinner plate.

The horn. The band exploded into sound it had been holding for twenty-four minutes. The town stood, sat, stood again. On the sideline, Aidan lifted his helmet and let air touch his face. He wasn't smiling; he was chiseling one from the inside.

Ms. Rivera was there before his heart could settle. "Pulse?"

"Ninety-one," he said truthfully.

"Honest," she murmured, as if pleased that the number and the boy's mouth matched. She handed him a honey packet. "Half now, half mid-third."

He tore it and swallowed sweetness that stuck to his teeth. Over his shoulder, he saw Karen with both hands at her mouth, John clapping in a way that looked like prayer. In the student section, Emily stood on the bench because she was small and the world was not, her notebook hugged to her like ballast.

Dempsey gathered them at the numbers before the march to the locker room. He didn't shout. He peeled the toothpick from his mouth and held it in his fingers as if he could point with quiet.

"This is what patience looks like," he said. "This is how it feels. It is not sexy. It is not loud. It is suffocating. You will suffocate them for twenty-four more minutes. Defense, keep the top on. Offense, steal the grass. No free yards, no free doubt." His eyes flicked to Aidan, then away, a courtesy. "And if your body says the word we agreed on, say it to me and no one else. We will move the huddle forward."

They broke with a low growl, that sound teams make when they are not finished with anything. As they jogged toward the tunnel, the band's drums matched their feet. The lights hummed. The town buzzed like a hive being told a secret. Aidan touched his wrist through the tape, felt the raised ridge of the letters, and let his breath find a rhythm that could carry him through twenty-four more minutes, through the rest of a night that would remember him whether he wanted it to or not.

Chapter Sixteen –
The Second Half

Halftime in the locker room was sweat and steam and voices half-hoarse from two quarters of noise. Jerseys clung wet, tape frayed, the faint sting of antiseptic drifting in from the trainer's corner. Helmets sat in neat rows, their decals scratched and chipped like scars.

Aidan dropped onto the bench, chest heaving. His ribs hummed with every breath, dull and deep, a drumbeat under his sternum. He forced himself to sip water slowly, ignoring how his hands trembled. Marcus leaned back beside him, towel around his neck, eyes blazing.

"They can't cover us," Marcus said. "Not for four quarters. Corners are already gassed."

"They'll blitz more," Aidan answered, his voice quieter. "Carter's been waiting."

Will slapped his shoulder pads from across the aisle. "Then we bury him. Play through us. That's why we're here."

Cruz, helmet still on, paced like a caged thing. "Defense is holding. Keep giving us time."

Coach Dempsey stepped into the center, toothpick gone, eyes sharp. "You're up nine. That's not safety—it's bait. They'll come out swinging to steal momentum. Hold the line. Offense, no panic. Defense, no free shots. Win first down, and they'll play our game."

He pointed at Aidan. "Stay smart."

Aidan nodded, but inside he was already rehearsing throws, counting steps, tracing coverages in his head. His ribs ached, his lungs burned, but his mind—his mind was sharp.

They ran back out into the lights, the crowd's roar doubling, the band thundering. Riverton's kickoff pinned them at the sixteen, the kind of small detail that changes a script.

First play: inside zone stuffed for one. The Riverton sideline barked. Second down: rollout, Carter barreling free, Aidan just getting it out to Marcus for a shaky three. Third and six, and the corner pressed, nickel buzzing. Aidan planted, scanned, and just as he hit the back of his drop—Carter arrived.

Helmet under his ribs again.

The air left him in a ragged gasp. The ball skittered sideways. Whistles. Fourth down.

He lay still for a second, the ache turning sharp, lightning across his side. He heard Rivera's voice on the sideline, Coach's whistle, Marcus shouting his name.

Truth. The word pressed against his wrist.

He shook his head, rolled to his knees, and pushed himself up.

"I'm good," he rasped, though his chest felt hollow.

The crowd roared in relief, though Karen in the stands clutched John's arm like it was the only thing keeping her upright.

Lincoln punted. Riverton took the ball at midfield, and Carter, emboldened, howled at the student section.

Defense answered with steel. Cruz filled the gap on first down, stuffing the back for a loss. On second, a corner blitz forced an early throw, incomplete. Third and long, Riverton tried a slant, but Cruz read it, knocking the ball down with a smack that echoed. Punt. The stadium breathed again.

Back on offense, Aidan huddled them close. His voice wavered at first, then steadied. "We need one drive. Slow it. Bleed them. Trust the grass."

They ran draw. Two yards. They ran stick. Four more. Third and manageable, and Marcus slipped the jam, snagging the ball at the sideline for a first.

The rhythm came back, even if every throw stabbed at his ribs. Out routes, flats, curls—boring football, beautiful football. Riverton grew impatient. Their safeties crept. Their linebackers cheated.

And then the moment arrived.

Single high. Boundary corner heavy on his heels. Marcus gave Aidan the look in the huddle: *now.*

Aidan nodded, but his chest tightened. Could he get enough on it? Could he trust his ribs?

The snap. Drop. Plant. Fire.

The ball spun through the lights, high and true. Marcus burst past the corner, stacked him, and the ball fell over his shoulder like a gift. Fifty-one yards. The crowd detonated, the band blasting mid-run, the town shaking.

Marcus pounded his chest, pointing back at Aidan. Aidan lifted a fist, but his knees wobbled as he jogged downfield. Rivera's eyes tracked him from the sideline.

First and goal at the eight.

Coach sent in a run, but Aidan checked at the line—saw the linebackers crowding, the safeties flat. He audible'd to a fade.

"Back corner," he mouthed. Marcus nodded.

Snap. Plant. Throw.

Marcus leapt, toes brushing paint, snagging the ball over a corner's helmet. Touchdown.

Fifteen-nothing, Lincoln.

The stadium was pandemonium. The band, the cheerleaders, the entire student section losing itself. The chant: **QB1! QB1! QB1!**

But on the sideline, Aidan sat on the bench, helmet in his lap, bent forward, chest heaving. His ribs screamed, pain radiating like fire. Rivera knelt in front of him.

"Say it," she urged softly. "Say the word."

He shook his head, teeth clenched. "Not yet."

Rivera frowned but said nothing, scribbling notes furiously.

Riverton struck back with anger. A slant for ten, a sweep for seven, a trap play that gashed the line for sixteen. Their quarterback found rhythm, hitting his tight end up the seam. Lincoln bent, bent again, until at the twelve, Carter bulldozed in as a fullback. Touchdown. Fifteen-seven.

The momentum shifted.

Back and forth they went. Lincoln punted. Riverton drove, stalled, kicked a field goal. Fifteen-ten. The crowd tensed, the sideline buzzed with nerves.

End of the third quarter, Aidan huddled them up. Sweat poured down his face, his chest ached, his voice rough. But his eyes—his eyes still burned.

"One quarter left," he said. "Ours to take. Nobody steals it from us."

Marcus clapped his shoulder pads. "Let's finish the story."

The fourth began with Lincoln grinding. Outs, ins, mesh routes. Marcus, the tight end, the back—they all took their pieces. But Riverton was relentless. Carter hit again and again, even if the whistle blew early. Each time, Aidan stood, a little slower, a little stiffer. Each time, he looked at Coach, at Rivera, at his wrist, and shook his head.

Truth could wait.

At midfield, with six minutes left, the play came. Riverton disguised, safeties showing two but bailing. Aidan saw it. He tagged the post. Marcus cut sharp, splitting the safeties, hands rising.

Aidan launched. The ball arced, slicing the night, and dropped into Marcus's chest. He sprinted thirty yards before being dragged down at the five.

The stadium erupted, shaking. Aidan bent, hands on knees, gasping. His ribs were knives, his vision spotted. Rivera shouted from the sideline. Coach barked, "Sit him."

Aidan stood. Shook his head. Walked to the huddle.

"One more," he rasped. "We finish it."

The call: zone read.

The snap. Aidan saw Carter crash, yanking to the back. Aidan pulled. Kept. Cut inside.

The linebacker met him at the two, helmet smashing ribs, pain flaring white-hot. But Aidan lunged, stretching, ball over the line.

Touchdown.

The stadium exploded. The band blared. Marcus hauled him up, shouting his name, teammates pounding his helmet.

On the sideline, Rivera checked him, hands firm. "Truth, Aidan. Say it."

His chest heaved. His ribs screamed. But he looked at her, at Coach, at the crowd chanting his number.

"Not yet," he whispered.

The game ended minutes later. Lincoln 22, Riverton 17. The town roared as one. Players stormed the field. Marcus hugged him tight. Will lifted him off his feet. Cruz bellowed to the sky.

But Aidan's body told a different story. His ribs burned, his vision dimmed, his legs shook. He raised his fist weakly to the crowd, forcing a smile.

And then he sagged, trainers catching him, Coach shouting his name.

The roar of victory turned into gasps.

Friday night had given Lincoln glory. But it had taken something from Aidan, too.

Chapter Seventeen – The Aftermath

For a heartbeat, the stadium didn't understand what it was seeing. The scoreboard still glowed with the win, the band still blared, cheerleaders still kicked in a rhythm they'd practiced since summer. Then Aidan's body told the truth his mouth would not—his knees softened, the helmet dipped, and he folded toward the turf as if the night had finally collected its fee.

Ms. Rivera was already moving. Trainers cut through the wave of teammates, voices suddenly flat and precise. "Clear space. Helmets off. Water down." Coach Dempsey's whistle punched one slicing note, and the chaos parted. Riverton's noise died into that odd visiting silence when the story stops being about them.

Marcus got there first, crouched so close their facemasks nearly touched. "Hey. I'm here," he said, like it was a promise with teeth. Aidan's breath came thin and ragged. He tried to say *I'm fine* and heard, himself, the lie. Rivera's hands found his ribs with the gentleness of someone who knows exactly where it hurts.

"Talk to me," she said. "Pain, same spot?"

"Yeah," he managed. Heat radiated under the pads, a throbbing tide. The lights overhead felt louder.

"Pulse is fast," she said to the assistant at her shoulder. "Get the cart. And call ahead."

Coach knelt opposite Marcus, not touching, just close enough that Aidan could see his eyes. "Truth?"

Aidan's jaw trembled. He wanted to toss a joke, wanted to bark a call, wanted to pretend the world could be willed back into rhythm. Instead he exhaled, tasted metal, and nodded once. "Truth," he whispered.

Dempsey's hand settled at the back of his helmet, a touch that understood both weight and mercy. "That's my guy," he said, and his voice stayed even as his eyes went glassy.

Around them, the town relearned how to breathe. Karen came down the steps without feeling her feet, John carving a path for her with a shoulder that had moved through crowds his whole life. When she reached her son, she didn't cry; she put one palm on his cheek and said his name like a litany until his gaze found hers. John stood behind them both, one hand on Aidan's shoe like he could tether him there.

The cart arrived. Aidan took the ride because bravado had stepped off the field five minutes before he had. As they rolled, the student section tried to rally, teetering between fear and faith. The band's drums faltered, then steadied, then stopped entirely when the cart turned toward the tunnel.

In the locker room the sound was wrong—too loud in one corner, too quiet in another, metal complaining with every bench shift. Marcus held the door, then trailed close enough to be scolded and not far enough to listen. Rivera's orders layered: "Pads off. Small sips. Ice wrapped, not pressed. Somebody call Patel."

Coach became a traffic cop. He intercepted wide eyes at the threshold, collecting helmets with one hand and sending boys toward showers with the other. "Give the man room," he said. "Celebrate out there. In here, we work." He caught Cruz by the bicep when the linebacker shouldered through. "He's in hands that know him," the coach said, quiet but unarguable. "Your job is to keep the door."

Cruz planted himself like furniture. Will hovered at a distance, hands opening and closing as if he could catch the hit he missed. The sophomore who'd drifted too close in walk-throughs stared at his cleats and swore he would learn a new shape for Sunday.

On the training table, Aidan lay with his pads peeled away and a blanket thrown over his waist, the cold creeping in as adrenaline leaked out. His skin shone with the uneven sheen of a boy who'd been a man for two hours. Rivera slid a cuff up his arm and watched the needle settle. "You can hate me later," she said, already reaching for the line kit. "Right now your body gets a vote. IV in. Breathe with me."

He did, because he could not do much else. In through the nose, out through the mouth. The pain edged back from white to bright. The room found focus. Karen's hand found his, the thumb-rub she had used on fevers and report cards alike. John stepped away to take a call and came back with his face set: the ambulance was coming the smart way, not the screaming way.

Dempsey crowded the head of the table and leaned until he was almost in the fluorescent lights. "Listen," he said to Rivera, but looking at Aidan. "If the hospital wants him monitored overnight, I'm there with donuts at dawn. If Patel says jump, we jump. If he says play—" He stopped. He wouldn't lie in a room full of truth. "We don't decide that tonight."

From somewhere deep in his chest, Aidan pulled a nod. "Biopsy," he said, the word chalk-dry on his tongue.

"Wednesday," Karen said, and the date sounded like a wall they could see but not climb yet. "We'll be ready."

Sirens did not wail; the ambulance arrived with the hush of the end of a parade. The EMTs moved with that particular mix of speed and boredom practiced on ten thousand calm emergencies. "Evening, folks," one said, and Aidan could have hugged him for the way he made it sound like a table at the diner. They slid him to their stretcher, counted together, lifted, turned.

"Do I ride?" Karen asked, already stepping forward.

"One parent," the EMT said, gentle but firm. John touched her elbow. "Go," he said. "I'll bring the car. Coach?"

"I'm right behind you," Dempsey said. "Marcus—"

"I'm coming," Marcus said, and then realized he'd said it out loud. He looked to Karen, to Coach, to the EMT whose answer would decide which parts of him stayed a boy and which grew up tonight.

"Lobby," the EMT said. "You'll beat us there anyway."

On the way out, the cart path had never felt longer. The locker room clap followed—palms on metal, on pads, on each other—a rhythm less like celebration and more like benediction. Cruz kept his post. Will said a soft sentence Aidan could not hear and would replay later without ever catching the words. A student manager pressed a folded towel into Karen's hand and said, "In case," because she was seventeen and nobody had trained her in the language for this but kindness.

The ambulance ceiling was a rectangle of white broken by vents and a jittery light. Karen sat at Aidan's shoulder and counted the streets without looking. The EMT checked vitals and slid questions in between bumps. "Pain scale?"

"It's football," Aidan said, which wasn't an answer and was exactly one.

"You're a funny one." The EMT tightened a strap and didn't argue. "You play the position?"

"Quarterback."

"Figures," he said, as if that explained everything—from the stubborn to the soft to the way the mother never took her hand away.

The emergency department knew them by now. A nurse with tired eyes smiled because she recognized the boy and because she hated that she did. They tucked him behind a curtain and the monitor took up that maddening beeping like an old habit. The pain meds moved in and smoothed the edges. The ceiling tile became the sky if he let it. He did not let it.

Dr. Patel arrived fast for a man with a service to run on a Friday night. He had his white coat on but his tie askew; he'd been working and would continue to. "I heard," he said, and squeezed Aidan's shoulder above the tape so it wouldn't hurt. "Let's take a look."

He asked questions the way good coaches diagram plays: one leading to the next. "Same pain? New pain? Breathing? Dizziness? Nausea? Did you pass out or choose the floor?" Aidan answered in the short form athletes prefer. Patel nodded, listening to the lungs, the heart, the story under the story.

"Good news," he said at last, translating. "No red flags right now. It looks like pain and fatigue and a body that is asking for mercy you did not grant." He let the humor sit. "The mass hasn't changed its mind about being there. The biopsy remains the next right thing. Tonight we manage pain, hydrate, watch."

Karen's eyes closed and held there like the last bit of prayer she had left. John arrived, breathless, having parked illegally in an act of civil disobedience he'd never attempted until now. He listened from just inside the curtain and looked like a man who had been told the bridge would hold for one more truck.

Coach hovered at the opening, big enough to block a view, small enough to make room for the family. He didn't step in until Patel stepped out, and then he slid into the chair beside Aidan like he'd been assigned it years ago. He set his cap on his knees and rolled the bill in his hands.

"I told them at midfield you're fine," he said, which could have been bravado if he hadn't added, soft, "and I meant it in the way that matters tonight." He sniffed, once, a sound that wasn't quite a laugh. "Defense took a picture with the band because they couldn't figure out what to do with their hands."

Aidan's eyelids slowed and lifted, fighting the warm drag of the meds. "We win?" he asked, because for a second the scoreboard in his head had been replaced by a ceiling tile.

Coach leaned in. "We did," he said. "Because you kept choosing boring beautiful and because a whole town remembered how to breathe when you asked it to."

Marcus slid in behind him, bouncing on his toes as if the floor might change its mind about holding him. "I told you," he said, pointing at Aidan's taped wrist, "if the corner sat, I was gone."

"You were gone," Aidan murmured. "Twice."

"And you threw it before I was open. Like always," Marcus said, and the grin cracked and the shine at his lashes threatened to slip. He coughed it back. "Coach says I can be loud in the lobby but not in here."

"Lobby needs you loud," Coach said, not turning. "Keep our boys from posting idiocy. Tell them we are not a rumor mill." Then, softer to Aidan: "Some folks outside want to know if they should light candles or barbecue. I told them to pray with their feet—go home, rest their voices, show up next week with lungs and love."

Patel returned with a nurse and a plan scribbled in a doctor's hand—orders that made sense to the staff and looked like a foreign alphabet to everyone else. "A couple of hours for fluids and pain control," he said. "If he stays stable, I'd rather you sleep in your own beds. Or attempt to." He glanced at Karen. "We can give him something gentle for that, too."

Karen nodded like a person who would decline the pill and watch her son breathe instead. John kissed her temple, a small public act that made Aidan's throat pinch in a new way.

There was a pause, the kind that only families and teams know how to fill. Coach stood to go because he understood about exits. He put a hand on Aidan's forearm, careful of tape, careful of lines. "You said it," he murmured. "That word." He swallowed. "That's a captain's thing."

"Felt like losing," Aidan whispered.

"It was winning," Coach said. "Don't confuse loud with brave."

When he left, Marcus took the chair, then gave it to Karen, then paced, then stopped, then dug in his pocket and pulled out something small and ridiculous—one of the rubber bands the team used to mark who had eaten pregame. He slipped it over Aidan's fingers like a kid swapping friendship bracelets. "For luck," he said, shamefaced, then lifted his chin as if daring anyone to make fun of a ritual that worked when nothing else did. "Text me when they cut you loose. I'll drive behind you like a secret service agent."

"You don't have a car," John said.

"I have a bike," Marcus countered. "And questionable judgment." He looked at Karen. "I'll ride slow, ma'am."

She almost smiled. "Thank you."

The room dimmed when the nurse hit the light to a softer level. IV dripped, machines hummed, the curtain breathed in and out when someone rushed past. The adrenaline that had held Aidan rigid all night dissolved. Pain receded to an ache he could catalog. The win took on the shape it would hold in memory: not the number on the board, but the way the huddle felt when everyone knew the same thing and decided to do it together.

His phone buzzed: a short message from a number not in his contacts.

I was there. You don't know me, not really. But you were so very brave in a way that didn't look like the movies. — E.

He stared at the letter, at the neatness of it, at the way she didn't say *quarterback* or *legend* or anything the town said when its mouth got big. He didn't write back. He tucked the phone under the blanket and let the quiet hold him.

Sometime near morning, Patel returned and nodded at the numbers in the chart like a coach nodding at a practice script. "All right," he said. "Let's send you home. We'll see you early next week. Rest. Hydrate. No heroics." He added, almost smiling, "I hear you've gotten good at that."

Aidan didn't argue. He watched the nurse pull the tape and the line, the small sting that said the night was ending. He dressed in the slow choreography of a boy with new bruises. Karen gathered papers like a librarian restoring order. John signed something and clipped a wristband free.

In the lobby, a few teammates had fallen asleep in chairs, heads tipped back, mouths open, a tableau of loyalty and poor choices. Marcus roused them with a whisper and a grin and a shove. They stood and tried to make their faces look like nothing had happened.

Outside, the air had rinsed itself. The stadium lights on the hill were dark now, the bleachers a silhouette against a sky thinking about dawn. Aidan paused on the curb and filled his lungs careful as a man counting china. Each breath arrived and left. Each one was a play he didn't have to call.

He slid into the car. Karen looked back twice before shutting her door. John checked his mirrors like there were more lanes to see than the road offered. They pulled away. Marcus pedaled behind them, ridiculous and steadfast, a blinking red light marking his promise.

At the corner where you could see the field if you craned your neck, Aidan did not look. He watched the traffic signal change and thought instead of the whiteboard in Coach's office and the word written in block letters that had become a rope he could hold. He pressed his thumb to the crease of the tape on his wrist, even though the letters had smudged, and felt for the shape of the thing he'd learned tonight.

Not invincibility. Not glory. Not even victory.

Truth.

Chapter Eighteen – The Diagnosis

The waiting room was too bright for the kind of news they had come to hear. It smelled faintly of burnt coffee and plastic flowers. Karen sat with her hands folded in her lap, knuckles white, lips moving in a silent prayer. John leaned forward in his chair, elbows on his knees, staring at a patch of floor like it could offer him answers.

Aidan sat between them, hoodie pulled over his head, earbuds in without music. He didn't want noise. He wanted the world muted, waiting with him. His ribs ached like they always did now, but the pain was background compared to the hammering in his chest.

He thought about football plays to distract himself. Second and seven, Riverton in man, safety cheating down—mesh beats it every time. He pictured Marcus cutting across the field, the ball landing just ahead of his hands. He replayed touchdowns, the chants of the crowd, the glow of the lights. He clung to it like film he could rewind.

"McAllister?" The nurse's voice cut through the waiting room.

Karen's hands trembled as she reached for his. John stood, steadying them both with a hand at the small of Karen's back. Aidan pushed his hood down and followed, his legs heavy, each step a countdown.

Dr. Patel's office was small, lined with shelves of medical books and framed photos of his own family. A soft lamp on the desk tried to make the room feel less like what it was. Patel stood as they entered, offering a smile that was kind but solemn.

"Please," he said, gesturing to the chairs. "Sit."

They did. The silence stretched as Patel opened a folder. Aidan stared at the man's hands, the way they moved carefully, deliberately, as if the act of turning a page could change the weight of what it carried.

Patel looked up. "The biopsy confirmed what we suspected. Aidan, you have a type of sarcoma. It's a rare cancer that develops in the soft tissue, in your case near the ribcage."

Karen's breath caught. John's hand closed into a fist.

Aidan's ears buzzed. The word *cancer* sat in the room like a living thing, crowding out air. He tried to hold it, tried to understand it, but it slipped through him like water through fingers.

"What does that mean?" Karen whispered.

Patel's voice was steady. "It means the mass is malignant. It is cancerous. The good news is that we found it earlier than most, because of the scans after your injury. That gives us options."

"Options," John repeated, the word heavy.

Patel nodded. "Treatment will likely involve chemotherapy. Possibly radiation. Depending on how it responds, we may recommend surgery to remove the mass. It's not an easy road, but it is a road."

Karen covered her mouth with her hands. Tears spilled freely now, hot and unchecked. John reached for her, his own eyes wet though he held them back.

Aidan sat still, staring at the folder on the desk. His mind replayed a single word: *malignant.* He knew the dictionary definition. He'd looked it up on his phone late one night when he couldn't sleep. But hearing it spoken, hearing it tied to his name—it was different.

"How long?" His voice cracked, thin and raw.

Patel's gaze softened. "Every patient responds differently. With aggressive treatment, many live long lives. But untreated..." He hesitated, searching for the line between honesty and cruelty. "It would progress quickly."

Karen sobbed. John rubbed his face with both hands. Aidan swallowed hard, ribs aching with the effort.

"So I can't play," he said flatly.

Patel's brow furrowed. "Aidan—"

"I can't play," he repeated, louder this time, as if saying it twice would make it real.

Karen reached for him, but he pulled back, shaking his head. "That's what you're saying, right? No football. No season."

Patel leaned forward. "I'm saying your health comes first. The risk of physical contact, of further injury—it could complicate treatment, even accelerate the damage."

Aidan's chest tightened. He pictured the field, the roar of the crowd, the taste of victory just a week ago. He pictured Marcus, Will, Cruz, the team rallying in the huddle. He pictured the state championship banner they all dreamed of. And then he pictured himself watching from the stands, powerless, forgotten.

"No," he said quietly.

Karen looked at him, startled. "Aidan—"

"No," he repeated, stronger. He met Patel's eyes, defiance burning through the fear. "I'm finishing the season."

Patel sighed, leaning back in his chair. "Aidan—"

"You don't get it," Aidan snapped. His voice cracked with fury and pain. "This is my last year. My last chance. If I stop now, if I just… quit, then what was all of it for? The practices, the hits, the late nights, the dreams? I can't just sit in a hospital bed while my team fights without me."

Karen shook her head, tears streaming. "Honey, please—"

"Mom," Aidan said, his own eyes wet now. "I have to. If this thing is going to kill me, it doesn't get to take football from me too. Not yet."

John's throat worked, words stuck. He looked from his son to his wife, torn down the middle.

Patel was quiet for a long moment. Finally, he said, "It's not the choice I'd recommend. But if you are determined, then we need to be careful. Very careful. We will monitor you closely. The moment your body says stop, you stop. No exceptions."

Aidan nodded fiercely. "Deal."

Karen broke then, sobbing into John's shoulder. John held her, eyes glistening, but when he looked at Aidan, there was a flicker of pride under the grief.

Patel closed the folder gently. "We'll start treatment as soon as the season ends. That's the compromise." He paused. "But Aidan—you must understand. The risks are real."

"I understand," Aidan said, though he didn't, not fully. He only understood one thing: Friday nights were still his.

As they left Patel's office, the hallway seemed longer than before. Karen clung to John, her steps shaky. Aidan walked ahead, jaw set, fists clenched.

In the parking lot, the evening sun cast long shadows. Aidan tilted his head back, staring at the sky. He felt small under it, smaller than ever. But inside, fire burned.

He whispered to himself, words only he could hear.

"Fourth and forever. That's what it is now. And I'm not punting."

Chapter Nineteen – Breaking the News to the Team

Coach Dempsey called it a players-only meeting, which in Lincoln meant exactly what it sounded like until it didn't. After practice the next day, when the last period bell had shaken its chalk dust loose and the sun slanted through the east windows of the field house, he blew his whistle and didn't say a word. The locker room quieted the way a church does when someone stands.

"Helmets on the hooks," he said finally. "Phones in the bucket." He pointed to a blue milk crate by the door. "All of them. Airplane mode when you get them back."

The boys grumbled and obeyed, one by one dropping rectangles of light into plastic. Marcus, already near the bucket, clanked his in first and gave the room a look that said *follow me*. They did. Cruz shrugged and emptied his pockets like he didn't much care for a world with or without phones. Will slid his phone in with a frown, then smirked when the sophomore next to him tried to tuck his under a towel and got caught by Coach's eyes.

Aidan waited by his locker, helmet hanging from two fingers, the red practice jersey draped over a knee like a flag. Ms. Rivera stood in the doorway and didn't enter, hands on hips, a silent crease between her brows. Karen had wanted to be here; Coach had said no, gently. John had said *this is their room*, and Karen had nodded while clutching the kitchen counter as if it were a rail on a ship.

When the bucket clicked full, Dempsey closed the door. He didn't stand on a bench or clear his throat or roll his toothpick. He just said, "Captains."

Will and Cruz moved first, taking positions on either side of Aidan and Marcus, making a small shape in the room that said *this is the center*. The rest formed a rough circle, some boys sitting on benches, some on the floor, backs against lockers. The old stereo squawked and was silenced. You could hear the soda machine hum in the equipment room.

Coach set his palm on the whiteboard, like he could ground the room by touching it. "There's something you need to hear," he said. "You're going to hear it from us, and you're going to hold it like you hold each other in a huddle. You will not make it a post. You will not make it a rumor. You will make it part of the way you work."

He looked at Aidan. He did not make a speech for him. He nodded once, and in that nod were all the hours on film, all the yes-sirs and no-excuses and the one small word that had remade a week.

Aidan stood. The red jersey on his knee slipped a little; he caught it and set it aside. He didn't climb, either. He stayed level with them, shoved his hands into the waistband of his shorts because they wouldn't keep still, and said, "I'm going to say this once, and then we can talk about football again."

The room shifted forward half an inch.

"I've got cancer," he said.

The word hit the tile and stayed there. For a second nobody breathed. Then a sound escaped someone's throat—small, involuntary—and the room exhaled in a hundred different ways: groans, swears, one whispered *no* that could have been anybody's mother.

Aidan kept going because if he didn't, he wouldn't. "It's in the soft tissue by my ribs. We found it because of the hit in the first game. We did the biopsy; we got the results." He looked at the floor and then back up. "It's real."

He waited for panic but got stillness instead, a kind of listening that pressed on his skin.

"I asked to finish the season," he said. "My parents said yes. Coach said yes if we follow rules. Treatment starts after. That's the deal." He lifted his left hand and flexed his taped wrist until the inside showed, the faint letters he'd written bleeding through the weave. "We made a word. You know it. If I say it, I sit. If Coach says it, I sit. No questions."

Marcus leaned his shoulder into Aidan's. It wasn't a dramatic lean. It was the kind you do when two people have carried something heavy up a set of stairs and need a second at the landing.

Coach turned to the whiteboard and wrote **TRUTH = RESPECT** in block letters that looked like he'd drawn them with a level. Underneath, smaller, he wrote **NO FREE DOUBT**. He capped the marker and faced the boys. "He's still your quarterback," he said. "Your job didn't change. It got clearer."

A hand lifted hesitantly near the lockers. It belonged to Jamal, the return man with fast feet and a slow smile. "Coach... what do we do? Like... besides block longer and shut up about it."

"You protect him," Cruz said before the coach could answer, his voice flat as a rule. "With your bodies, with your brains, with your mouths. You don't let a man in your gap and you don't let a leak out of your phone."

Will nodded. "You keep your feet right and your eyes right. That's it. That's everything."

A sophomore, the same one who had learned about red jerseys the hard way, swallowed. "Is... is he going to die?" The room reacted— groans, a *hey man*—but the kid's face was naked. He could not put the word away after hearing it once.

Aidan spared him the walk back from it. "Everybody dies," he said, and the corner of his mouth flicked because he couldn't help himself, because he was seventeen and stubborn. "I'm not planning it for this fall."

Laughter broke something that had needed breaking. It wasn't loud; it was enough.

Ms. Rivera cleared her throat in the doorway. "Since we're doing truth," she said, stepping in now, clipboard hugged to her chest like a shield, "here's some more. He checks in with me every morning and after practice. If I say he sits, he sits. If I say no contact, that doesn't mean *little contact*. It means zero. If anyone tests that, you run until your legs file a complaint. If he says the word, you treat it like a snap count—everyone moves to the next thing. You will not hover over him like bees."

"Thank you, Ms. Rivera," Dempsey said, and a few boys smiled at her rank in the room, which was not on the depth chart but was higher than any of them.

Another hand. Cruz again, but this time he didn't wait to be called. "We need a code," he said. "For the field. In case he needs space without making a sermon out of it."

Coach pointed with his chin. "Make one."

Cruz thought for exactly one second. "Blue two," he said. "Means we slow it down, huddle, get a sub ready, get the play in with the clock like we own it. Means we buy him a breath without blinking."

"Blue two," Will repeated, rolling it around like he could memorize it by taste. "Got it."

Aidan nodded. "Blue two."

Someone near the back—Micah, the kicker with a mop of hair and a good heart—raised his hand halfway and then spoke anyway. "Uh, my uncle had it. Not the same kind. We, um… we shaved our heads as a family. For him." He looked like a boy asking permission to touch a live wire. "We could... I don't know... we could do something. For you. If you want."

Aidan pictured the hallway at school, the photographs, the way eyes did the math of pity. "Maybe later," he said, as gently as he could. "Let's play first."

Micah nodded and looked relieved, like he'd been prepared to start buzzing boys in the shower room that second and didn't really want to.

Coach held up a hand. "What he needs is what we've been doing. Boring beautiful. You want to honor him? Win first down. No free yards. No free doubt." He let the words sit. "Also: some people will find out. Parents, teachers, folks who need to know how to move around him. You keep it off the internet. If I see screenshots, we'll find out who, and you will wish my cussing was the worst of your day."

Marcus finally spoke, his voice low and steady. "Some of you are going to be scared. That's normal. Some of you are going to want to turn every play into a tribute. That's not helpful." He looked around until he found each set of eyes. "We do our jobs. That's how we carry him. That's how he carries us."

"Say it again," Will said, and Marcus did, and then someone else did, and soon it didn't sound like a command but like a thing they remembered.

Aidan took a breath. It hurt. He took another. It still hurt. He talked anyway. "I'm not going to be who I was in August," he said. "Not every snap. I'm going to get tired sooner. I'm going to look at Coach and Ms. Rivera more than you want me to. I might say the word you hate and sit. When I do, you don't make it a story. You make it a series. Next man. Next call. Next thing."

He found Jamal again. "And if I throw a ball you can only catch with a miracle, do your job." Jamal grinned, eyes bright. "Yes, sir."

Cruz slapped the top of a locker with an open palm. "Who are we?"

"Brothers," the room answered, softer than usual but deeper.

"Who do we protect?"

"The man to our left and right."

"Who are we?"

"Lincoln."

It wasn't loud. It didn't have to be.

They broke and it didn't feel like a break so much as a rearrangement. Boys drifted by Aidan one at a time, quicker than hugs and longer than a nod. Will pressed his forehead to Aidan's for a half second and said, "No free rushers." Jamal bumped him lightly with a fist and said, "You throw it, I'll find a way." Micah said nothing and handed him a Gatorade he didn't want and then looked relieved when Aidan took a sip because it gave them both a thing to do.

When the room thinned to captains and Coach and Rivera, the air changed. The door opened; you could hear the weight room again, the clank of plates, boys trying to make themselves into something that could carry more. Dempsey sank onto the bench like he'd only just now admitted he needed to sit. He blew out a breath and looked at Aidan without the middleman of a team.

"Proud of you," he said simply.

Aidan shrugged one shoulder because he couldn't shrug the night. "They asked if I was going to die."

"They asked the right man," Coach said. "You gave them the right answer."

Rivera stacked her clipboard on an overturned bucket and said, "You did more than that." She pulled a small roll of different tape from her pocket—black instead of white—and handed it to him. "For your wrist next game. If you don't want people to read the word, write it where only you can feel it. Sometimes that's enough."

He took it, thumb smoothing the edge. "Thanks."

"Don't thank me," she said, and almost smiled. "Eat. Hydrate. Sleep." She looked at Coach. "He needs out of here in ten."

"Go," Dempsey said, waving them toward the door. "Home. Family. Homework. Whatever keeps you from becoming a statue."

Marcus slung his bag over a shoulder and jerked his head toward the exit. "Come on."

In the hallway, where the wall bore the photographs of boys who had been them in other years, they slowed. Fluorescents hummed, a custodial cart squeaked. Somebody had left a practice script taped crooked to a door. The edges curled.

"A bunch of them are going to cry later," Marcus said without judgment. "Cruz won't, but he'll buy somebody a burger and not mention it."

"Will probably already texted the line group chat: if anyone misses a lift, he'll eat them," Aidan said.

"Accurate." Marcus shoved him with his shoulder, gentle. "You okay?"

"No." Aidan thought about making it a joke. He didn't. "But I will be on Friday."

"That counts," Marcus said.

They stepped into the evening. The sky had gone that flat Midwestern gray that sometimes meant rain and sometimes just meant you couldn't see the stars tonight. A breeze pushed the flags on the visitors' side a little. From the field, you could hear a pair of sophomores running routes on air, their voices high and earnest, the ball making that pleasing thup in good hands.

In the lot, Karen waited with the car. John leaned against the hood like he had in college, the posture of a man who hadn't yet figured out how to hold his hands in a world where the boys he loved were telling hard truths. Marcus veered toward his own ride, a hand-me-down sedan that coughed on cold mornings, then turned back.

"Hey," he said. "Before you forget: Emily gave me something for you." He reached into his backpack and produced a folded page, lined and torn from a notebook, her tight printing marching straight. He held it out and then pulled it back a fraction. "You want it?"

Aidan's gut tightened in a way that had nothing to do with ribs. "Yeah."

Marcus gave it over like he was handing off a reverse. "She said no pressure. Also she said she doesn't know football but she knows narratives, which felt like a threat."

Aidan laughed, quick and surprised. He didn't open the note right there. He slid it into his wallet with the index card she'd drawn on, both pieces settling against the leather like ballast.

At home, after Rivera's demanded plate of food and a shower that stung the places tape had left behind, he sat at his desk and finally unfolded the paper. It was not a speech. It was a list.

Things you can control:

— How you breathe before the snap.

— Whether you say your word when you need it.

— Who you trust with the space between plays.

— Writing down the small things so you don't forget your own life when other people ask for the big headline.

At the bottom, in smaller letters: *I'll be in the stands. I don't know how to cheer right. I'll learn. — E.*

He read it twice, then set it under the lamp. He wrapped his wrist in the black tape Rivera had given him, the letters pressed invisible into the underside, and sat for a minute with his palm against the desk, feeling the word without showing it to anyone.

The phone buzzed once. The captains' group chat, Will's name at the top.

Will: *Blue two is in. We're locked. No leaks. No free rushers. No free doubt.*

Cruz: *We hit first. We hit last.*

Marcus: *We breathe together.*

Aidan typed slowly.

Aidan: *Truth, when I need it. Friday, we play our brand.*

He set the phone face down. The house made its normal sounds—dishwasher, weather, his mother moving in the kitchen like she and time had to be in the same room or one of them would go wrong. He sat with the weight and the lightness, with the thing that had found him and the things he had chosen, with a team that now knew and had not run.

In the dark of his room, when the quiet reached the place where it could hold him, he spoke the word one more time, not to sit out a series, but to name what the next weeks would ask.

Truth.

He let the air out and felt, in the emptiness it left, enough space for Friday.

Chapter Twenty –
The Return to Friday

By the time the bus turned down Laurel Avenue, Friday had already taken the town by the shoulders. Lawn chairs staked out places along the chain-link, grills smoked behind pickup beds, and kids in blue hoodies chased each other in surges that moved like fish under a dock. From the back row, Aidan watched it all pass the windows and felt the familiar pinch under his ribs. It wasn't fear. It wasn't quite pain. It was the knowledge that the lights were about to do what they always did: tell the truth of a week.

Northfield wasn't Riverton—less swagger, more system. On film they'd shown a lot of quarters, patient corners, linebackers who stayed married to their keys even when the ball flirted elsewhere. Coach had said they were a mirror: "They'd rather cut you with paper than punch you in the mouth." Paper could bleed you out just the same.

The bus door sighed and the boys spilled into the tunnel, the way they always had, except not. Every pair of eyes in the locker room now knew what lived under the tape at Aidan's ribs. The secret wasn't a secret to them anymore; it had become shape, rule, rhythm. Truth meant sit. Blue two meant space. No free doubt meant you set your feet and did the next thing right, and the next, and the next.

He pulled the game jersey on—blue, heavy, the number trimmed in white that glowed even under the fluorescent hum. At his locker, he unrolled the strip of black tape Ms. Rivera had slipped him after the team meeting and pressed it against his left wrist. The letters he wrote there were for him alone now; the word became texture under skin.

Marcus dropped onto the bench, helmet in his lap, tapping the crown with two fingers like a drummer warming up. "They show two high, I'm eating curls," he said. "Single, I'm gone. You pick."

"We'll take the grass until they beg us not to," Aidan said. "Make boring look beautiful."

"Coach poetry," Marcus said, mock solemn, then checked his laces anyway.

Out at the numbers, Northfield's band tuned with the distracted authority of people who'd played the same charts for a decade. The Greyhounds warmed up in tidy lines. The captains met for the toss, gripped palms that had no right to be this cold in October, and watched a coin flash, disappear, and decide. Northfield deferred. Lincoln would have the ball first. The student section barked their usual nonsense. It landed differently in Aidan's chest tonight—lighter, somehow, because it wasn't everything.

Karen and John found their seats—farther down than usual, closer to the rail. John carried two hot chocolates and a pocket full of plans. Karen carried a knot behind her sternum and tried not to braid it into every breath. Two rows up, Emily Hart wedged between a pair of marching band parents and hugged her notebook like a life preserver. She didn't wear face paint. She didn't need the armor.

The kickoff tumbled and settled into Jamal's arms at the four. He knifed up the hash to the twenty-six, got grabbed by a jersey that should have been a flag and wasn't, and flopped onto the paint with a grin like he'd planned it. Offense jogged. Aidan rubbed his thumb across the ridge of his wrist tape and brought them in.

"Trips right," he said, just like always. "Sixty-two. Eyes up. Tempo."

Northfield showed quarters on the first snap, safeties reading his shoulders, backers at five yards with their chests squared like teachers

116

at the front of a classroom. The ball came up, came out. Out route for seven. The band's drumline didn't bother to cheer. Boring football didn't impress drums.

Second and three. Duo into a light box—four became six when the back fell right. First down. Will's hands were easy and mean, his feet quiet. On the next snap, Northfield thieved a slant with a nose tackle swim that looked too pretty for a boy that size. Second and twelve. Aidan checked to stick, hit the tight end on his outside shoulder, set up third and manageable. Then mesh—Marcus drifting and settling in the shadow of the umpire, the ball floating into his chest like an apology for what patience costs. Move the chains.

The drive ate turf and time. Out. Draw. Curl. Sneak. The crowd murmured as if they'd wandered into a library by mistake. At the eighteen, the field compressed. Northfield squeezed the red zone like a throat, bracketed Marcus with a nickel and a safety, and dared somebody else to matter. Aidan took the dare. He found the tight end on a leak into the flat. Six. Another leak. Three. Third and short turned into a run that went nowhere. Field goal. Three-nothing isn't a song anyone sings, but the scoreboard blinked the number, and the band honored it with a bar out of respect.

Back on the sideline, Ms. Rivera appeared to his left hand like she'd been manufacturing herself out of steam. "Rate?"

"Eighty," he said. She didn't write it. She made him say it again without looking at his watch. "Eighty-two," he corrected. She arched a brow and scribbled. "Salt," she said, and he obeyed.

Cruz and the defense worked with their own kind of patience. Northfield loved split zones and bubbles that made you tackle in space. The first series gave them exactly that—three clean stops, a punt that rolled like a guilty conscience to the Lincoln thirty. Second series, the Greyhounds found a crack on a trap that gassed ten. Then Cruz engaged a gear that looked like anger and was really faith: fill, shock, shed, stuff. Third and six, the quarterback tried to roll away from his own limitations. Cruz ran him into the boundary and made him remember the fence line.

End of one: three-nothing. The student section booed boredom out of habit. Dempsey saluted boredom like an old friend.

Between quarters, Aidan rolled his shoulder and found the tug under his ribs running a little tighter than he wanted to admit. He glanced at the sideline. Coach stared at the field like it owed him money. Ms. Rivera's eyes made that little squint she did when a boy's mouth and his pulse did not tell the same story. He shook out the feeling and let it be named later.

Start of the second, Northfield walked a safety down and dared Lincoln to remember it had legs. Aidan tagged a zone read with a keep that existed only if the end crashed. The end did. Aidan pulled and slid before the backer could turn him into a motivational poster. Booing from the kids who wanted more blood. A small nod from Coach. Marcus clapped once, hard.

Two plays later, the Greyhounds blinked the wrong way. The boundary corner's weight edged inside just enough for Aidan to recognize pride disguised as leverage. He wanted the hole shot like a kid wants sugar. He checked grass instead. Three yards. The student section sang something obscene to the math. Aidan smiled inside his helmet and counted it as a win.

They crossed midfield on small bites and one audacious little wheel to the back that lifted the student section enough to remind them why they'd come. Red zone again. Stuck again. Nine-nothing when Micah banged it clean.

Northfield answered with their only swagger of the night: a double-move that turned Jamal around and drew breath from the stadium like a siphon. Forty-one yards and a dead silence that made the concession stand refrigerators loud. The Greyhounds finished the drive with a naked boot that fooled nobody and still worked. Nine-seven after the kick clanged in.

On the next series, the pocket squeezed. Somebody missed. Somebody else missed in a better way. Carter had worn number fifty-two the week before for Riverton; Northfield's version wore forty-four and lacked the violence but not the geometry. He ducked under Will, got a finger on Aidan's hip, and pulled. The turf came up fast. The pain came old and new. He lay there long enough for Ms. Rivera to take two steps and for the crowd to take none.

He rolled, breathed, pressed his mouthguard against his molars until plastic tasted like citrus. He stood. He nodded at Coach. He found Marcus's eyes. The hand signal came without drama—index and middle finger together, tapping the thigh.

Blue two.

The offense huddled. The play clock slowed because it had been asked to. They repeated a concept with different people in different spaces and stole six yards the way thieves do it in daylight. The next play, screens left then right, marionetting linebackers into grass they hadn't planned to stand in. Cruz, from the defensive huddle on the sideline, barked the cadence along as if he could will air into Aidan's chest. Ms. Rivera put her clipboard down and didn't touch him because the rules said don't, and because sometimes care is a thing you do at the speed of trust.

Two snaps later, third and eight. Time for an answer. Aidan wore the same face he wore in algebra when he didn't want Mr. Tanner to see the panic. He took the snap, felt the pocket, moved without bragging about it, and threw a dig that shouldn't exist against quarters when a backer has done his homework. It existed anyway because the ball said so and Marcus's hands co-signed. First down. The crowd stood without knowing why they'd stood.

Two plays after that, they finally lied to Northfield at the right speed: sail concept away from a safety who'd been disciplined since August. Marcus sold the post so clean the corner sent a thank-you note. The ball arced to the sideline at twelve yards deeper than it had any right to be. Toe-tap. Whisper of rubber. Six. The band found a melody. The clock found mercy. Halftime wandered in with a 16–7 lead and the scent of popcorn grease.

In the tunnel, Coach caught Aidan by the elbow and ran a finger along the edge of his wrist tape as if he could read the word through his skin. "You call it, I answer it," he said, quietly. Aidan nodded and was grateful not to be told he looked pale.

Halftime was orange slices that tasted like church, a quick scalding rinse of water, Cruz cussing only in nouns, Will promising violence with a voice so low it could pass for a prayer. Ms. Rivera had him drink a bottle that insisted it was fruit and was only salt. He swallowed and felt his stomach threaten a revolt. He loved her enough to keep it in.

Northfield came out of the break with script and stubborn. Bubble, bubble, a slant that finished angry. Third and short, they took a shot at the boundary over Jamal's head because they'd watched film, too. Overthrown by two feet and the whole town added those two feet to the list of mercies it would name at bedtime. Field goal. 16–10.

Lincoln's next drive was the beginning of something you don't write about in the paper but remember anyway. Four plays, three of them for four yards and one of them for two. The crowd died of impatience and lived of relief. The student section tried to chant and failed. The line stayed where it should. The backs slipped where they weren't expected. The throw always arrived two beats before a hit that never got there. A drive like that isn't bravery. It's remembering you can be boring and still be right.

Midway through the third, Aidan felt the floor move under him. It was nothing. It was everything. The world went a half-step to the left and then politely righted. He blinked. On the next play he forgot which foot started his drop and recovered with a hitch that made Coach's toothpick do a small, unhappy wag. Ms. Rivera took a step into the white. He looked over, and for the first time that night, he didn't nod back.

He looked at Marcus instead and said it—soft, so soft only a huddle could hear.

"Truth."

Marcus didn't flinch. He clapped his hands and yelled "Blue two!" with a grin so big the defense probably figured he was lying. Dempsey subbed from the sideline without making it theater. Eli Torres—quiet sophomore, good legs, hands that trembled when he signed the phone bucket sheet the first week of August—sprinted in with eyes doubling as headlights.

Aidan put the ball in Eli's stomach and the word in his ear. "You've had this all week," he said. He meant it. Eli nodded like he'd been waiting to be told that and not waiting to be asked to be somebody else. The snap came. Aidan jogged to the sideline without dragging his feet and took the paper cup Ms. Rivera had waiting like she'd conjured it.

Eli handed off twice, threw once for three to a tight end who looked astonished and then embarrassed about his astonishment. Third and short turned into a sneak that didn't need an adult. First down. The sideline didn't hold its breath. It breathed like a person who'd practiced.

Two snaps later, Aidan returned, felt his legs like forgiveness, and finished the series with two throws that would never make a reel and will live in Will's memory as holy. The drive stalled at the thirteen and Micah chipped it. 19–10. The band played, not tentative anymore.

Northfield scored once more before the night would let them stop—too many bubbles and then a post that arrived in the only place a ball can be thrown when a safety tries to be everywhere. 19–17. The crowd discovered a second voice, lower, less choir and more engine.

Four minutes left. The ball at Lincoln's twenty-seven. Aidan huddled them, his breath a metronome that took effort to set. "No time travel," he said. "We stay here. Grass, grass, grass."

First down: duo for four. Second: stick for five. Third and one: a hard count that nobody bought and a sneak that dared them to find the spot under a pile of knees. First down. Northfield burned a timeout and tried to borrow momentum from the official's hands. It didn't work.

Two plays later, second and nine, the corner finally took the bait he'd been too disciplined to taste. Marcus didn't even flash a look this time. Aidan did. The call came in with the slightest tap of a finger across the facemask. The hitch looked like a hitch. The go looked inevitable relative to it. Aidan threw it from a pocket that Will had cut out of stone. The ball fell over a hand that would forever be convinced it had touched it. Thirty-six yards. The stadium turned lightheaded and then remembered to stand.

They didn't get greedy. Draw for two. A screen that tore six out of a defense that thought it had learned. Third and two on the Northfield twenty. The stands shook and begged for a kill. Coach tapped his wrist. Two-minute planet. The call in Aidan's helmet said *win first down; win the game.* They did, with a slant that asked for less and got exactly what it asked for.

Northfield spent their last timeout. Aidan leaned his helmet against Marcus's for half a second because the world was loud and he liked the feel of the plastic cooling his skin. "One more," he said. "Make it hurt."

They trapped into a loaded box for three. They trapped again for two because the math said they shouldn't and the town deserved to see what stubborn computation looked like. Third and five, forty seconds, no timeouts for the Greyhounds, ball on the thirteen. Aidan wanted to throw a fade so pretty it would write itself on air. He sent Eli in instead and said, "Keep it if the end sleeps."

The end slept. Eli kept. Two yards. Fourth and three, twenty-two seconds. Coach pointed at Micah and then at Aidan. The message said, *ice this thing.* They did. 22–17—somewhere a scoreboard had been told to respect a pattern.

The kickoff was a squib that murdered clock. Northfield's last throw met Cruz's hands like a dog meets a gate. The horn sounded not like grace but like a due date met with exact change. The boys trotted, not sprinted. The band wheezed and celebrated. The crowd roared and then exhaled so slowly the bleachers seemed to lower a half-inch.

On the sideline, Ms. Rivera put a hand to Aidan's shoulder and didn't ask. He gave her a number anyway. "Ninety-two."

"Honest," she said. "Good." She pressed a bottle into his palm and then, low enough that only he heard it, "Proud."

He laughed once because he'd never heard her say that to anyone. "Don't tell Coach."

"Coach already knows," she said, and moved on to a guard who looked ready to cramp into a caricature of himself.

John and Karen didn't try to get to the rail. They knew better than to fight the river at the edges. They stood in the aisle and clapped until their palms stung. Karen cried. John's eyes were watery in a way that did not embarrass him. He put his hand on the small of her back and felt the bones of a person who had forgotten to eat and would insist she wasn't hungry.

In the scrum, Marcus found Aidan and pointed to his wrist. "You used it," he said. It wasn't an accusation. It was a string tied to a finger in case you forgot something important later.

"Yeah," Aidan said.

"And the world didn't end."

"Nope."

"Good to know," Marcus said, and slung an arm around his shoulders like a mantle.

In the locker room, the noise was rowdy but not wild. Boys sang off-key. Someone banged a helmet against a locker until Coach told him to find a better instrument. Dempsey didn't give a speech so much as a verdict: "Workmanlike," he said. "Smart. You suffocated them and you didn't apologize for it."

He didn't look at Aidan when he added, "You did a captain's thing." He didn't have to.

The captains' group chat lit ten minutes after the showers cooled and the socks had been located.

Will: *We ate clock. Dinner was tasty.*

Cruz: *Defense owes offense fries for that third-and-eight dig.*

Marcus: *Offense owes defense shakes for bailing out Jamal on that double move.*

Jamal: *I will accept a small frosty and your forgiveness.*

Micah: *Three for three, if anyone wants to notice.*

Aidan: *Blue two worked. Truth worked. See you at film.*

He sat on the bench long enough to feel the building empty under him. He pulled the black tape off his wrist slowly, not in one satisfying yank but the way you unstick something you plan to use again without tearing. He folded it, felt the letters just barely impressioned on his skin, and pressed his thumb there until the warmth returned.

On the walk to the parking lot, he checked his phone. One message from an unknown number, which wasn't unknown anymore.

I learned one cheer: "First down." I used it a lot. — E.

He typed a response and then didn't send it, not because he'd changed his mind but because the night didn't need words to close. He slid the phone into his pocket and let the cool settle over his jersey as the stadium lights clicked off in banks, the field surrendering back to regular grass in increments.

The town still didn't know. Or it did, in that way towns know—half whispers, half prayers, half respect for the line between a boy's body and other people's stories. It would know soon enough. For one more week, the page stayed turned to the part where football was still a thing he could hold.

At the corner by the exit, he stopped and looked back at the end zone painted with the school's name. Fourth and forever. Some nights, the math bent. Some nights, the play was a series of right-sized truths, one after another, until the clock ran out and what remained wasn't glory so much as proof: you can choose how to be brave.

He took a breath. It hurt. He took another. It hurt less. He walked to the car where his parents waited, Marcus idling behind them in a coughing sedan like a tail he'd promised to be. The door shut. The night followed them home, not heavy this time, just full.

Chapter Twenty-One – The Ripple Effect

Monday morning arrived with the kind of silence that made Aidan think the whole world had decided to hold its breath. The house smelled faintly of coffee and pancakes, but he knew Karen hadn't eaten. She never ate on Mondays anymore. She hovered, fussed over his backpack, checked if he had his water bottle, then stopped herself mid-motion and folded her arms tightly as if holding them still could stop her heart from racing.

"Don't overdo it," she said.

"I'm going to school, Mom," Aidan replied, sliding the strap over his shoulder. His ribs protested under the weight, but he didn't show it. "Not basic training."

Her mouth opened, closed, and then softened into something like surrender. John kissed her temple on the way out, thermos in hand, giving her that look that said *I'll watch him when you can't.*

The walk into school was the same as always and completely different. Posters from the Friday night win still clung to the hallways—**Lions 22, Greyhounds 17!**—but the whispers traveled faster than any announcement.

"That's him—"

"—heard it's cancer—"

"—still playing?"

Aidan kept his eyes forward, focusing on the linoleum tiles, counting every fifth one like he used to in freshman year when nerves got loud. Marcus fell into step beside him, earbuds dangling, a wall of calm in motion.

"They don't know," Marcus muttered.

"They know enough," Aidan said.

"Not the word. Just… something."

Aidan nodded. The difference mattered. To him. To his parents. To Coach. Words were heavier than whispers.

First period English, Mrs. Reynolds passed back essays with a smile too tender to be casual. Aidan tucked his paper into his binder without looking at the grade. The boy two rows over glanced at him too long, and Aidan felt the weight of it like a hand pressing between his shoulder blades.

At lunch, Emily sat down across from him. Not beside Marcus, not at the edges, but directly in front of him. She pushed her glasses up with her thumb, her notebook open to a fresh page.

"You don't have to write about me," Aidan said.

"I wasn't," she replied, unbothered. "I was writing about how people pretend not to look at things they can't handle."

He blinked at her. "You mean me."

"I mean everyone. But if the shoe fits…" She tapped her pen against the page. "You're still you. That's what they don't get."

He let out a breath. "Feels like they're all waiting for me to… break."

Emily's gaze softened. "Then don't give them a show. Give them football. Give them Friday. The rest is none of their business."

Marcus leaned over, stealing a fry. "I like her," he said. "She's bossy in the right way."

"Thanks," Emily muttered, though her cheeks flushed.

After lunch, Cruz found Aidan by the lockers. "Heard the sophs want to shave their heads. For you."

Aidan groaned. "God help us."

"Already told them no. Said it'd make us look like we lost a bet. You're welcome." Cruz smirked, then added more seriously, "We've got you. Just keep calling plays."

By the time practice rolled around, the tension had seeped into the locker room. Boys moved sharper, quieter, like they'd stepped into church. Coach noticed immediately.

He blew his whistle once, and the sound cracked like thunder. "Stop looking at him like he's glass!" His voice filled every corner. "He's your quarterback, not your caution sign. You want to protect him? Block your gap. Stay in phase. Do your job. That's it. Nothing extra. Nothing less."

The room exhaled. The tension shifted into energy. When they hit the field, Aidan barked cadence with his usual authority, and the first snap felt like football again, not theater.

Still, Ms. Rivera's eyes never left him. She tracked every movement, every throw, every time his hand pressed into his ribs. When he finally doubled over after a rollout, catching his breath a second too long, she jogged over, clipboard in hand.

"Truth?" she asked quietly.

"No," he said, straightening, though sweat dripped into his eyes.

"Blue two then?"

"Not yet." He managed a crooked smile. "Save it for Friday."

That night at dinner, Karen pushed peas around her plate, appetite gone again. "I can't stand it," she admitted. "Knowing he's out there while—while this thing is inside him."

Aidan set down his fork. "Mom, I'm still me. I'm not the cancer."

Her eyes filled. "You're my son. I don't want to lose both."

John reached across the table, taking her hand. His other hand found Aidan's wrist, strong and steady. "We walk this together. Day by day. Play by play. That's all."

Aidan swallowed hard and nodded. For once, he didn't argue.

Before bed, his phone buzzed. A text from Emily.

People stare because they don't know what else to do. Let them. You don't owe them answers. Just… be Aidan.

He stared at the message for a long time before typing back.

Trying. One Friday at a time.

When he set the phone down, the black tape still pressed against his wrist. He traced the letters underneath with his thumb. Truth.

Friday would come again. And when it did, the whispers would fade into noise, the stares into shadows. On the field, there was only grass, only plays, only the next breath. That was his world, and he wasn't ready to leave it yet.

Chapter Twenty-Two – The Rivalry

By Thursday night, the week had tilted toward Easton the way a compass needle settles: inevitable, a little stubborn. Easton wore orange and black and a chip on its shoulder for reasons that had nothing to do with geography and everything to do with old games people still argued about at reunions. This was the one circled since summer—the rivalry that made even reasonable adults forget they had jobs in the morning.

In the hallways, posters bloomed with bad puns and spray paint. **SQUASH THE TIGERS. PAWS OFF OUR HOUSE.** Someone hung a banner over the cafeteria that read **EAT EASTON** until the custodian, white-haired and loyal to grammar, added a comma with a strip of tape.

By homeroom, the not-quite-secret was no longer content to be a whisper. A blog post—anonymous, sanctimonious—had appeared overnight: *Lincoln's QB playing through "health scare"? Should he?* The word *cancer* wasn't written, but it hovered in the negative space, larger for being unsaid. Phones glowed. Jokes curdled before they formed. Teachers confiscated screen time with gentler hands than usual.

Aidan saw the headline on a classmate's phone, glanced, and kept walking. Marcus stepped between the screen and his quarterback like a cloud erasing sunlight. "Delete that," he told the kid, not mean—final.

At lunch, Emily slid into the seat across from Aidan and set two index cards on the table. On one, she'd drawn a tiny lion with a number four on its chest, squinting like it needed glasses. On the other, three words in tidy block letters: **Just play ball.**

"That's the whole lesson plan?" Aidan asked, cracking a smile.

"That's the whole sermon," she said. "You okay?"

He considered lying. He didn't. "Nervous," he said. "Tired of being a headline I didn't write."

"Then give them a better story," she said simply. "The one with first downs and boring beautiful and a win we'll be insufferable about for a year."

He laughed, and for a second the room sounded like any lunchroom in any town where Friday night still meant something.

Coach kept practice clipped and unsentimental. "They live in quarters, then bail to three when you guess," he said, pointer tapping the whiteboard like a metronome. "Patience makes them twitch. Twitch gives you grass. Breathe with your feet."

Cruz led the defense like a man escorting a friend through a crowd. "Eyes right," he barked. "Hands violent. No free slants. We hit first and we hit last." Will sent GIFs of brick walls to the line group chat with the caption **be ugly** and got a dozen thumbs-ups and one confused exclamation point from a freshman he would pull aside later and educate.

Ms. Rivera doubled down on the rules without doubling her voice. "Check-ins," she told Aidan. "Morning, after school. Hydrate like a job. Truth without apology. Blue two without drama." He nodded, and she made him say the nod out loud: "Yes, ma'am." It was easier to obey a sentence that had real words in it.

Friday arrived on the back of a flat gray sky that promised rain and decided to be theatrical instead. The bus to Easton rumbled with a contained energy, a pressure cooker, a thousand jokes that died before they wore out their welcome. Out the windows, the rival's stadium rose in a wedge of concrete and memory. The field gleamed artificial and smug. The Tigers' student section had already colonized their bleachers with stripes and megaphones and a sign that read **CAN HE EVEN PLAY?** in orange block letters someone thought were clever. A few faculty members tried to confiscate it. The students shrugged, and the sign migrated three rows up like a stubborn species.

"Give me that," Coach Dempsey told a volunteer in an Easton polo, and the man did, because the voice was the one referees obeyed without enjoying it. The sign disappeared under the bleachers like bad weather.

In the tunnel, helmets in hand, the team formed the circle that was older than any of them. The chant that belonged to Lincoln rose and fell. Aidan stood with the captains and let the sound pass through. He taped his left wrist with the black strip Ms. Rivera had given him; the word he pressed under it was the only prayer he trusted. Marcus leaned in close and bumped his helmet once. "Grass," he said. "Then the sky."

Easton's band did what bands do when they know you hate them. Their drumline found a rhythm designed to get under skin. The announcer welcomed *YOUR EASTON TIGERS* like he'd been paid by the exclamation point. The captains met at midfield. Easton's quarterback—tall, smirking—offered a hand and a comment meant to be quiet: "You sure you should be out here, Four?"

"Ask your safety," Aidan said, and let the coin decide the rest. Lincoln deferred. The Tigers wanted the ball. Of course they did.

Cruz set the tone on the first snap—filled and folded and found a helmet with his shoulder like physics class, not murder. Second down, the Tigers tried to get cute with a jet sweep that ended up a yard behind where it started because Jamal tackled everything smaller than a truck. Third and long, Easton took the shot: a post over the top, a prayer with too much arc. Their receiver got hands on it and Cruz got hands through it. Punt. The student section booed boring disguised as fear. Lincoln's sideline breathed.

Aidan jogged onto Easton's turf and felt the difference under his cleats—harder, a little slick, like it had no interest in mercy. He rubbed his thumb across his wrist and gathered the huddle. "Trips right. Sixty-two. Let's make them hate how quiet we can be."

First throw: out route for six. Second: stick for four. First down. The Tigers rolled late to buzz the flat. Aidan checked to a slant. Three. The boo birds tested their throats; the Lincoln stands found their polite clapping voice. It was a rivalry—sound mattered. Aidan took it out of the equation. Draw. Duo. Mesh. The clock ticked like a metronome someone had set to "patience."

At the Easton thirty, third and seven, the Tigers disguised two deep and arrived with five. Will stoned the end; the back got enough of the blitzer's thigh to change an angle. Aidan climbed the pocket the way you're supposed to and threw a dig across his body only because the shoulder and the foot agreed beforehand. Marcus secured it, turned through a tackle, and fell on the twenty-two like a man completing a plan. Two plays later, they were at the eleven. The red zone clamped.

"Take the points if they make you," Coach said in his ear from the sideline, the frequency that belonged to men allowed in your helmet.

Aidan faked a hard count that didn't move anybody and threw a curl that did. Fourth and two. He looked to the sideline; Dempsey tapped his wrist. Deny the urge to be interesting. Micah's kick split the uprights so clean the net didn't bother lowering its standards. Three-nothing.

The Tigers answered with noise and movement and a quarterback who thought his legs were smarter than Cruz's eyes. They weren't. Three-and-out, again. Will and Cruz chest-bumped at the sideline like elks with restraint. The offense went back to work. More grass. A screen called only to remind Easton that math existed. Then a little wheel to the back because the outside backer guessed and guesses cost more in October. They were at the thirty-five as the quarter turned.

In the stands, Karen wore two sweatshirts and held a third like a shield. John offered her hot chocolate she didn't need. They shared a look parents share when they're watching the same person live two lives at once. Two rows behind them, the blog author—unidentified but obvious—typed a new headline and got a stern word from a principal who was tired of tearing down what teenagers built on Friday nights.

Emily found her spot at the fifty, pencil behind her ear, index card in pocket. She watched the student section across the way unfold a banner that read **FOURTH AND NEVER** and felt something like anger and not exactly justice burn in her sternum. She started a chant—clumsy, off-beat—that failed magnificently and still did the job. The Lincoln bleachers stood up for no good reason except the one that counted.

Easton struck first in the second quarter. They found a soft spot on a switch release that made Jamal look like he'd missed a page. He hadn't; the Tigers had written a new one. Twenty-nine yards later, the orange and black section invented a hymn. Two plays after that, their running back slipped a tackle and landed in the paint. Seven-three. The Tigers' band played something brassy and cruel. A Tiger in the front row cupped hands to mouth and yelled, "How's your chest, Four?" Security looked for a reason to care; found none.

Aidan stood over the ball at the twenty-five and let the sound wash and recede. He wanted the hole shot like oxygen. The boundary corner's feet admired the hash; the safety's split was not perfect. Marcus's stance said *now.* Aidan's ribs said *later.* He threw the out for seven. Boring beautiful. The boos came like gnats. He wiped them away with a stick route that broke laughter out of the Lincoln sideline because of how predictably effective it was.

By mid-quarter, Easton had grown impatient. Their end lined up two inches wider, eyes eating backfield. Their nickel cheated. On second and six, they sent five and changed their minds too late. Aidan slid left, felt the tug in his side and named it *not now,* and found the back underneath for four. Third and two. Hard count bought nothing. Inside zone got two and exactly that. First down. Coach's thumbs-up read like a masterclass.

At the Easton fourteen, the play called itself. The Tigers had bracketed Marcus so firmly he could feel their breath. The tight end, meanwhile, had been uninteresting all night. He delayed, chipped, bled into the flat, and found a square of air that had not existed on film. Aidan feathered it over a linebacker's eyelashes. The tight end turned and extended the ball over the pylon like a man placing a book back on a shelf. Touchdown. Ten-seven.

The game tightened. Easton moved the ball with swears and screens; Lincoln answered with tempo and unremarkable excellence. Ms. Rivera handed Aidan a salt cap at every change of possession like a Eucharist that tasted like a swimming pool. He took it, grimaced, breathed. On a roll right late in the half, the Tigers' end got free and took a rent payment under Aidan's ribs. The world went bright at the edges. He got up slowly enough that three different kinds of love— coach, trainer, mother—walked toward the white line.

He looked at Coach and shook his head. He looked at Rivera and didn't lie. "Blue two," he mouthed to Marcus.

Eli trotted in, hands perfect on his first snap because there are moments you can practice. He kept once when the end crashed like a fool and earned three. He handed off twice behind Will's hip and earned eight more. The drive stalled at the thirty and Micah banged it high and true as the horn wagged its little tail. Thirteen-seven at half. The Tigers sulked toward the tunnel; Cruz laughed once like he had heard a joke only he understood.

In the locker room, Dempsey didn't let the words pile. "They're waiting for you to blink," he said. "Keep your eyes open. No free yards. No free doubt. Defense, top stays on. Offense, the grass belongs to you if you take it like you own it. Don't go shopping for fireworks."

He turned to Aidan in the hush after the noise. "You say it if you need it," he said. "And if I say it, you don't make me the bad guy."

"Truth," Aidan said, and Ms. Rivera watched the way the syllable moved in his throat the way a mechanic watches a belt.

Third quarter, Easton came out like men who'd been promised steak if they flipped the script. They ran kick-out into the boundary, then booted away from Cruz and prayed he was human. He wasn't; he chased it down anyway. Third and five, they tried a slant under a rubbing route the refs let be clever. Jamal got an ankle. Fourth and one at the Lincoln forty-two; the Tigers went fast. Cruz anticipated fast. The running back met a helmet at the line that contained history. Turnover on downs. Lincoln's section sang on a note only relief finds.

Aidan's first throw of the half was a checkdown for four. His second was a curl for eight. His third was an incompletion he threw into the band, earning him a look from a clarinetist with a sense of self. He apologized with a glance he hoped said *next time I'll aim for trumpet.*

Midway through the quarter, he felt the floor shift again. Not as sharp this time, more like a boat you hadn't realized had left the dock. He blinked. He tapped his thigh—blue two—and gave Eli a look that said both *I trust you* and *don't be cute.* Eli wasn't. He kept them on schedule, hit a stick, handed off into mismatches Will created by torque and ill will. When Aidan came back in, the ball had moved eleven yards and the air had cooled behind his teeth. He finished the drive with a sail that asked Marcus to be exactly where he was. Field goal. Sixteen-seven.

Easton would not die politely. Early fourth, they dialed up a slot fade against quarters that had been honest all night. It worked because high school football allows a thing to be right on paper and wrong in a heartbeat. Sixteen-fourteen after the kick and a botched gator-chomp parody from the visitors' section nobody appreciated.

Four minutes, forty-eight seconds. Ball on the twenty-three. Rivalry games are supposed to have romance. Coach gave them math. "First downs," he said into the helmet. "Win two of them and they don't have time to forgive themselves."

Aidan huddled them with breath that came efficient and thin. "Grass until they cry uncle," he said. "Blue two if I call it. Truth if I say it."

First down: duo for four, because Will decided it. Second: stick for six, because Marcus knew where to sit. First down. The Tigers burned a timeout to dramatize their despair. The band's drumline miscounted and found itself anyway.

Second set: draw for three. Out for five. Third and two near midfield. Easton stacked the box like men who wanted a story to tell in a bar. Aidan hard-counted and smiled inside the helmet when a nose flinched—a learned flinch, a muscle memory of fear. No flag. Fine. He looked left, right, then at Marcus.

"Now?" Marcus whispered.

"Not yet," Aidan said, and took the slant for three and the right to keep the ball.

Easton's last timeout vanished. One-seventeen. The student sections were hoarse and inventive. Karen clutched John's sleeve enough to make fabric a rosary. Emily stood on the seat because she was small and courage sometimes needs height.

Second and eight on the Tigers' thirty-six. Aidan felt his lungs argue. He pressed his thumb to the tape, felt the ridges of a word through skin. He looked at Coach. Coach didn't blink. He looked at Rivera. She didn't step. He looked at Marcus. Marcus nodded once: *now.*

The boundary corner, who had been dutiful all night, betrayed himself. His hips stole a half-step downhill when they shouldn't. The safety counted something and miscounted. Aidan didn't admire it. He dropped, planted, and threw the hole shot where it would be. Marcus stacked, separated, and didn't get cute at the sideline; he caught and fell, gift-wrapping the clock. The stadium sound wasn't joy yet; it was a promise to try for it.

Two kneels kept honest by angles and bruises. The horn arrived like a punctuation mark that had been earned. Sixteen-fourteen, Lincoln. The Tigers marched off with the grim dignity of men who intend to be angrier in the morning.

On the field, bodies slumped and whooped and found water bottles like talismans. Dempsey shook exactly one referee's hand and saved his commentary for another life. Cruz hugged Jamal in a way that looked like violence and felt like a heartbeat. Will found the nose tackle who'd flinched and told him, "Next time, breathe," because he had been taught to make better football players out of enemies.

Ms. Rivera appeared and wrote a number on her clipboard before she asked. "Ninety-four," Aidan said, honest enough. "It's coming down."

"Truth used?"

"Once," he said.

"And the world?"

"Still here."

She nodded. "Eat something that isn't salt."

John and Karen made it to the rail as the crowd thinned to family and people with reasons. Karen touched Aidan's cheek and didn't say *I told you so* or *please stop* or *I can't survive this.* She said, "I love the way you throw the ball to where it's going to be."

"That's football, Mom," he said, and John laughed watery.

Near the fifty, a boy in Easton orange approached with his helmet under his arm and his mouth full of apology. "Hey," he said, not meeting Aidan's eyes. "What our section did—that was... not it."

Aidan nodded once. "Play better," he said—not cruel—and shook the boy's hand like a person who kept the world small when it wanted to expand into nonsense.

Emily waited at the bottom of the bleachers until the traffic of reunion thinned. When she stepped onto the track, she didn't wave or call; she stood where he would see her if he was looking. He was. She handed him an index card with a lion and a number four and a tiny exclamation point that looked embarrassed to be there. On the back: *First downs are a love language. — E.*

He laughed, and the ache in his ribs softened into something he could carry home.

On the bus, Will sent a single text to the captains' thread.

Will: *We didn't blink.*

Cruz: *We hit first. We hit last.*

Marcus: *Grass, cry uncle.*

Aidan: *Truth. Friday again soon.*

Out the window, Easton's stadium fell behind with the care you give to a mirror—reluctant to leave but relieved to be done with the person it showed you. The road unspooled black and certain. Next week had needs; tonight had already been met. He pressed his thumb to the tape and felt the word there without needing to read it.

The rivalry would be remembered for the score, for the hit Cruz made on fourth and one, for the sign nobody would admit they were proud of tearing down. For Aidan, it would live as a series of right-sized choices: a slant instead of a sermon, blue two instead of bravado, a hole shot only when the math finally asked for poetry. He leaned his head against the cool window, closed his eyes, and let the bus carry him through the dark toward a town that, for now, knew how to hold its boys without squeezing the air out of them.

Chapter Twenty-Three –
The Town Knows

Saturday mornings in Lincoln usually belonged to recovery. Boys slept late, parents dragged themselves to soccer games for younger siblings, and the town's main street wore a quiet coat of exhaustion. After a rivalry win, though, the silence never lasted. Signs sprouted in shop windows—**WAY TO GO LIONS!**—and waitresses at the diner wore blue ribbons in their hair. Someone painted **QB1** on the hardware store's window in washable paint that would last longer than anyone intended.

But this Saturday, the air felt different. Less celebration, more watchfulness. The whispers that had lived in hallways and behind cupped hands at school had seeped out into church foyers and supermarket aisles. Everyone seemed to know, and no one knew how they were supposed to act.

At the diner, a pair of older men nursed coffees at the counter. "Kid's tough as nails," one said, shaking his head. "But cancer? My God."

His friend stirred sugar into his mug. "I heard it's rare. Serious. You think Coach ought to let him play?"

"He's seventeen. Let the boy live."

"You let him play, and something happens out there—it's on Dempsey."

They both fell quiet when the bell over the door jingled and Karen walked in for takeout pancakes. Her smile was polite, but her eyes said she'd heard enough. She gathered the bags quickly, thanked the waitress, and left before her composure cracked.

At church the next morning, the pews filled with glances more than hymns. Karen sat with her hand laced through Aidan's, John on his other side. The pastor spoke of strength, of endurance, of faith in valleys, but Aidan felt every sideways glance like a stone in his shoe. When the final hymn ended, people approached in clusters.

"We're praying for you."

"Stay strong, son."

"My cousin had chemo. If you ever need advice—"

Karen smiled through tears, John nodded with dignity, and Aidan shook every hand, but by the time they reached the parking lot, his jaw ached from clenching.

"Feels like they're already at my funeral," he muttered.

Karen gasped. "Don't say that."

"I'm not dead, Mom. But they look at me like I am." He pulled the hood of his sweatshirt up and walked faster toward the car.

On Monday, the school newspaper came out. Emily's byline sat on the front page beneath a photograph of the team huddled in the Easton end zone. The headline read: **Our Quarterback, Our Brother.**

Aidan found a copy on his desk first period and flipped it open. Emily hadn't used the word *cancer*—not once. She wrote about leadership, about courage, about the way a team could learn more from patience than glory.

"Aidan McAllister is still our quarterback. He is still the same boy who throws touchdowns, teases his best friend, and groans at cafeteria meatloaf. He is not a headline. He is not a diagnosis. He is ours."

He read the last line three times. By the time class started, half the room had read it too, and for once, the glances that came his way didn't sting. They steadied him.

At lunch, he found Emily at her usual spot, scribbling notes in the margin of a math worksheet. He dropped the paper in front of her.

"You didn't have to."

She looked up, eyes sharp behind her glasses. "Yes, I did. They were going to talk either way. Now at least they have words that aren't poison."

He swallowed. "Thank you."

Her smile was small, but real. "You're welcome."

Practice that afternoon carried an edge. The team had read the article, too. Will slapped Aidan on the back harder than usual, muttering, "Our brother," like it was a battle cry. Cruz barked louder, daring anyone to make a joke. Even the sophomores, who usually drifted through drills like leaves in wind, moved with purpose.

Coach Dempsey watched it all, arms folded. When practice ended, he gathered them.

"Word's out," he said. "Doesn't change the field. Doesn't change your jobs. The town can pray, the papers can write, the whispers can gossip. In here? We work. We block. We tackle. We trust." His gaze swept across every helmet, then landed on Aidan. "He's still your quarterback. That's not charity. That's football. You want to honor him? Do your job."

The boys broke with a roar that rattled the cinderblock walls.

That night, Karen sat at the kitchen table, the newspaper article spread in front of her. She traced Emily's words with her fingertip.

"She's right," she whispered. "He's still our boy."

John set a hand over hers. "He's more than that now. He's theirs too."

Karen's eyes filled again, but this time the tears weren't just fear. They were pride, tangled with sorrow.

Upstairs, Aidan lay on his bed, phone buzzing with texts he didn't have the energy to answer. He pulled the black tape from his wrist and smoothed it flat on the nightstand. Tomorrow, he'd write the word again. Tomorrow, he'd practice again. Tomorrow, he'd walk back into whispers that had finally said his name out loud.

But tonight, he closed his eyes, and for the first time since the diagnosis, he didn't feel like he was carrying it alone.

Chapter Twenty-Four – Playoff Push

By Monday morning, the bracket lived on every locker, taped crooked over geometry tests and college flyers. The state association's PDF looked like a family tree and a threat: threads of names tightening toward a single box that said **CHAMPION** in a font too cheerful for November.

Lincoln drew the sixth seed, home against Westfield, a team that dressed like they'd been raised in a weight room and called themselves the Mustangs because no one in Westfield had ever met a mustang and therefore could mythologize one. They were the kind of first-round team that thought momentum was a personality trait. Film showed a defense that lived in quarters, got nosy late, and sent pressure from places that made offensive coordinators pretend they didn't see.

Coach Dempsey pinned the bracket to the corkboard with a thumbtack that went in like a promise. "November football is about the same five boring things," he said at Monday's after-school meeting, not turning to face them yet. "Win first down. Own the ball. No free yards. No free doubt. And—" he tapped the board "—we get really good at saying *next*." He turned then, toothpick trapped at the corner of his mouth, eyes bright and unsentimental. "They're strong. We're smarter. We'll make them hate how long the night is."

The weight room smelled like rubber and old victories. Will ran the line through a circuit that looked like punishment and felt like religion. "Feet first," he told the freshmen who hadn't yet learned that hands are liars. "Hips second. Hands last. That's the order if you want to keep our guy standing." He didn't have to point at Aidan to make the sentence land.

On the other side of the wall, Cruz worked the defense until the air turned metallic. "Eyes! Hands! Finish!" he barked, somewhere between drill sergeant and older brother, holding the unit together with volume and the belief that tackling is ethics.

Ms. Rivera cornered Aidan by the scale, not apologizing for the way she watched numbers like a hawk. "Down two," she said, neutral and worried. "That could be sweat. Could be stress. Either way—salt, sleep, food." She pressed a Tupperware into his hands like she'd packed it for a second son. Inside: rice, chicken, a slice of banana bread with a sticky note that read **EAT.** He rolled his eyes and obeyed. She smiled without showing teeth. "Morning check, after-practice check. You skip, I tell your mother, and she will find a new octave."

At school, Emily's column had unclenched something. Teachers stopped speaking to Aidan in italics. The glances softened from *what if* to *we've got you.* Somebody tied blue ribbons to the light poles along Main Street; somebody else added a hand-painted sign outside the barber's that read **BORING BEAUTIFUL** like they'd discovered a new theology. The blog stopped sniffing around and posted a list of best concession stand hot chocolates instead, which was a mercy for everyone.

Tuesday's practice arrived under a sky that had decided to be steel. The field felt harder, even the rubber pellets stingier. Aidan wore the red non-contact jersey at the start like Coach had asked—warmup periods only—and hated it the way you hate something that saves you. When they switched to team, he pulled on the blue and breathed easier. The installs were clean. The openers script went up on the whiteboard in thick block letters:

- *Trips Rt 62 Smash*

- *Duo / Check to Inside Zone*

- *Mesh Tag Wheel*

- *Sail vs. Quarters*

- *QB Draw from Empty (Slide at 7)*

"Tempo on two," Dempsey said, tapping the board. "We won't go fast. We'll go first."

Marcus jogged back to the huddle after a rep and bumped Aidan's shoulder pad. "Corners are nosy on smash," he said, grinning. "Sell the flat, I'll eat the corner."

"Only if you chew," Aidan said. The banter came easy, even when breath didn't.

By Wednesday, Westfield had sent a small convoy of dads with camcorders to ring the fence at practice because that's how November works—espionage disguised as parenthood. Coach put the walk-through on the grass practice field and ran team inside the gym with taped hash marks just to be rude. "If a Mustang dad can run a camcorder from a pull-up bar," he said, "I'll hire him."

At home, Karen folded laundry like she was smoothing crumpled weeks, stacking blue socks and towels, building small towers of normal. Aidan sat at the counter chewing pasta like a man completing a task, ribs humming under the tape, phone face down. John leaned on the far side of the island, breaking down film silently on his tablet, glancing up when Aidan winced and pretending he hadn't seen. "Mike—Will—will wash that end past the pocket," John said softly, almost to himself. "Step up and hitch. Don't widen. You widen, you invite physics."

"I know," Aidan said, and he did, and still he appreciated hearing his father turn care into coaching because it hurt less that way.

Thursday night brought the quiet. The line group chat devolved into memes about pancakes. Cruz sent a clip of an NFL linebacker

146

misreading split zone with the caption **don't be this guy**. Marcus texted Aidan a single play card photo and a single word: *now?* Aidan typed back: *later.* Emily sent an index card photo—tiny lion, number four, and beneath it: *November is made of clocks.* He stared long enough that the black tape on his wrist warmed under his skin. He slept badly, which is to say like every boy who's ever had a Friday.

Game day split the town into three kinds of people: those who arrived at the stadium two hours early with blankets and thermoses; those who did not attend because superstition required them to circle the block listening to the radio; and those who claimed indifference and secretly checked the score every five minutes. The lights popped on in banks, chasing the gray away. Breath steamed in small, visible prayers.

In the locker room, Dempsey spoke without raising his voice. "They'll try to shorten the game. We shorten their patience. You will get bored before they get beat if you're not careful. Don't. Work the problem." He looked at Aidan then, only long enough to make an agreement. "Truth is a tool, not a surrender."

"Truth is a tool," Aidan echoed, and Ms. Rivera nodded once, as if he'd said it for her.

Warmups were routine and treasonous for how normal they felt. Aidan's first twenty throws spun true. His next five wobbled like a lie and he fixed his shoulder slot, tucked his elbow, exhaled. Marcus's hands sounded like clean punctuation. Will's feet whispered on pass set. Cruz found a rhythm slapping his thigh pad that his unit adopted like a drumline. Westfield's band practiced a song that sounded like a dare. The Mustangs' student section chanted **OVER-RATED** with the full sincerity of children who had never rated anything.

Captains at midfield. Westfield won and deferred. The coin clinked, a small sound, and the night moved.

The first series belonged to the defense, which is to say to Cruz. Westfield tried to bully Duo into a box that refused to be bullied.

Second and eight became third and ten on a TFL that would have looked like violence if it hadn't been so clean. Westfield's quarterback rolled right into a teacher he hadn't met and threw a ball that hit the pep band's bass drum. Punt.

Lincoln's offense jogged on. Aidan rubbed his thumb across the ridge of tape on his wrist—private liturgy—and brought them in. "Trips right. Sixty-two. Eyes." The Mustangs presented their quarters look honest on snap one. Out route for seven. Draw for three. First down. Will clapped once, the way a man claps when a hammer behaves.

Westfield sent pressure early, trying to knock the script out of Aidan's hand. On second and long, the nickel snapped off the corner and came free. Aidan felt him before he saw him—the air changes when a man decides to arrive—and replaced the blitzer with the ball, flipping a quick out that became eight yards and annoyed a defensive coordinator. Third and two. Hard count. The nose flinched and the ref pretended he didn't. Fine. Duo for three, thank you Will, advance the story.

They reached the red zone being relentlessly unremarkable, and the red zone punished them for it. Two runs for four. A slant broken up by a linebacker with too much caffeine. Micah jogged out. Three-nothing, not a song, still a score.

The Mustangs answered with tempo disguised as variety. They found a soft curl, stole six, then got greedy and tried a double move that Jamal defended with a fingertip and an apology. Third and four, Westfield's quarterback kept on zone read into Cruz, which is like checking if a door is locked with your face. Punt.

The second quarter turned mean in the way playoff football does when both teams realize the paper bracket had been lying to them about how this would feel. Aidan took a real shot under the ribs on a rollout that the end sniffed late. The world tilted then righted. He stood, counted to three, and nodded toward the sideline like a man acknowledging a sunset. Ms. Rivera took a step and didn't breach the white. Dempsey pointed at his temple—think first.

"Blue two?" Marcus asked in the huddle.

"Blue two," Aidan said, and Eli slid in on a sub so casual the Mustangs thought it had been planned for them. Eli handed off twice behind Will's hip and kept a third time when the end crashed out of habit. Three yards. First down. The student section grumbled because blue two didn't look like romance; the coaches loved it because it extended breath.

On the next series, Aidan returned. He ran the tempo like a man turning a key. Smash stole seven. Stick stole five. A screen to the back asked a linebacker to decide and punished him for deciding wrong. At the sixteen, Westfield spun to three late and tried to bait a throw inside leverage. Aidan checked it away. Two plays later he found the tight end on a leak past a nosy safety for six. Ten-nothing. The band remembered how to be a problem.

The Mustangs pulled three back with a field goal born of stubbornness. Ten-three at half. The locker room smelled like oranges and iron and November. Dempsey didn't waste sentences. "They have two good calls left," he said. "We have all of ours. Suffocate them with correctness." He raised a finger in Aidan's direction without assigning blame. "You do not try to prove a point. You are the point."

Aidan's ribs radiated heat in slow pulses. Ms. Rivera pressed a cold pack wrapped in a towel into his side with the care you use on a newborn and a bomb. "Rate?" she asked.

"Ninety," he said.

She looked at the watch. "Eight-six," she corrected, but smiled anyway. "That's honesty with flavor."

The third quarter took on the shape of a chess game played with shoulder pads. Westfield moved the ball in jerks—four, three, negative two, panic—and punted into wind. Lincoln's offense ate clock and protein—five, four, third and one, sneak—until they didn't,

149

and Aidan threw a ball into the marching band again to the clarinetist's visible disdain. "I'll aim for tuba next time," he muttered to Marcus, who snorted and told him to throw it where band kids weren't.

Midway through, the Mustangs finally hit the one good call Dempsey had predicted remained: a slot fade against quarters that had settled into bored honesty. It landed like a coin dropped in the only grate on the block. Touchdown. Ten-ten. The visitor's section howled like it had been practicing.

On the sideline, Karen's hands found each other and didn't separate. John leaned forward in the way of men who think proximity is control. Emily stood on the seat again, pencil behind ear, her index card already lettered in block ink she'd decided was good luck: **FIRST DOWNS ARE A LOVE LANGUAGE.** She didn't hold it up yet. She wasn't the loud kind of brave.

The next drive was the one the bracket will not record and the boys will remember. First play: draw for four. Second: stick for five. Third and one: hard count, nothing, dive anyway, Will moving a human with economy. First down. The clock unspooled like thread. Then, on second and eight, the end beat the chip and arrived exactly where Aidan's ribs could least afford arrival. The world went too bright. He landed curled around the ball because some instincts are born in August and survive every month after.

He lay there long enough for Ms. Rivera to say his name and make it a question. He coughed, then laughed because it hurt, then said it: "Truth." The word was small and enormous.

Marcus clapped once like a man starting a metronome. "Blue two!" he yelled conversationally, which was the only tone that didn't make it a sermon. Eli took three snaps that were all correct. Aidan drank water like obedience and counted seventeen seconds until the floor stopped rolling. When he returned, he threw a curl before he was technically allowed to and found Marcus sitting like a man who had reserved that exact seat in the secondary hours ago. First down. The crowd roared like a pot remembering how.

Fourth quarter, ten-ten and the temperature dropping like a dare. Dempsey tapped his wrist at Aidan after a run went nowhere. "Two first downs, and they'll run out of night," his mouth said around the toothpick. Aidan nodded and made the quarter smaller.

First down: out route for seven. Second: duo for three and decisive spot. First down. The linebackers edged. Marcus gave Aidan the *now?* look and Aidan tilted his chin: *not yet.* Second set: sail away from a buzz safety, body quiet, ball confident. Twelve yards. Westfield burned a timeout to consult with their gods. The gods suggested they blitz. They did. Aidan replaced the blitz with the ball again, this time to the back on an angle that felt like theft. The ball reached the thirteen with two minutes and a small lifetime left.

On first down, Aidan wanted a fade so pretty it would make the scoreboard blush. Coach's voice was in his ear: *Don't go shopping for fireworks.* He ran duo into a loaded box for two and the right to stay himself. On second, he rolled left to change the picture and tucked under a hand he felt but didn't fear. Slide at seven. The boos— some from children who believed quarterbacks should be brave in ways that got them broken—washed and went. Third and three, Marcus was bracketed like a museum piece. Aidan found the tight end again on a delay that existed only if the defensive end thought he was smart. He did. First down at the nine.

Westfield took their last timeout to make content of their sideline. Dempsey pointed at Micah, then at Aidan. The message was a sentence he'd taught them in August: *Win first down; win the game.* Duo for two. The Mustangs crowded paint. Aidan looked to the boundary and saw the corner's heels too close to truth. He did not throw the hole shot. He handed off and let Will write the last line with his feet. Third and goal at the five and twenty-three seconds. Micah jogged. The stadium held its lungs. The kick was clean; the net behaved; the scoreboard remembered obedience. Thirteen-ten.

The kickoff was a squib the front line murdered with their shins. Westfield tried one play from their forty-two because hope is not rational and hit the middle of the field where Cruz kept a ledger. Time expired politely.

There was no dogpile. November teaches you economy. The boys hugged each other like men at a train station and found water. Ms. Rivera wrote a number on her clipboard because she trusted her pen more than her heart. "Ninety-five," Aidan said before she asked. "Coming down."

"Truth used?"

"Once."

"Good." She squeezed his shoulder. "Eat."

The handshake line was honest. Westfield's quarterback said, "See you on film next year," and meant it like a curse and a compliment. Will told a nose tackle he respected his hands because respect is how linemen say *I love you* after sixty snaps. Jamal found a kid he'd tackled into philosophy and told him to keep his head up—literal, not metaphor—because tomorrow's practice would be brutal if he didn't.

At the rail, Karen's face was wet and luminous. She touched Aidan's cheek with mittened fingers and said, "You were patient," like a woman thanking someone for returning what was hers. John hugged his son in public and did not apologize for it. "Next," he said, that single word doing everything a longer speech would have fumbled.

In the locker room, steam rose, and somebody sang two bars of a victory song and forgot the third. Coach didn't speechify. He stood on the bench, looked at the bracket taped to the corkboard, and drew an X through Westfield with a black marker. The squeak made the room feel small and safe. "Tuesday, six a.m. film," he said. "Glenwood or St. Mary's—whoever thinks they're ready. Hydrate. Homework. Be boring. Be beautiful."

When the room thinned to captains and the hum of the soda machine, Aidan sat on the bench and waited for the tremble in his hands to be private and then to pass. The high, clean pain under his ribs settled to a sullen ache. He stood to toss his wrist tape and didn't. He smoothed it instead, the letters he'd pressed there earlier leaving a faint impression he could feel with his thumb.

Marcus slumped beside him, hair damp, grin lazy. "One down," he said.

"Three to go," Aidan said.

"Math major," Marcus teased, then sobered. "You said it when you needed it."

"And we didn't punt the night."

"Look at us," Marcus said. "Grown."

Aidan laughed, the sound catching and smoothing. His phone buzzed on the bench—captains' thread lighting up.

Will: *We ate the line. Second helpings Tuesday.*

Cruz: *Defense owes nobody anything. Still buying fries for the stick on third.*

Micah: *I like November.*

Aidan: *Truth worked. Blue two worked. Next.*

A second buzz—a number he didn't save because he didn't have to.

November is made of clocks, Emily's text read. *You just used them better. — E.*

He typed: *First downs are a love language,* and stared at it, then sent it, then turned the phone face down because the night didn't need more words to mean more.

On the way out, he passed the bracket again. The next box wore two names separated by a thin line: **Glenwood / St. Mary's**. He didn't

153

trace it. He didn't need to. The road narrowed. The lights would get brighter. His body would ask for mercy he'd learned to give in small, correct doses. The town would make more signs. Coach would say fewer words with greater accuracy. Ms. Rivera would keep a ledger the universe respected.

He pressed his thumb to the ridge of the tape one more time, felt the shape of the word through his skin, and walked into November like a boy who understood that some courage is loud and some is quiet and the kind that wins in playoff weather is usually the second kind.

Chapter Twenty-Five – Glenwood

The film had warned them, but film never moved this fast. By the second snap, Lincoln knew Glenwood didn't play the same game Westfield did. The Rams wore black and gold, but they might as well have been dressed in lightning. Their receivers were long, their linebackers closed space like the field had been tilted in their favor, and their defensive end—number 55—moved like someone had wound a spring too tight.

Coach Dempsey had said it all week: "They don't want patience. They want panic. Don't give it to them."

Easier in the classroom than under playoff lights.

The opening kickoff boomed into the end zone, no return. Aidan gathered the huddle at the twenty-five. His ribs hummed, already taped tighter than a present no one wanted, but his eyes found Marcus and steadied.

"Grass," he said. "One blade at a time."

First play: Duo. Will buried his man, the back slid for four. Second play: stick for six. First down. Boring beautiful.

Then Glenwood showed its teeth. First and ten, the Rams sent a safety on a delayed blitz Aidan barely picked up. He slid left, released late. The ball floated longer than he liked. Marcus snagged it, turned up field, and was hammered by a corner who looked carved from granite. Gain of two. Second and long.

By third down, the Rams had ears for cadence. They timed it, jumped the snap, and swallowed the pocket whole. Aidan went down hard under number 55, helmet rattling turf. He lay still long enough for Marcus to curse and Will to haul him up. He nodded once, ribs screaming. Punt.

Glenwood's offense wasted no time. First snap: slant for twelve. Second: screen that unfurled like ribbon, seventeen more. The Rams' quarterback clapped once, grinned at the sideline, and hit a seam route that split Lincoln's safeties. Three plays, six points. Their band roared like an army had arrived.

Karen's nails dug into John's sleeve. "They're too fast," she whispered.

"They're just boys," John said, though his eyes tracked the Rams like they were shadows in a dream.

Emily stood a few rows down, notebook closed, hands clenched around her thermos. She glanced back once, met Karen's eyes. No words. Just shared fear.

The next drive, Aidan found rhythm in quicks. Out. Hitch. Slant. Each release came earlier, faster, his arm working like a piston. Marcus settled into soft spots, Cruz's younger brother—called up from JV for special teams—snagged one across the middle for seven. The chains moved.

At midfield, Glenwood sent six. Aidan saw it, replaced the blitz with the ball again, dumping to the back who darted through a crease for twelve. The crowd exhaled, remembering how noise worked.

Then, on second down at the thirty-three, disaster flirted. Aidan dropped back, scanned, and number 55 ghosted past Will for once, the angle perfect, the hit brutal. Helmet under ribs, body folded, ball loose. Fumble.

The stadium gasped. The Rams recovered. Aidan curled on the turf, coughing, air refusing to return.

"Truth?" Ms. Rivera was already at the sideline.

He shook his head violently, staggering upright. "Not yet." His voice cracked like glass.

Marcus caught his arm, eyes burning. "You don't have to be a martyr."

"I have to be a quarterback."

Glenwood turned the fumble into points three plays later. Deep post. Touchdown. 14–0. The scoreboard glowed cruel.

Lincoln's sideline huddled, jittery. Coach didn't shout. He leaned close. "They're daring you to be stupid. Don't. Breathe. Boring beautiful."

Aidan nodded, though every breath scraped fire.

The next series, he slowed it down. Duo. Duo again. Short stick. Curl. First down. The Rams smirked, waiting for a mistake. He gave them none. At the forty, he checked to mesh. Marcus and the tight end crossed, defenders collided, Marcus sprung free for twenty-three. The crowd roared, the band remembered how to play.

Red zone. First down: incomplete. Second: draw for two. Third and long.

The Rams showed blitz again, disguising nothing. Aidan took the snap, felt pressure, and lofted a ball to the corner of the end zone. Marcus rose, toes brushing paint, hauled it in. Touchdown.

14–7. Lincoln was alive.

The rest of the half was survival. Glenwood's speed stretched the defense, but Cruz's tackling clinic kept the bleeding to field goals. 20–7 at halftime.

In the locker room, boys slumped, sweat dripping, lungs burning. Coach stood at the board, drew two circles and a line between them.

"They want us wide. We go narrow. They want panic. We give patience. They want a highlight. We give them homework." He tapped the marker on the board. "One blade of grass at a time."

Aidan sat wrapped in ice packs, shivering. Ms. Rivera knelt beside him, whispering, "Truth is still there. Say it when it owns you."

He nodded. His thumb rubbed the tape on his wrist. The word pulsed like a heartbeat.

The second half was a war. Lincoln's first drive: twelve plays, fifty-eight yards, all small bites. Out, curl, draw, stick. The Rams blitzed; Aidan bled them. Marcus caught everything in reach, Cruz's brother chipped in two key grabs. At the five-yard line, Aidan pulled on a zone read, kept, dove across the line. Touchdown.

20–14.

The crowd exploded. Karen wept openly. Emily stood on her seat, yelling words she hadn't meant to yell.

But Glenwood answered. A wheel route down the sideline, seventy yards, silence. 27–14.

Fourth quarter. Ten minutes. Lincoln needed two scores.

The huddle was quiet, breaths clouding in the cold. Aidan looked at Marcus, then the line.

"We're not done." His voice was hoarse, but the fire lived. "We're not done until the clock says so." And they weren't. Ten plays, eighty yards, culminating in Marcus slipping between brackets for a fourteen-yard touchdown. 27–21.

The Rams stalled, forced to punt. The stadium buzzed like an engine.

Three minutes left. Ball at the twenty. Season in his hands.

First down: curl for five. Second: draw for three. Third and two. Duo. Will crushed his man. First down.

Then it came. Glenwood sent six again. The end had a free run. Aidan saw it late, planted, launched a deep shot to Marcus. The hit came under ribs, brutal, lights exploding. The ball spun thirty yards, Marcus leapt, snagged, landed at the Rams' twenty-five. The crowd detonated.

But Aidan didn't rise. He lay on the turf, motionless, gasping for air that wouldn't return. Ms. Rivera sprinted. Coach dropped to a knee.

Finally, Aidan rolled, coughing, hand clutching ribs. He waved them off weakly, staggering upright.

"Truth?" Rivera asked.

He pressed his hand to his tape. Shook his head. "Not yet."

Two plays later, he hit the tight end on a seam. Touchdown. 28–27. Lincoln up, twenty seconds left.

The Rams tried desperation. Cruz picked off a pass at midfield, cradling it like a child. The horn sounded. The stadium shook.

Lincoln had beaten Glenwood.

In the stands, Karen collapsed into John's arms, sobbing with joy and terror. Emily pressed her hands together like prayer, whispering, "He did it," over and over. On the field, Marcus grabbed Aidan, half-carrying him to the sideline. "You're insane," he said, tears mixing with sweat.

"I'm your quarterback," Aidan rasped.

Coach met him at the numbers, eyes wet though his voice stayed steel. "Next week," he said simply.

Aidan nodded, ribs screaming, body begging for rest. But the fire still burned. November wasn't over.

Chapter Twenty-Six – The Semifinal (Expanded)

By Tuesday the bracket had thinned to four names, two on each side like finalists waiting to be invented. On Lincoln's half: **St. Mary's**— private school, crisp uniforms, a tradition that traveled like its own weather. Their film looked like catechism: quarters that pattern-matched without panic, linebackers whose feet never lied, a quarterback who could hurt you with his eyes and then with everything else.

"They feed on mistakes," Coach Dempsey said, tapping the laser pointer at the whiteboard where St. Mary's alignments glowed. "So we starve them. No sugar. No free yards. They don't get a story unless we write it."

The week felt shorter even though every day stretched. Ms. Rivera's clipboard became a clock: weigh-in, pulse, hydration, salt. "Down a pound," she said Wednesday, neutral and not. "That could be socks. Or it could be your body doing the math. Eat."

She handed him a little thermos. "Broth," she said before he could grimace. "Warm goes down easier when the ribs complain."

He drank and felt the heat spread like a small argument he wanted to lose.

At home, Karen folded towels with unnecessary precision and tried not to read the articles that now included Aidan's name with too much room around it. John toggled between HUDL and patience, replacing panic with technique. "When they spin to three late," he said, drawing with his finger on the counter because the tablet was in the other room, "don't go hunting. Take the hitch. If the corner cheats, you'll know. But he won't. He's a math student."

Aidan nodded, not because he needed the reminder but because he liked the sound of his father's voice when it treated fear like a coverage to be solved.

Emily left a small envelope in the McAllisters' mailbox on Thursday evening with a sticky note that read **no doorbell, just luck**. Inside were three index cards: a tiny lion running through snow; *No free doubt* in block letters; and, last, in small script, *You don't have to be the headline to be the hero. — E.*

Karen found the envelope and, after reading, stood a long time at the sink. When Aidan came in from a walk-through, cheeks pink from the dry cold, she held the cards out. "I like her," she said, undecorated. "She writes like a coach, not a fan."

"Me too," he said, and the admission felt simple and good.

The semifinal was at a neutral site—the old college stadium on the edge of town, concrete poured when men wore hats to games, the kind of lights that hummed loud enough to be part of the crowd. The air had teeth; the forecast flirted with flurries and then decided to deliver show instead of promise. As the buses rolled in, a dust of snow began to pin-dot the turf, catching in face masks and eyelashes.

"You'll want to be heroes," Coach said in the tunnel, voice low because cold made loud sound brittle. "Don't. Be right. It's enough."

Cruz had a towel tucked into his belt like a banner. Will rolled his shoulders, the tape on his fingers white against the night. Marcus flexed his hands and shook them once like he was flinging off last week. Aidan taped his left wrist with the black strip and pressed the letters into the underside where only he could feel them. He breathed in through his nose, out through his mouth, felt the ache hum and settle.

The captains strode to midfield. St. Mary's kids had that clean-shaven, efficient look like someone had arranged them by ruler. The coin flashed, flipped, decided. Lincoln received. The band played a brave version of the fight song through scarves. The student section's poster game had matured—no taunts, just a line of hand-painted signs that said **TRUTH, NO FREE DOUBT, BORING BEAUTIFUL,** and, tucked between them, Emily's neat **FIRST DOWNS ARE A LOVE LANGUAGE** in a blue mittened hand.

The opening kick settled into Jamal's arms; he brought it to the twenty-seven and slipped on a new seam of snow that made the crowd gasp and then laugh, relieved it was just gravity. Aidan jogged to the huddle and rubbed his thumb along the tape ridge.

"Trips right. Sixty-two," he said. "Eyes. Tempo."

St. Mary's showed quarters with outside leverage like a textbook. Out for seven. Duo for three—first down. Smash for five. Draw for two. The cold made the ball feel like a rock and his ribs feel every breath. He narrowed his world to cadence, steps, shoulders. When the Crusaders sent a weak-side pressure, he replaced it with the ball to the back in the flat and stole eight. Not pretty. Beautiful enough.

At the Crusaders' thirty-four, the field tightened as if offended. Aidan tagged mesh and watched the inside backers "banjo"—switch responsibility mid-route like a dance they'd practiced in church. The sit was covered; the wheel was shaded. He threw the checkdown and took the boos like vitamins. Third and six. He found Marcus on a dig right at the stick, and the safety arrived exactly then, the sound like two batons striking, the ball glued by hands that refused to be negotiated with. First down. The band tried exuberance and found only endurance.

Red zone. If patience had a smell, it would be cold rubber and breath in November. Two runs for four yards. A slant broken up by a corner teaching film in real time. Micah trundled on, the ball barked, the kick went through polite and centered. Three-nothing, Lincoln, in a quarter where it had felt like both teams had been grading papers.

St. Mary's answered with the thing film promises and you can't stop hating: RPOs into empty spaces because their quarterback's eyes and feet had an alliance. First down, glance route behind a linebacker's step. Second down, zone read kept at exactly the right wrong time, seven yards. Third and three, orbit motion, fake, throwback to a tight end who looked like confession. The drive ended with a quarterback draw called from a huddle and executed like a sacrament. Seven-three, Crusaders.

On the sideline, Ms. Rivera appeared, unsmiling and attentive. "Rate?"

"Ninety-ish," he said.

She looked at the watch. "Eighty-eight. Good-ish." The corners of her eyes softened. "Call it if you need it."

"Tool, not surrender," he said, and she gave a small salute with the pen as if she'd been waiting to hear him say it back.

The second quarter eased into being like a joint you've warmed. Lincoln stole five here, four there. St. Mary's stole six and paid it back with a penalty that made their coach's jaw flex. The snow fattened, not real, not a problem, just enough to make the world picturesque and footing suspect. On a second-and-ten, the Crusaders spun to one-high late. The boundary corner's heels got greedy. Marcus's stance whispered *now*. Aidan shook his head. Not yet. He hit the pivot for four and made third-and-short look like chess. The boos were fewer now, the adults catching the rhythm the kids always resist.

They crossed midfield and stalled at the thirty-eight, got nothing on a hard count, and punted to pin. The Crusaders climbed out methodically, the quarterback jogging like a man not interested in frostbite, and then they got cute—double pass into a field that had too much white in it. Jamal picked it in the snow like a boy finding a coin and slid out of bounds on a laugh. The stadium warmed fifteen degrees.

Two minutes to half. Two-minute drill was Aidan's favorite problem even with fingers that couldn't quite remember summer. He hit Marcus on out-and-up for twelve and toe-tap. He found the back on an angle for nine he rode to eleven because his hips argued with physics. He looked backside and hit the tight end sitting between zones like a man sitting between arguments. Timeout. Twenty-six seconds. Ball at the nineteen.

The call came in, something they'd drawn on a napkin in June and installed in August for a week like this: sprint out right, throwback left—*Leak Storm*. St. Mary's bit, because good teams bite if you feed them enough correct. Aidan sold it without hurry, shoulders open, hips telling a small lie, then reset and threw back to a tackle-eligible who had all the subtlety of a truck and two soft hands he'd practiced in secret. Touchdown.

Ten-seven, Lincoln, into the half. The tunnel air pressed close and smelled like wool and oranges. Coach's talk was spare: "Top stays on," to defense. "Take the grass until they invent sky," to offense. He turned to Aidan with the water bottle most men ask permission to drink from. "I've got no ego about rotating you. If I say *Eli*, you nod and breathe. If you say *truth*, I nod and don't teach it a lesson."

"Deal," Aidan said. He meant it, and something unlaced between his shoulders.

Ms. Rivera tightened a bandage and made him sip broth again. "Not my favorite vintage," he said, and she huffed a laugh, the kind that refuses to be charmed by its own existence. "Rate?"

"Ninety-one," he said, honest. "Nerves."

"Good nerves," she allowed. "Don't wait until they're bad."

164

The third quarter arrived with a wind that had found its voice. St. Mary's adjusted cruelly: more motion to corrupt Cruz's angles, more glance to punish the tiniest overstep. The Crusaders took the kickoff and turned it into seven by increments and then one knife—quarterback keep off tackle, a defensive end fooled by gravity and a fake he'd seen too often. Fourteen-ten, Crusaders.

On the next series, Aidan felt the world rock under him, a boat's small warning. He blinked, tapped two fingers to his thigh.

"Blue two," Marcus called, easy as weather. Eli trotted in like a promise kept. Three plays of competent correctness—duo, stick, draw—became a first down. Aidan drank water and counted breaths. Ms. Rivera's eyes did their math and didn't panic aloud.

He returned, found the rhythm again. Out. Curl. Hitch. At the Crusaders' forty-three, he wanted the hole shot because everything in his body wanted a shortcut out of wind. The corner's hips weren't lying. He checked away and took five. The adults cheered out of proportion. The kids groaned and then smiled because the scoreboard didn't move and the clock did.

Deep in the third, St. Mary's sacked him on a well-timed green dog that made Will swear in a dialect that sounded like love. The ribs flared hot, a struck match. He rolled and laughed because it hurt and said it: "Truth."

Blue two ate a minute. The punt wriggled into the corner. Cruz, who had been a metronome, turned into a sentencing judge—fill, fit, finish—and St. Mary's found third-and-forever and a punt of their own.

Fourth quarter, fourteen-ten, and the sky deciding whether to snow in earnest. Coach tapped his wrist. "Two first downs," his mouth said. "They'll run out of absolutions."

First down: duo for four, Will moving a man the way carpenters move stubborn studs—with patience and leverage. Second: stick for six and a stare from a linebacker who admired the audacity of boredom. First down. The band found a beat they could keep even with numb fingers.

Then the bad thing—just a little one—arrived. Third and six at midfield, the end swam and arrived under Aidan's ribs with malice that wasn't personal and hurt like it was. The world strobed. He lay there too long. Ms. Rivera and Coach and Marcus all moved at once with the choreography of people who had rehearsed something no one wanted to perform. He sat up, coughed, tasted metal he did not name.

"Truth," he said, before either could ask.

Eli took them the last inch of a first down with a sneak that could have been called humility. Two more snaps ate snow and time. Punt. Pin. St. Mary's started at their eight and learned what it feels like to breathe with a hand on your chest. Jamal made a tackle that felt nostalgic and mean. Cruz arrived where the ball wanted to be and asked it to justify itself. Third and long. The quarterback tried to invent room and found a sideline that had other ideas. Punt.

Two-fifteen on the clock. Ball at the St. Mary's forty. The stadium's noise condensed, less roar than intent.

Aidan's breath came thin but regular. He rubbed the tape, felt the word, didn't need to read it to be guided by it. "Grass," he said. "Then sky."

First down: hitch for five. Second: draw for four. Third and one: hard count got a flinch and, this time, the flag. First down without bruise. The Crusaders' coordinator looked like a man who had mislaid a favorite pen.

Twenty-nine yards. Wind in his face. He rolled right, not to run but to change the picture, and hit Marcus on a sail at twelve, the ball sticking like a sentence finished.

Fourteen yards. One timeout each side. Coach's voice in the helmet: "Win first down." Duo for three. The clock took a polite sip. Second

166

and seven. The safety cheated a half-step toward Marcus because he was not a fool and yet was a man. Aidan didn't punish pride; he rewarded geometry. The tight end delayed, nudged, leaked—again—and opened a window at eight. Aidan threw it with shoulders quiet and hands sure. First and goal at the six. St. Mary's took their timeout to ask the night for advice.

Dempsey pointed—Micah, then Aidan—and mouthed without drama: *Three plays for three yards; kick if you must.* Aidan nodded, happy to be boring in a world that kept offering him reasons to be loud.

First down: duo for two, anger in pads, patience in feet. Second: roll left behind Will pulling, Waterfall, and slide at the one because the safety had announced violence. Booing from children. Clapping from parents. Third and goal, twenty-three seconds, and he could feel the hole shot like a song in his teeth.

He handed off. Will and the right guard folded a man and a half into a shape that left exactly the space the back needed to fall into the end zone like a book finding its shelf. The place exhaled joy. There was no flag. Micah's extra point kissed through, demure.

Seventeen–fourteen. Twenty seconds. Squib, shins, scramble. St. Mary's got one throw—one—with four seconds and a wind that had turned treacherous. The ball climbed and spun and fluttered. Cruz went up like a man climbing into a photograph and batted it down with the absurd gentleness of a person blowing out a candle. Horn. Lincoln.

The hug at the rail was messy and public. Karen cried without apology. John held both of them like a man who had been practicing for a different future and chose this one instead. Ms. Rivera breathed in a way he had never seen her breathe at a game—not managing, not measuring, just breathing.

On the field, Aidan bent with his hands on his knees and laughed because it hurt less than anything else he could have done. Marcus crashed into him from the side and then eased, foreheads touching. "Next week," he said, reverent and ridiculous.

"Next week," Aidan echoed.

The handshake line tasted like respect and winter. St. Mary's quarterback, a kid with decent eyes, said, "You make boring look like art," not snide. "Go win it."

"We'll try," Aidan said, because arrogance felt wrong in snow.

In the locker room, they sang exactly one verse of something and forgot the rest on purpose. Coach didn't climb a bench. He walked to the bracket, now taped to cinderblock, and drew a black X through **St. Mary's** with his pen. The sound was secular and sacred. Then he drew an arrow to the last box, just the one, and wrote in block letters the thing the town had been thinking and no one had yet said aloud on a wall:

STATE FINAL.

He turned and found Aidan's eyes last. "Tuesday," he said, voice like a plan. "Six a.m. Truth travels with us."

The room thinned. The steam lingered. Ms. Rivera handed Aidan a paper cup and didn't ask for a number because she trusted his face. He beat her to the sentence anyway. "Ninety-three. Coming down."

She nodded. "Eat."

He peeled the black tape from his wrist slowly, folded it twice, felt the faint letters on his skin, and pressed his thumb there until warmth returned to more than his hand.

His phone buzzed before the captains' thread did—Emily.

You didn't buy fireworks. You made a cathedral out of first downs. — E.

He typed and erased twice, then sent: *We starved them.* A second message arrived before he could pocket the phone:

One more. I'll bring a louder index card.

Outside, the snow had thickened into something worthy of the name. The stadium lights haloed each flake so the world looked like it was clapping. The buses idled. Boys carried coolers and helmets and the last of the doubt out into the night. Aidan paused at the doorway and looked back at the chalked word on the wall—**STATE FINAL**—like a door he would walk through and a thing he'd been running toward since August with a hundred friends and the ache of a bargain he was still keeping.

He stepped out into the snow and let it sting his face. He took a breath that hurt. He took another. He put his hand over his ribs and felt the tape's ghost and the letters there, not visible and more present than anything else.

Truth.

Chapter Twenty-Seven – State Final

The buses rolled before sunrise, two convoys lit by yellow beams and escorted by the kind of silence that means everything has been said. The boys wore travel sweats, headphones, hoods up. Some dozed. Some stared out at frost that crawled across farm fields like lace. In the front, Coach Dempsey sat straight-backed with a clipboard he didn't look at. His toothpick rode the corner of his mouth like punctuation.

Aidan sat by the window, ribs bandaged so tight it felt like breathing through gauze. The black tape on his wrist warmed under his thumb. He didn't write the word yet. He'd do that in the locker room, the ritual saved for the moment before the lights. Marcus snored beside him, earbuds blaring faint tinny drums, head bumping against the glass.

The stadium appeared after an hour like a revelation—newer, bigger, meant for college Saturdays and suddenly theirs. The scoreboard's blank face loomed, waiting to decide what would be remembered. By the time the buses pulled into the lot, the parking fields already brimmed. Half the town of Lincoln had made the drive; the other half would be glued to radios and TV.

Inside the locker room, the air smelled of fresh paint and history. The walls gleamed white. The benches were sturdy and indifferent. Jerseys hung like armor. Each one bore weight heavier than the stitching.

Coach didn't speechify. He stood at the front, toothpick tucked in his hand, and said, "Same field. Different paint. Don't let the crowd lie to you. It's still football. It's still you."

He looked at Aidan longer than the others. "You made a bargain. We've kept it honest. Tonight, you play it out. Truth if you need it. Blue two if you must. No free doubt. The rest will take care of itself."

The boys clapped once, hard.

Ms. Rivera taped Aidan's ribs one final time, her hands efficient, her eyes not. "How's the pain?"

He smirked. "I'll call it halftime."

"Don't joke," she said, but the corner of her mouth betrayed her. She pressed the roll of tape into his palm when she finished. "For luck."

He used it. Black strip across his left wrist, letters pressed beneath the fabric: **TRUTH.**

Kickoff was thunder. The other side—Ironwood, dressed in crimson and white—returned with a swagger that matched their reputation. Their quarterback was a senior with scholarship papers already signed. Their line averaged thirty pounds heavier per man. Their fans filled half the stadium and then some.

But the first defensive series belonged to Cruz. Fill, shock, shed, finish. Ironwood gained two, then lost one, then watched their quarterback's third-down throw fall incomplete. Punt.

The crowd split in half—half jeering, half exploding. Lincoln's sideline came alive.

Aidan jogged out, Marcus to his right, Will pounding his chest like a war drum.

"Grass first," Aidan told them in the huddle. "Sky later."

First down: Duo for five, Will swallowing a defensive tackle. Second: stick for four. Third and one: sneak. Chains moved. The student section roared **BORING BEAUTIFUL** until their voices cracked.

They crept across midfield, each snap a small theft: hitch, curl, draw. At the thirty-two, Ironwood sent heat. Aidan slid, replaced the blitz with a dump-off to the back, eight yards. At the twenty-four, Marcus raised his eyebrows—*now?* Aidan shook his head. *Not yet.*

Red zone. First down: nothing. Second: mesh, Marcus clearing traffic, snagging seven. Third and short: Duo again. First down at the twelve. The drive stretched, deliberate, like a sermon.

On second down, he found Marcus on a dig that stopped on a dime. Touchdown. Seven–nothing, Lincoln.

The crowd erupted. Karen clung to John's arm, tears already streaming. Emily stood on her seat, index card in mittened hands: *FIRST DOWNS ARE A LOVE LANGUAGE.*

Ironwood struck back in four plays. Slant. Zone read. Out route. Then a seam route their receiver caught in stride for forty. Touchdown. Seven–seven.

Back and forth it went. Lincoln's patience against Ironwood's power. Ten–seven after a field goal. Ten–ten after another. Fourteen–ten when Aidan pulled on zone read, kept, and dove across the line, ribs screaming, Ms. Rivera chewing her lip on the sideline.

By halftime: 17–17.

The locker room buzzed with adrenaline and cold sweat. Boys sucked oranges dry. Cruz barked like a man who'd learned a new language just to shout in it. Will sat silent, fists clenched, face pale with focus.

Coach said three sentences. "They're strong. We're smarter. Forty-eight minutes is a long time to be smart."

Aidan sat with his head bowed, whispering the cadence under his breath. Ms. Rivera pressed another salt cap into his hand, her pen hovering over the clipboard. "Rate?"

"Ninety-three."

She glanced at the watch. "Ninety. Hold it."

Third quarter. Ironwood leaned into muscle. Their line surged, their back pounded, their quarterback darted. A ten-play drive ended in a plunge. 24–17.

Lincoln answered with patience: curl, draw, hitch. At midfield, Aidan rolled right, threw deep. Marcus leapt, snagged, came down at the twenty. Three plays later, the tight end leaked across the middle. Touchdown. 24–24.

The stadium shook.

The rest of the quarter was defense and bruises. Cruz flattened a pulling guard. Jamal undercut a slant. Ironwood's linebacker slammed Aidan so hard the air left his chest in a wheeze he couldn't disguise. Ms. Rivera stood at the white line, hand twitching toward the field, but he waved her off.

"Truth?" Marcus asked in the huddle.

Aidan touched his wrist, breathed. "Not yet."

Fourth quarter. 27–27. Ten minutes. The season dangling on the smallest mistakes.

Ironwood drove first. Their quarterback scrambled, juked, dived. Field goal. 30–27.

Lincoln got the ball with five minutes. The huddle circled, faces pale with frost and belief.

"We've been boring all year," Aidan said. His voice cracked, then steadied. "Now let's be beautiful."

First down: curl for six. Second: Duo for three. Third and one: sneak, legs churning, Will pushing behind. First down.

At midfield, Ironwood blitzed. Aidan saw it, lofted a ball to Marcus. Thirty yards later, out of bounds at the twenty. The crowd lost its mind.

First down: draw. Two yards. Second: out route. Five. Third and three.

Coach's voice in his helmet: *Patience. No free doubt.*

The play call came: zone read. Aidan took the snap, read the end, pulled. He tucked the ball, ribs screaming, legs pounding, broke one tackle, then another. The end zone opened.

Ten yards. Five. He dove, stretched, broke the plane. Touchdown.

33–30, Lincoln.

The stadium exploded—noise, color, prayer. Karen sobbed into John's chest. Emily screamed his name, hands shaking with her index card clutched tight.

But the hit came late. Number 52, Ironwood's linebacker, barreled through. His helmet drove into Aidan's ribs as he lay across the goal line. The sound was ugly, final.

Aidan didn't move.

The crowd roared, then stilled. Ms. Rivera dropped her clipboard and sprinted. Coach Dempsey followed, his face stripped bare. Marcus tore his helmet off, screaming his name.

On the turf, under the lights, with the scoreboard frozen at **Lincoln 33, Ironwood 30**, Aidan lay motionless.

The game ended not on celebration, but on silence—the kind that holds both triumph and grief in the same trembling hand.

Chapter Twenty-Eight – The Hospital

The ride to the hospital blurred into sirens and fluorescent light. Paramedics swarmed the field, kneeling in the end zone where moments before victory had been carved. They cut Aidan's jersey, pressed oxygen to his mouth, wrapped straps across his chest as if containment could hold life in. Marcus and Cruz stood at the sideline, helmets dangling in their hands, faces hollow, while Ms. Rivera rode in the ambulance with him, her clipboard left behind on the turf like shed skin.

The crowd hadn't moved. Ten thousand people, frozen between joy and horror, stared at the scoreboard that still read **Lincoln 33, Ironwood 30.** The band's instruments hung silent at their sides. The only sound was Karen's voice, broken, screaming her son's name as John gripped her waist to keep her from collapsing.

The hospital smelled like antiseptic and grief. Fluorescent lights buzzed too bright. Karen and John ran through sliding doors, their coats half-open, escorted by a nurse with the kind of face that knew how to be urgent and gentle at once.

"He's in trauma bay three," the nurse said. "The doctors are working. Please—wait here."

Waiting felt like betrayal. Karen paced, fingers knotted in prayer. John sat rigid in a plastic chair, hands clasped tight, jaw locked. Emily arrived minutes later, hair tangled from the wind, cheeks flushed from the run up the hill from the stadium. She hesitated at the doorway until Karen saw her, then opened her arms without hesitation.

"He'd want you here," Karen whispered into Emily's hair.

Marcus, Cruz, and Will came soon after, still in their pads, sweat drying cold on their skin. Coach Dempsey trailed behind, hat in his hands, eyes shadowed. Ms. Rivera appeared from the double doors, her scrubs smeared, clipboard replaced by rubber gloves. She pulled the gloves off slowly, as if each tug might buy her another moment before she spoke.

"He's stable," she said at last, her voice steady but tight. Relief rolled through the room, bodies sagging, air filling lungs again. "He's breathing. We've stopped the bleeding for now. He's going upstairs for scans."

Karen collapsed into John's arms, sobbing. Marcus clapped once, sharp, like he was trying to anchor the room. Cruz bent over, hands on knees, whispering thanks into the floor.

Ms. Rivera's gaze settled on them, softer now. "But it's serious. His body... it's tired. He's fought longer than most ever could."

Hours passed. Machines beeped, footsteps echoed, time stretched. The boys fell asleep in corners, helmets resting at their sides. Emily never moved from her chair, notebook clutched in her lap like armor. Karen held Aidan's hand whenever she was allowed into the room, whispering Bible verses, telling stories from when he was small—his first steps, his first catch in the backyard, the night he begged to stay up late to watch the Super Bowl.

John sat on the other side of the bed, stroking his son's hair, repeating the same quiet refrain: "You did it. You did it, son."

When Aidan stirred, eyelids fluttering, the room leaned forward. His lips cracked into a faint smile.

"Did we win?"

"Yes," Karen whispered, tears spilling. "You won, baby. You won."

Marcus stepped closer, voice breaking. "State champs, Four. Scoreboard still says it."

Aidan exhaled, the ghost of a laugh caught in the sound. He tried to lift his wrist, the black tape still there, the word smudged but legible. Ms. Rivera helped him, pressing his hand gently against his chest.

"Truth," he whispered.

The room swallowed tears and silence together.

By morning, the whole town knew. Cars crowded the hospital parking lot. The chapel filled with classmates, teachers, neighbors. The mayor dropped off coffee for waiting parents. The diner sent trays of sandwiches. Lincoln had always rallied for touchdowns and trophies; now it rallied for a boy lying in a hospital bed, his heart fighting to keep its rhythm.

Inside, the team gathered around him in shifts. Cruz promised he'd wear number four next season. Will swore the line would never let another quarterback take a free shot as long as he breathed. Marcus sat longest, telling jokes until his throat hurt, pretending Aidan would laugh again at the punchlines.

Emily finally laid her index cards on the nightstand: the lion, the motto, the line about first downs. She added a new one in fresh ink: *You gave us more than football.*

Karen read it, pressed it to her lips, and wept.

Late that night, monitors beeped slower, breaths shallower. Doctors spoke gently, words wrapped in mercy but edged in inevitability.

John took Karen's hand. Marcus reached for Cruz, who reached for Will, a chain of boys holding each other upright. Emily laid her head on the rail, her tears darkening the sheet. Ms. Rivera stood in the corner, hands clasped, eyes closed, whispering a prayer she hadn't intended to say aloud.

Aidan opened his eyes once more, gaze drifting over them all. His lips moved, soft, almost inaudible.

"Thank you."

Then the monitors flatlined, and silence filled the room.

Karen's scream broke it. John held her as if the weight of grief could be carried by muscle alone. The boys buried their faces in each other's shoulders. Emily gripped the index card so tightly it bent.

Coach Dempsey stepped forward, his voice low, steady, reverent.

"He gave everything he had. And it was enough."

Chapter Twenty-Nine –
The Funeral (Expanded)

The gym couldn't hold them, so the town moved the service to the field.

By noon the stands were a quilt of blue coats and wool hats, the railings dressed with ribbons, the fifty-yard line edged with chrysanthemums from the florist who'd done every homecoming for twenty years. The state trophy sat on a table draped in a simple cloth—someone had tucked an index card beneath it that read **FIRST DOWNS ARE A LOVE LANGUAGE** in tidy block letters.

They set Aidan's helmet and his cleats on the table beside the trophy, scuffed and stubborn. The number four jersey lay folded, the white numerals bright even under winter light. The scoreboard, for once, was on in daylight: **LINCOLN 33, IRONWOOD 30.** No clock. Just numbers.

The band warmed quietly, not to perform so much as to keep their hands from going numb. The cheerleaders stood with arms linked, bows subdued. Teachers took their places along the track and tried not to count students who should have been in class. At the top of the home bleachers, a row of old-timers from the diner—men who had played when face masks were smaller and practice water was rationed—took off their caps and didn't put them back on.

The pallbearers were boys. Will and Cruz on one side, Marcus and Jamal on the other, two seniors behind them who had learned in

179

August how not to flinch and learned in November when to. They wore suits and sneakers because dress shoes weren't built to cross turf. When the hearse door opened and the first corner of the casket showed, the whole home side rose without being told.

Karen walked behind, one hand on the polished wood like it might float away without her, John's hand steadying the small of her back. Ms. Rivera came next, scrubs traded for a dark coat, her clipboard absent for the first time anyone could remember. Dr. Patel stood with her, tie straight, eyes tired, the expression of a man who had told truths for a living and preferred not to today.

They set the casket on a platform at the fifty, the place where Aidan had clapped his hands and brought the huddle in a hundred times, where he'd looked left and right and said *grass* and meant it. The pastor stepped to a microphone on a stand that had grown up out of the paint like a stem. He said welcome and a Psalm and a line about running with endurance. He kept it short because he understood the grammar of grief.

The mayor read a proclamation that declared **Aidan McAllister Day** and announced the creation of the **Fourth and Forever Scholarship**, to be given every year to a student who made boring beautiful in whatever they did—medicine, music, diesel mechanics, debate. People clapped, then cried, then clapped again because crying alone in a crowd feels like drowning.

Coach Dempsey spoke without notes. He stood with his cap crushed in his hands and looked at the casket the way he had looked at walls with whiteboards—problem, plan, respect.

"He was not a miracle," he said, voice low and even on the PA. "He was a boy who made the right choice, then another, then another, until a season turned into a life we could be proud of. He didn't give speeches. He called plays. He said *truth* when lesser men would've said nothing and hoped to sneak by." He turned his head, finding the line of boys in their suits. "He was our quarterback. Not because he threw a pretty ball—though he did—but because he trusted the boring things. First down. Ball security. Eyes right. No free doubt." He exhaled once, a sound like a whistle that didn't need a whistle. "He taught me that a person can be brave without being loud. We will carry that forward. We will make him ordinary on purpose by doing our jobs the right way, on the field and off."

He stepped back. Will walked forward next, a large boy trying to be smaller out of courtesy. He didn't trust the microphone at first, then found it. "We promised him no free rushers," he said, voice thickening once and then clearing. "We couldn't stop everything. But we can stop some things from here on. If a kid gets pushed around in our hallway, he's got five linemen for life. If a teacher needs help moving boxes, we're there. If somebody needs a ride home or a tire changed or a couch carried up the worst stairs in town, call the group chat. We got you. That's our protection now."

Cruz went next and didn't bother with a microphone. His voice carried like it always did. "He hit first and he hit last," he said, and half the team huffed a laugh at the familiar cadence. "But what I'll remember is when he said *truth* and we all moved. That's leadership. That's family. That's how we'll run it. He's not here to set the edge. We are."

Marcus stood with both hands on the podium because if he didn't hold something he might float away. He looked at the helmet, then at Karen, then at the student section where Emily sat with her notebook closed on her lap, hands on top, as if keeping her words from scattering.

"I was supposed to run the routes and he was supposed to throw it where I'd be," Marcus said. He smiled despite himself. "Usually I was there." The crowd gave him the mercy of a small laugh. "Here's the thing: he threw things to where they were going to be, not where they were. Passes. People. Nights. He saw a little ahead and he asked us to get there. When we did, it worked. When we didn't, he didn't blame—he came back to the huddle and gave us grass again." His throat tightened. He let it. "He made me better in ways I can't run on a route tree. I don't know how to pay that back except to keep showing up when the easy play looks prettier."

He stepped away before he could become a different person. On the way past the casket, he set a small thing on the wood: a slice of the black wrist tape, letters indented but unreadable if you didn't already know.

Ms. Rivera didn't intend to speak. Then she did. She walked up with her hands empty and her posture that of someone who has had to be right more than she's wanted to be.

"He was my patient," she said simply. "And my headache. He could charm a pulse down ten beats if he thought it would buy him another series." Laughter. She smiled at the casket like she wanted to scold it one last time. "He listened when it mattered. That matters. He chose truth. That saved him more times than you think, and it saved the people around him, too." She looked out at the boys, at the town, at the parents who had started counting breaths in their sleep. "Take care of your ordinary. Eat. Sleep. Go to your checkups. Say the hard word when you need to. That's not small; it's holy."

At the pastor's nod, Emily rose. She wasn't on the program. No one needed a program to know she would stand. She walked to the microphone with her pencil behind her ear by reflex and her index cards in her coat pocket like talismans.

"I didn't know what football was for," she said, and the band kids nodded involuntarily. "This season taught me it can be a language. Aidan taught me first downs mean love—small, right choices that move you toward the good thing when the good thing doesn't want to be moved. He refused to be a headline in the worst sense. He became one in the best." She pulled out one card, read without looking at it because she had written it into herself. "We say heroes are loud. He wasn't. He was patient in a way that made bravery quiet enough to sit with. I'm grateful to have known him even in the margins."

Karen stepped forward last. The wind lifted the edge of her scarf and the microphone caught the sound of cloth. She touched the helmet and then her son's jersey the way mothers touch fevered foreheads and homecoming boutonnieres and the top of a head bowed over homework.

"I don't have words for the way the house sounds," she said, and no one breathed. "But I have words for him." She turned toward the casket. "You made me braver than I knew how to be. You told the truth even when I didn't want to hear it, and you kept your bargain longer than I knew anyone could. You were kind. You were stubborn. You were patient. You were ours." She lifted her chin, backbone a visible thing. "Thank you for letting this town love you out loud."

When she stepped away, the pastor nodded to the band director, who lifted a hand. The band played the fight song once, quiet as it could be and still count. On the last note, the scoreboard went dark, then blinked back to **33–30** because someone in the booth had decided that was part of the liturgy now.

The team stood and formed two lines from the fifty to the gate. As the pallbearers lifted, each player stopped and pressed something on the casket—wrist tape, a towel strip, a patch with a number 4 they'd worn on their sleeves since the semifinal. The procession walked under a tunnel of upheld hands, not like a celebration, like a promise.

The hearse took the slow route out of the stadium, looped once around the track, then eased onto Main Street. People lined the sidewalks all the way to the church, blue ribbons tied to every lamppost. Signs didn't shout; they thanked. Children sat on their fathers' shoulders and didn't ask many questions because adults had faces like civics lessons.

At the cemetery, the ceremony was short. The earth was hard and honest. The pastor said dust and breath and hope that sounded like muscle and mercy at the same time. When it was time, Karen set the folded jersey into the crook of the casket's flowers, fingers lingering on the four. John placed the helmet carefully on top for a moment and then handed it to Marcus, who held it like it could still call a huddle.

After, people did what people do when they can't fix a thing: they cooked. The church hall tables bowed under casseroles and pies and something unidentifiable that had probably been an act of love at some point in its journey. People told stories that were small enough to carry—*He carried my groceries when my wrist was in a cast. He stayed after and threw to my little brother for half an hour. He signed a program and wrote "do your homework" and my kid did it.* Laughter broke through the surface of grief in bubbles and then settled again.

The scholarship jar on the edge of the table filled and then overflowed. Someone pulled a proper box from a closet. Then two boxes. By sunset, there was talk of an endowment, and the banker from the second pew nodded like a man who could make numbers behave if given purpose.

In the late afternoon, the field drew people back the way ponds draw kids with sticks. The maintenance crew had chalked a small **4** in the corner of the end zone where he had fallen, small as initials carved into a tree. The sun slid behind the bleachers and turned the air the color of steel. Marcus wandered out to the paint and sat with his knees up and his hands on his shins. After a minute, Will lowered himself beside him. After another, Cruz dropped like a weight, elbows on knees.

They didn't talk for a while. The silence wasn't empty; it was full of everything they'd already said aloud and the more important things they'd said with how they'd blocked and tackled and waited.

"We still have lifts," Will said eventually, because you have to point at something.

"Yeah," Cruz said. "And a freshman who takes the wrong angle on every outside zone."

"And a JV receiver who thinks 'now' means every play," Marcus added, the smile tugging at the corner of his mouth. "We'll teach him later."

They sat until the lights popped on in banks, late by habit, because the field forgot it was done for the year and reached for night out of instinct. Ms. Rivera crossed the track with a paper bag and tossed it to them—sandwiches, water, a packet of salt she pretended not to have included. "Eat," she said, then nodded at the chalked **4** and didn't explain herself. She didn't have to.

Emily walked the edge of the track and didn't step onto the turf, staying where she always stayed—close enough to see, far enough to tell it true. She waved once when Marcus glanced over. He tipped the helmet in his lap like a hat. She took an index card from her pocket, the last blank one she'd kept, and wrote slowly: *We will keep moving the chains.* She set it under the state trophy earlier; now she tucked a corner under the edge of the scoreboard ladder, a private vow.

Night came in fully. People filtered home in ones and twos and then none. The maintenance man—white-haired, proud of grammar— made one more slow lap and, on a private impulse, turned the scoreboard lights off and then back on, as if saying *goodnight* properly mattered.

In the weeks that followed, the town learned new routes. The scholarship fund reached a number that made the banker wipe his eyes. The school board voted to retire the number **4**—they hoisted it to the rafters of the gym on a Tuesday afternoon with the band playing warm-ups and the custodians leaning on their carts, and no one thought less of themselves for crying at two o'clock on a school day. A decal went on the field house door: **TRUTH** in block letters, paint plain and permanent.

Coach put a framed printout on his office wall: **NO FREE DOUBT.** He hung the state championship photo next to it—boys mid-yell, confetti caught in the wind, the scoreboard a fact. He kept the toothpick, finally, in a drawer and not in his mouth. Sometimes that's what change looks like.

Spring found the practice field soft again. Freshmen tripped on lines because that's what freshmen do, and a sophomore with good legs and hands that had stopped trembling took snaps in seven-on-seven while Marcus stood behind him and said, "Now means later unless the corner forgets to be humble." Will taught footwork to a guard who'd been born stubborn and would someday be useful. Cruz put a hand on a kid's shoulder and adjusted it a half-inch toward whatever was right.

In the stands, Karen sat with a thermos and a book she didn't read. John timed sprints on a phone he'd pretended to dislike. Between drills, Ms. Rivera walked the sideline and made boys drink water and didn't apologize for how mundane care can be. Dr. Patel came once, stood with his hands in his coat pockets, watched two plays, nodded like a man filing a report in a quiet room where the pen scratches mattered.

When August rolled around, the grass was the color it is when you have believed in something long enough to see it again. The boys in blue huddled at the numbers on a day so hot it made steel soft. Marcus clapped them in once, out of habit he couldn't argue with, and said the only thing he could: "Grass."

On the bleachers, Emily balanced a notebook on her knee and wrote a lede she'd been practicing since winter: *Lincoln returns a team that knows how to choose the next right thing, even when nobody's watching.* She chewed the end of her pencil, then added a line under it, not for print but for herself: *Some stories don't end; they widen.*

And on the inside of one wrist—two, three, eventually twenty—the tape pressed letters against young skin not because the boys needed instruction but because they liked the weight: a word you say when you need it, when a promise matters, when a town is watching and when it isn't. Truth.

Chapter Thirty –
The Empty Locker Room

Monday's bell rang like nothing had changed. It echoed off the same cinderblock halls, bounced along the trophy cases, and skimmed the blue ribbons tied to every stair rail. Kids still sprinted the last twenty feet to beat the tardy. The vending machine still ate a dollar and gave back regret. But under the noise there was a seam of quiet, like the building had learned a new way to hold its breath.

Posters had bloomed over the weekend—some formal, some scrawled in marker:

Thank you, #4.

No Free Doubt.

Boring Beautiful.

Somebody taped a printout of the scoreboard—**33–30**—to the office window. Someone else, probably the white-haired custodian with grammar opinions, added a strip of tape under it: **Final**.

At lunch, the table where the captains usually sprawled stayed half full and too neat. Will stacked trays as if the geometry might help. Cruz didn't sit; he hovered, telling a sophomore to eat, telling another to stop pretending fries were a food group. Marcus had his hands hooked in his hoodie pocket, knuckles gone pale. He didn't touch the fries at all.

Coach Dempsey's text hit the captains' thread at one-oh-five: **Field house. After last bell. Phones in the bucket.**

After last bell, they went.

The locker room wasn't empty—not with thirty boys and the hum of a soda machine—but it felt like it was. Helmets were lined in ranks. Shoulder pads slept on metal shelves. Someone had scrubbed the tile until it remembered August.

And there—third row, second stack from the door—his locker. Nameplate still clipped to the lip: **McALLISTER, A.** The practice jersey hung where it had been left after Tuesday's walk-through. The tape roll sat on the shelf, half-used, black. A sharpie, uncapped and dried, lay like an extinct species. Someone had folded a towel into a square too precise for boys. Somebody had placed his wristband on the hook, the elastic tired, the shape familiar.

Nobody crowded it. They formed a perimeter you couldn't see and wouldn't cross.

"Phones," Coach said, and the clink of glass in plastic started the way rain starts on a porch roof. The blue milk crate filled. He set it by his foot like a promise to give them back later.

He didn't stand on a bench. He didn't carry a speech. He stood square in front of the state championship photo now framed on the far wall. Confetti looked like snow someone had decided to color. The scoreboard glowed in the corner of the picture like a steady star.

"We're here because teams do not end at funerals," he said. "They change shape."

He let it sit.

"First order," he said. "McAllister's locker stays as it is through spring ball. Not a shrine—don't you dare build a shrine in here. It's a workplace. But names matter. That one hangs until we decide together where it lives next. We'll retire the number in fall. Until then, the space stays as a reminder that ordinary work turns seasons into something worth remembering."

He turned, found the faces he needed—seniors who had a few breathless months left of being seniors, juniors who were pretending they weren't already men. "Second: the job list. Will, you're still a captain. Cruz, you're still a captain. Marcus—" a flicker of something softer, "—you're still a captain, even if it feels like the word doesn't fit right today. You three divide the winter board. Lifts. Study hall sign-ins. Ride lists. If a freshman misses, you put a body on his porch—not a text—a body."

A hand went up—Micah, already back to being the kid who turns kickoffs into punctuation marks. "Coach… the jersey? The patch?"

"We'll keep the four on our sleeves through spring workouts," Coach said. "We'll take it off when it becomes decoration and not discipline. You'll know the difference."

Ms. Rivera stepped in from the doorway, not her usual sideline silhouette. No clipboard. A simple sweater and the look of someone who had slept three hours and could fake seven.

"Five minutes," Coach said, ceding space with a nod.

She didn't climb anywhere either. She took the spot in front of Aidan's locker and didn't pretend not to know it. "Grief is physical," she said. "You're going to feel tired at noon. You're going to forget to drink water. You're going to think you're sick and you might just be sad. Eat anyway. Sleep anyway. If you wake up at two a.m., that's a thing bodies do right now. Text someone useful, then put the phone down."

She lifted a hand before the chorus of *we're fine* could start. "We're doing check-ins the way we did with him. Not because you're fragile. Because you're a team and teams carry. If you need to say the word—" she tapped her own wrist, a ghost of black tape there, "—say it. In the hallway, in my office, on a jog past the math wing. It still counts off the field."

Cruz's jaw worked. "You got hours for kids who don't like offices?"

"I've got a bench by the trainer's door," she said. "And a coffee lid I can draw a play on while you talk."

A laugh cracked the room's stiffness. It helped.

Coach took it back. "Calendar," he said. "This week: lifts Tues/Thurs, film on Friday—not game film. Identity film. We're going to watch ourselves do the boring beautiful things. If you don't like seeing yourself block correctly on a big screen, get over it. Next week: leadership groups start. You're going to teach middle schoolers how to move their feet and how to apologize when they get it wrong. That's not charity. That's legacy."

He looked toward the open door, as if he could see through the hallway, into the school, into town. "We have a scholarship meeting with the board on Wednesday. If you're asked to speak, you talk about effort and homework before you talk about touchdowns. Understood?"

Heads bobbed. Some throats clicked. Marcus's eyes kept flicking to the third row, second stack.

Coach set the milk crate on the floor. "Grab your bricks," he said, meaning the pieces this team was built from. "Then go do your homework."

No one moved. Not yet.

Will stepped forward and put his palm flat to the cool metal of the locker door—just once, like checking a stove before bed. He turned, cleared his throat in a body too big for subtlety. "Line room, five minutes," he said to his herd. "We're making a list. Teachers who need chairs lifted. People who need rides. We're filling his calendar."

Cruz slapped the side of a locker with an open hand. "Defense, we got a winter seven-on-seven league that thinks it's cute. Let's teach."

Marcus didn't call receivers. He walked to the equipment cage and spoke to the manager instead. "Leave his gloves where they are," he said quietly. "And put a fresh roll of black tape on the shelf. Not to use. To know it's there."

He turned and found Coach watching him.

"Say it out loud once," Coach said, not a command. A permission.

Marcus took a breath that did not feel like a knife for the first time in days. He tapped his own wrist. "Truth," he said, and the word didn't break him. It steadied him.

The room exhaled.

They drifted to their corners—the line room, the whiteboard with magnets, Ms. Rivera's bench-that-wasn't-a-bench yet. Boys wrote down teacher names. Someone texted the middle school AD, got a thumbs-up sticker in response, and decided stickers might be allowed in leadership work. Jamal started a sign-up for snow shoveling because he'd seen Mrs. Fischer's steps and decided the season didn't end at the fifty.

On his way out, Marcus passed the open door and nearly collided with Emily. She stopped short, pencil behind her ear, a notebook clutched against her coat. She didn't look past him. She didn't look into the room.

"I'm not coming in," she said, as if he'd asked. "I'm here to ask if I can… if I can write about the scholarship meeting. For the paper. Not a profile. A process."

Marcus's mouth twitched. "Coach'll say yes if you spell *boring* right."

"I know how," she said. She glanced past his shoulder once, quick, at the row of lockers. "How are you?" It wasn't a throwaway. It wasn't a headline.

He answered the way boys do when they've decided to practice the truth. "Hungry," he said. "Mad. Okay. Not okay. You know."

"I do," she said. "Mostly the hungry." She fished something from her coat pocket and handed it over. An index card, of course. **We keep moving the chains** in her neat block letters. "For the corkboard," she said. "Or the milk crate. Or the trash. Whatever works."

He turned it over. On the back, smaller: *Call me if nobody else answers.* A phone number. He nodded once. "Thanks."

She went. He tucked the card into his wallet with the others—a small, strange weight he'd grown used to carrying.

Down the hall, Karen stood in the main office with a cardboard box she didn't want. John had one too. The secretary whispered I'm sorry twice, like an apology could line the inside of corrugated. Inside were the detritus of a life at school: the photography club's permission slip he hadn't turned in, a locker combination on a Post-it, a math quiz with a 97 and a doodle of a lion in the margin. Karen touched them all like relics, like tools. She didn't cry in the office. She cried later, in the car, and John put his hand on the gearshift and didn't shift until she nodded.

The school board meeting Wednesday went past into **Old Business** because grief must obey agendas. The banker stood up and said the number in the scholarship account out loud and had to sit back down again. Ms. Rivera presented a one-page plan titled **Aidan McAllister Grant: Criteria**—attendance, effort, service. Coach added a single line in his block print: **No free doubt.** Karen spoke last and said one sentence that would live on the application forever: "Show us the small, right things."

Back in the field house on Friday, the projector hummed like summer. Coach labeled the film session **Identity** in the HUDL folder. He didn't show touchdowns first. He showed first downs. Ten snaps in a row of Duo for three, of stick for five, of a curl reached for with quiet hands. He paused after the seventh clip. "This is what we celebrate," he said. "This is what we teach."

Someone sniffed. Someone laughed at himself for sniffing. It was fine.

After film, they went as a unit to the locker row and stood without making a circle that would have felt too formal. Ms. Rivera set a small shadow box on the empty bench—black tape, a piece of white towel, a strip of the state championship confetti, the smallest lion sticker someone had peeled off a band kid's case and replaced later with apology. There was room for more, but not many things. That was on purpose.

Coach looked at the nameplate one last time and slid it free. He didn't hand it to Karen because she wasn't there; he didn't hand it to himself because that wasn't the job. He handed it to Marcus.

"Hang it in the receivers' room," he said. "Eye level. You keep it there until we put it up in the gym."

Marcus took it like a ball with a story attached. "Yes, sir."

On his way out, Marcus pressed his palm to the cool metal one more time. Will, passing, did the same. Cruz didn't; he thumped his own chest once and pointed at the tape in the shadow box, a vow he didn't need to say.

The last sound in the room wasn't a speech. It was the ordinary noise teams make when they decide to keep going: the clang of two locker doors, the swish of a broom, the soft slap of a winter hat against a boy's head. Coach killed the lights. The dark didn't feel empty.

Out on the track, Emily stood with a small crowd at the rail. Someone had chalked a **4** in the corner of the end zone again, small as a signature. A freshman wideout—Eli, nerves still showing at the edges—jogged a route on air and caught a ball he'd tossed to himself. He looked embarrassed, then did it again with intention.

"Grass," Marcus called from the doorway, just loud enough to carry. "Then sky."

Eli nodded like he'd been given a script. He took three steps, planted, turned—boring, beautiful—and kept his hands quiet the way he'd been taught.

Inside, the shadow box sat on the bench in the third row, second stack. The tape inside it made no sound at all, which was the point. The boys didn't need it to speak to remember what it meant.

And the field, as it does, waited.

Chapter Thirty-One –
The Scholarship

Winter deepened in Lincoln, the kind of cold that creaked through the gym rafters and left boys stamping their feet before sprints. Snow pushed against the field house doors, and salt buckets stood sentry in every hallway. Basketball owned the gym now, but the football team's presence lingered in banners, taped wrists, and the faint smell of tape and sweat that no janitor's mop could erase.

But the scholarship—that was new.

The school board set up folding tables in the auditorium for the first official meeting. Karen sat in the front row, hands clasped tight, John beside her, posture upright in a way that looked military and reverent. Coach Dempsey wore his best jacket, the one that didn't quite fit across his shoulders anymore, and Ms. Rivera brought her clipboard back out, though this time it held nothing but a few neat forms.

Emily sat three rows back with her notebook balanced on her knees. She wasn't reporting; she was recording. She wrote phrases like *ordinary heroism* and *no free doubt* in margins while her pencil tapped nervously.

The mayor opened the proceedings, voice trembling even though he had given speeches a hundred times before. "The Aidan McAllister Scholarship," he said, "is not for touchdowns. It's not for the loudest or the most celebrated. It's for the student who makes the next right choice, day after day, when nobody's watching. It is for the small, steady courage that changes teams, classrooms, and families."

Karen stood when invited, her voice thin at first, then gathering. "We want this to honor the way he lived, not just the way he left us. Show up. Work hard. Be kind. That's all we're asking. That's everything."

A hush filled the auditorium.

When the floor opened for nominations, the first name came from Marcus. He stood, hands shoved into his pockets, and spoke awkwardly into the microphone. "Freshman. Quiet kid. Name's Trevor. He stays after practice to help managers carry water. Nobody asked him to. He just does."

Cruz added another. "Sophie from the band. She tutors kids before first period, then plays at every game like it matters more than Friday night."

Will, blunt as always, nominated a junior lineman who had worked shifts at the diner to help pay for his own cleats. "He never said a word about it," Will muttered, "but he earned it."

Each story folded into the next until the scholarship felt less like money and more like a mirror the town held up to itself.

By the time the vote ended, the envelope went to a sophomore named Leah—the daughter of a factory worker, a girl who balanced school, her little brothers, and still showed up early to help teachers set up labs. She accepted with wide eyes and whispered, "I'll try to be worth it," into the microphone.

Karen hugged her afterward, tears hot on her cheeks. "You already are."

That night, the field sat under snow. The number **4** chalked in the end zone was buried but not erased. Marcus, Will, and Cruz stood at the rail anyway, breath steaming, watching the empty stadium lights burn against the cold.

"He'd like Leah," Cruz said finally. "She's tough."

"Yeah," Marcus agreed. He pulled a folded index card from his coat pocket—Emily had slipped it into his hand after the meeting. On it, one line: *Ordinary is holy.*

He tucked it back, the paper worn soft.

"Spring's coming," Will said, voice low. "Grass first."

"Sky later," Marcus finished.

They stood together in the cold, not for a ceremony, not for closure, but for the simple act of not leaving.

Because legacy wasn't in speeches or trophies—it was in showing up, again and again, when the snow melted and the field asked for footprints.

Chapter Thirty-Two – Spring Ball

The thaw came the way most mercies arrive—quietly and later than you wanted. The snow withdrew into the shady edges, leaving the practice field the color of wet bread. Cleats snapped mud and stitched it back again. The first whistle of spring didn't sound like autumn's metal certainty; it sounded like a body remembering how to breathe.

The field house reintroduced itself: cinderblock cool to the touch, the hum of the soda machine, the faint ghost of tape and sweat that even winter couldn't bleach. The shadow box still sat on the bench in the third row, second stack—black tape, a square of towel, a confetti scrap that refused to stay flat. In the receivers' room, the nameplate hung at eye level above the depth chart: McALLISTER, A. It didn't glare. It watched.

Coach Dempsey walked out with a laminated practice script and a whistle he didn't use much anymore. "It's April," he said, voice low over the crowd of boys in blue. "Nobody wins a game in April. We win habits. Boring beautiful. No free doubt. Helmets on."

The helmets found heads with the clatter of a hundred small promises. Will herded the line to the far right hash, where sleds waited, heavy and smug. Cruz claimed the defense with a clap and a towel tucked into his belt like a banner. Receivers clustered by the numbers. Marcus tugged his gloves on, flexed his fingers, and looked at the freshman wideout who had been caught practicing toe-taps in the hallway mirror for a month.

"Route tree is a language," Marcus said, easy. "First, you learn to say hello without tripping."

The kid nodded, eyes too wide, legs too springy. Over Marcus's shoulder, Eli jogged out carrying two footballs and the kind of nervous that tastes like pennies. He was taller than he'd been in November, still all elbows when he forgot himself. When he didn't, his feet were quiet, his hands even quieter. The red QB jersey looked new and unavoidable.

Ms. Rivera set a cooler on the white line with a thud. "Hydrate," she announced, as if she were calling an audible. No clipboard today—she had memorized more numbers than she could admit—but the trainer's bag bumped against her hip like punctuation. She scanned faces and postures and the spots where tape peeked from beneath sleeves. She watched Eli longer than she meant to.

Indy periods broke the field into stations. On the far end, Will squared freshmen in front of the sled. "Hat under hands," he told a guard who wanted to be a bulldozer and was currently a shopping cart with aspirations. "Feet first. Hips second. Hands last. If your hands go first, you're telling lies your feet have to clean up." He demonstrated with the economy of a man who'd moved a human on live television and found it less interesting than getting the steps right.

Cruz set cones at angles that made no sense until boys missed them. "Eyes," he barked. "If your eyes go on vacation, your body follows. Strike, shock, shed. Finish with quiet feet." He made them do it slower than they wanted, which made them breathe louder than they liked.

Receivers ran alphabet, then arithmetic. Slant, snap, come back to me like you meant to. Curl, sit, don't admire the ball. Out, cap your route at the right depth even when your lungs are lying about what right is. The freshman who wanted every play to be now took three choppy steps and flared too early. Marcus put an open palm up—not a stop sign, a metronome.

"Now means later," he said. "Sell grass before you ask for sky."

The kid tried again. The second time his hips told the truth. Marcus nodded. "There you go." He clapped once, the way Aidan had, and the sound went through the line like a current.

Seven-on-seven turned the middle of the field into geometry. The defense pattern-matched with clean minds and messy hands. Eli took the first rep too fast, sailed a curl because his eyes moved before his shoulders did, and exhaled audible at his own mistake. He caught Rivera watching him and looked down, thumb pressing the ridge of the black tape wrapped around his wrist—a strip he'd started wearing in January without announcing it to anyone.

"Again," Coach said, and Eli nodded, eyes settling. He hit the out for five because five was right, not because it was pretty. He checked the draw just to make the linebackers hesitate in May, the kind of cheap truth you can spend later. He found Marcus on a stick where Marcus had been every Tuesday since he learned he could be.

On the third rep, the world tilted a half-inch, the way a field does when you remember the people who aren't on it. Eli blinked and made the smallest fist with his left hand. He didn't need a stadium or a huddle.

"Truth," he said under his breath.

He stepped back. Coach raised an eyebrow but didn't make it a lesson. "Blue two," Marcus called, conversational, and the second quarterback jogged in with more certainty than talent. Three snaps of competent correctness, then Eli slid back to the front and hit the angle route to the back, who looked startled to be included in April and then delighted.

From the bleachers, a small audience had formed that wasn't exactly a crowd. Karen sat in the first row with a thermos tucked into both hands, spring wind lifting the edge of her scarf. She hadn't planned to come the first day. Her feet had brought her. John stood at the rail with his elbows on cool metal, counting steps the way fathers count breaths. Near the fifty, Emily balanced her notebook on her knee and wrote a line she'd rewrite twice before she liked it: *Spring is the part of the story where grief learns to lift with two hands.*

She didn't stay behind the glass of the press box. She stayed where she could hear the cadence. A freshman tripped on an agility ladder and laughed at himself before anyone else could. Will barked and then grinned and then showed him how to keep his toes out of the squares without thinking about it. Cruz adjusted a sophomore's angle by half a shoe and the kid made a tackle on air that felt like apology for every missed step since January.

Coach moved through it all with the patience of a man who had decided to shepherd instead of direct. He tapped Eli's elbow and tilted it two degrees. He told the corner to keep his hips honest and his eyes nosy. He whistled only once, to stop the universe, because a freshman safety led with his crown into a bag. He walked the boy back to the bag and taught him how to keep his chin up and his neck safe and his future available. "We hit first," he said softly. "We don't hit wrong."

Halfway through, Ms. Rivera fished a roll of athletic tape from the cooler lid and tossed it to Marcus, who caught it one-handed and wrapped his fingers where California in February had decided to live in a Midwestern April. "Eat," she told Jamal, and he bit into a banana like he had been caught stealing a base. She handed Eli a small paper cup. "Salt," she said, not because he needed it, because ritual tells the body it is remembered.

Down near the numbers, Leah—the scholarship winner—arrived with a stack of flyers to hand Coach for the middle school clinic next week. She hovered at the edge until Marcus waved her in like she belonged, which she did. Will pointed at a box of water jugs like a man assigning dignity. Leah picked one up without looking self-conscious and made the rounds with the ease of someone who'd carried heavier things in smaller rooms.

"Clinic's Tuesday," Coach told the team, voice above a murmur. "We're teaching sixth graders how to move their feet and tell the truth to themselves when they want to be fancy. Put your names on Rivera's sheet if you can be useful."

Hands went up and names went down. Cruz drew a smiley face next to his name because he enjoyed confusing paperwork.

They set a ball at the twenty for a late-practice script, the kind that turns air into film if you pay attention. First call: duo. Will's feet were poetry written by a carpenter. Second: stick to the tight end, who caught it and remembered to tuck the point without looking at his hands. Third: out for four. The chains clacked, not because anyone had brought them out, because the voice on the sideline learned how to make that sound.

"First down," Emily called out of habit that felt like prayer. Heat rose under her cheeks. A few heads turned and smiled. She shrugged. "Practice counts."

They hurried to the line and slowed it down because they'd decided that pacing is leadership. Eli checked the weak-side pressure that only existed in his head and replaced it with a ball to the back at the right time. Marcus ran a seam for no one just to remind the world he could. The freshman wideout ran a curl like a man signing his name carefully, and the ball found him at the moment his pencil would have lifted. He secured it, turned, and took two honest steps up field before he let himself smile.

On the sideline, Karen wiped her eyes and then laughed at herself for wiping her eyes. John rested his hand on the rail and felt it warm under the sun he hadn't noticed arriving. Ms. Rivera wrote nothing on nothing and watched everything. The white-haired custodian with grammar opinions shuffled by and straightened a cone by an inch because he could.

When the whistle blew to end it, nobody sprinted to the locker room. They drifted, then gathered, then stood in a shape that had a hole in it and didn't. Coach didn't talk long.

"Good start," he said. "We were boring on purpose. We will keep being boring until we can be beautiful without accident." He pointed toward the end zone nearest the road, where the chalked four from winter had been rained into a ghost. "Touch the corner on your way in," he added, "not because it's magic. Because it's practice."

The boys jogged that way, hands brushing paint that wasn't there, something like an amen.

Emily waited until most had gone before she climbed down to the track. Marcus was halfway to the gate, helmet swinging from two fingers. She fell into step beside him.

"How'd it feel?" she asked, pencil behind her ear like a flag.

"Like April pretending to be October," he said. Then he looked back at the field. "Like we're allowed to try again."

"You are," she said. "You kept your promise."

He made a face. "Which one?"

"Show up." She tapped the edge of her notebook. "Also teach the freshman that 'now' is a scheduling word."

He laughed, quickly. "He'll get it."

They reached the gate. On the other side, the town sagged into afternoon—bikes, dogs, a mailbox with its red arm up like it had something to say. Karen stood by the fence and waved, the way mothers do when the world gives their sons back to them, even for an hour. John lifted his chin. Coach collected stray pinnies like a farmer gathering tools before rain. Cruz argued good-naturedly with Jamal about whether a towel could be lucky. Will carried a sled farther than anyone had asked him to.

Eli hung back on the numbers, the practice ball tucked in the crook of his arm. He looked at the receivers' room door, then at the empty square of sky above the far bleachers, then at the black tape on his wrist. He pressed his thumb to the ridge.

"Truth," he said—not to sit, not to bail, not to make a point. Just to name the thing that would make the next rep right.

He jogged in, caught the door with his free hand, and let it swing for the boy behind him who didn't know yet how someone holding a door can feel like coaching.

The field held the day a little longer before it let it go, the way good places do. The ruts in the grass would green over. The cones would stack. The shadow box would catch dust and a few glances. The nameplate would keep its place until the gym rafters asked for it. And tomorrow, and the day after, and the day after that, boys would come back and move their feet and their eyes and their small, ordinary courage across the yard.

Grass first. Sky later.

Chapter Thirty-Three – The Season After

Summer wrapped itself around Lincoln like a damp blanket. The air smelled of cut grass and grilled burgers, cicadas buzzing so loud they drowned out thought. Baseball season sputtered, band rehearsals filled parking lots, and football waited in the weight room.

The field house stayed busy. Morning lifts bled into linemen flipping tires, receivers running routes on air, Cruz timing sprints with the whistle he'd "borrowed" from Coach. The shadow box still sat in its spot, and every boy touched the bench on the way past without looking like they were touching it. Rituals grow when no one calls them rituals.

Coach had warned them: "Next season won't feel like last season. Don't make ghosts do your work." But ghosts hung around anyway. They showed up in the cadence Eli practiced, the black tape on his wrist, the way Marcus clapped once before huddles. They lived in Karen's thermos at the rail, in John's quiet presence at the back of film study, in Emily's pencil scratching lines that she pretended were just for the school paper.

The first team meeting of August filled the auditorium. Helmets gleamed in the lobby, jerseys folded neat in cardboard boxes. Coach stood at the podium, chewing the inside of his cheek before he began.

"We start a new year," he said. "The scoreboard's back at zero. The trophy's in the case. It won't win you a yard in September. What will:

feet, hips, hands. Homework done. Hydration. The ordinary. We know this."

He paused, let his eyes sweep. "We carry number four with us. But not like a statue. Like a tool. He'd hate a statue. You know that. You honor him by doing the small things right until people get bored of watching. Then you do it again."

A hum rolled through the room, something between grief and agreement.

Practice started hot and stayed hotter. The turf burned under cleats. Helmets steamed when they came off. Eli threw ball after ball until his arm ached, his ribs wrapped in tape less for pain than for memory. Marcus taught freshmen how to sell routes with their eyes, Will cursed through sled pushes, Cruz turned tackling drills into poetry and bruises.

After one scrimmage, Emily stood by the fence, notebook in hand. Eli jogged over, sweat dripping, a grin flickering through his exhaustion.

"You writing about us again?" he asked, pulling his helmet off.

"Maybe," she said. "Or about you."

He frowned. "I don't need a story."

"Neither did he," she said gently. Then, before he could answer, she handed him an index card. In neat letters: *The next right thing.*

He slipped it into his wristband. Didn't thank her out loud. Didn't need to.

The season opener came under orange light, late August sky thick with heat. The stands filled—townsfolk, teachers, classmates, families in lawn chairs pressed against the fence. The band hammered the fight song, louder and sharper than usual.

Karen stood with John at the fifty, both of them in blue, both of them clapping when the captains jogged out. Eli wore red, the quarterback's jersey. He looked smaller than the job, then larger once he set his jaw. The coin flipped, clinked, settled.

The first drive was messy. A false start, a dropped snap. Second drive, better: stick, draw, curl. First down. The student section roared.

By the second quarter, Eli found Marcus on a seam, the ball spinning true. Touchdown. The crowd erupted, and someone lit sparklers at the rail though it wasn't legal. The scoreboard glowed: **7–0.**

Cruz sacked their quarterback two drives later. Will pancaked a man who outweighed him. Leah waved from the concession stand, handing out nachos, and Emily scribbled furiously, her pencil racing faster than the plays.

Lincoln won that opener 20–7. The handshake line was honest, the hugs at the rail tighter than August deserved.

In the locker room after, Coach kept them standing. He tapped the whiteboard with the marker's blunt end.

"One and oh," he said. "Not state champs. Not history. Just one and oh."

He pointed at Eli, who still had tape dusted on his wrist. "You looked nervous. Good. You looked patient. Better."

Then he looked at the whole room. "We keep showing up. That's the work. Grass first."

The boys, sweating and spent, echoed him: "Grass first."

And from the corner, where the shadow box caught the faint light of a bare bulb, it almost felt like an answer.

Chapter Thirty-Four – The First Loss

The September air cooled, but Lincoln's practices burned hotter. Two wins stacked in the ledger, both hard-earned, both messy enough to remind the boys that football never bowed to ghosts or slogans. The town buzzed again—newspaper clippings, diner talk, kids in the hallway flashing "boring beautiful" like a handshake.

But the third Friday brought Millbrook. Bigger roster. Faster skill. A team that treated huddles like inconvenience and tempo like religion.

The stadium was electric, but uneasy. Karen sat with John in the same seats as always, thermos between them, both bracing for the night. Emily perched with her notebook open, pencil steady. Leah worked concessions, pausing between orders to glance at the field.

From the opening whistle, Millbrook made their statement. A screen pass went for twenty. A slant turned into forty. Lincoln bent, then broke on a quarterback draw that left Cruz swiping air. Touchdown.

The home crowd groaned.

Eli gathered the huddle at the twenty. His hands shook once on the ball, then steadied. "Grass first," he said. "Don't care what the scoreboard says. Grass first."

They answered. Duo for four, stick for five, sneak for one. First down. Marcus pulled a hitch for eight, Jamal added a jet sweep for seven. The crowd found its rhythm again, stomping bleachers. At the thirty-five, Eli dropped back, saw the safety creep, and lofted one deep. Marcus caught it in stride, end zone in sight. The roar cracked the night. Tie game, 7–7.

But Millbrook wasn't rattled. They answered in three plays. Then again. By halftime: 21–7.

The locker room buzzed with frustration. Helmets slammed, curses hissed. Coach didn't shout. He wrote one word on the whiteboard: **Patience.**

"They're daring you to panic," he said. "Don't."

Second half. Lincoln fought. Cruz forced a fumble. Will opened a lane wide enough for a truck. Eli hit Marcus on a slant for six. 21–14. Hope returned.

But Millbrook crushed it with a 12-play drive that drained minutes and hearts. 28–14. Lincoln clawed back once more—Eli sneaking at the goal line, ball stretched across paint. 28–21. Four minutes left.

The crowd stood. The band blared. Cruz roared at his defense.

And Millbrook broke them. A fade down the sideline, caught with fingertips. A dagger of a run up the gut. Touchdown. 35–21. Final.

Silence lingered after the horn. The boys trudged off, sweat mixing with disappointment. The scoreboard glared its cold truth.

In the locker room, no one spoke at first. Eli sat with his helmet between his knees, tape still tight around his wrist. Marcus dropped beside him. "Not your fault," he said quietly.

Eli looked up, eyes sharp. "Then whose?"

"None of ours. All of ours. That's football."

Coach stepped in, hat off, hair damp with sweat that wasn't his own. "Look at me," he said. Thirty pairs of eyes lifted. "You played hard. You lost. We'll lose again someday. But if you let this loss write your story, you've missed the lesson. It's not the scoreboard that defines you. It's the next snap."

He pointed at the shadow box tucked in the corner. "He wouldn't have asked for wins. He would've asked for work. Tomorrow, we work."

The boys nodded. Some angrily. Some tired. But they nodded.

That night, Emily wrote under the yellow glow of her desk lamp:

The scoreboard said defeat. The lesson said patience. Lincoln's boys carry a shadow, but they will have to learn—over and over—that legacy isn't a shield against losing. It's a compass pointing them back to the field after.

She set the pencil down and whispered into the quiet, "Grass first."

Chapter Thirty-Five –
The Bounce Back

The Monday after Millbrook felt heavier than the score had been. The hallways buzzed with whispers about the loss, students shrugging it off like it didn't matter—*just one game*—but the team carried it like weight plates stacked on their backs.

The film session was brutal. Millbrook's speed looked even faster on the projector, their discipline sharper. Missed tackles replayed in slow motion, blocks that slid off showed up in unforgiving clarity. Eli sat in the front row, jaw clenched. Every overthrow looked bigger on screen, every decision too late.

Coach didn't yell. He rewound, clicked pause, and circled angles on the screen. "See this step? Too wide. See this shoulder? Too high. You're giving them grass they didn't earn."

He let the silence hang. "We fix feet, we fix everything else."

Practice that afternoon ran different. Will barked at linemen like he'd taken the loss personally. "Low man wins! Get under! You give me flat hands again, you're running." They didn't argue. They lowered hips and hit the sled until the squeal of metal echoed across the field.

Cruz paced the defense like a drill sergeant. "No free yards! None! If you see daylight, kill it. If you see space, fill it. Millbrook made us chase. We don't chase—we dictate." He slammed his shoulder into a pad, then grinned. "Let's hunt."

Receivers ran crisp routes until their lungs burned. Marcus grabbed Eli's jersey after one rep, forcing eye contact. "Don't wait for me to be open. Throw me open. Trust me."

Eli nodded, breathing hard, thumb pressing the ridge of his tape. "Truth," he muttered.

"Damn right," Marcus said.

By Wednesday, the rhythm had changed. Eli's passes snapped sharper, his cadence steadier. The line moved as one. The defense swarmed. The practices weren't just intense—they were clean.

On Thursday, Emily caught a glimpse of the field from the bleachers. She wasn't supposed to be there—band rehearsal had wrapped early—but she watched anyway. The sun dipped low, orange against the grass, painting the boys in long shadows. Eli lofted a perfect seam ball, Marcus snagged it midstride, and for a moment it felt like November again.

Emily scribbled in her notebook: *They're writing their own chapter now, not copying his.*

Friday night came with the smell of popcorn and autumn's first bite in the air. The stands buzzed but cautious—after Millbrook, nobody knew which Lincoln team would show up.

They answered fast. First drive: duo, stick, hitch. First down. Marcus on a slant for twelve. Eli faked the handoff, rolled right, and zipped one to Jamal in the flat. Touchdown. The crowd roared, relief washing over the bleachers.

The defense fed off it. Cruz stuffed a run at the line, then chased the quarterback into a hurried throw. Interception. Another score followed—Marcus toe-tapping in the corner of the end zone, Eli pumping a fist but staying calm. 14–0 by the end of the first quarter.

The opponent tried to claw back, but Lincoln's patience smothered them. Will and the line ate clock with run after run. Eli refused risky throws, checking down and smiling when boos trickled from kids in the stands who wanted fireworks. Coach clapped once from the sideline—boring, beautiful.

Final: Lincoln 28, Riverton 10.

The locker room shook with music and laughter, the weight of Millbrook falling off like sweat. Eli sat on the bench, tape frayed on his wrist, Marcus beside him.

"That's how it's supposed to feel," Marcus said.

"Yeah," Eli breathed, a grin breaking wide. "One blade at a time."

Coach stepped in, holding up the game ball. He didn't toss it to the star receiver, didn't hand it to Cruz. He walked it over to the line and set it on Will's lap.

"Protection," he said. "That's where it starts."

The boys clapped, loud and long.

Later that night, Karen walked out of the stadium arm in arm with John. She looked up at the scoreboard one more time, then whispered, "He'd be proud."

Emily, notebook under her arm, walked behind them, smiling softly. She'd already written the lede in her head: *After loss, Lincoln remembered. They returned to their language—boring, patient, beautiful—and found themselves again.*

Chapter Thirty-Six – Midseason Grind

October crept in on a wind that made metal bleachers sing. The stadium light poles wore halos on damp nights, and the track took footprints like a ledger. By now, the new season had shed its glitter. The rhythm was Tuesday-film, Wednesday-hurt, Thursday-sharp, Friday-true. Saturdays were for laundry and aches. Sundays were for pretending homework didn't come with a whistle.

Coach called the stretch "the honest part."

He was right. The glow of the opener was gone, Millbrook was a scar that no longer itched, and every opponent felt less like a villain and more like a mirror. You won first down; you were a genius. You lost it; you were a cautionary tale. Most weeks, you were a little of both and the scoreboard forgave your sins by ten points or punished them by three.

Eli learned the math. He stopped hunting seams on first and ten and discovered five-yard outs could build cathedrals. Marcus taught the freshmen the difference between "open" and "NFL open," and then reminded Eli he could still throw him into open if a corner fell asleep. Will's ankle turned once on bad turf and he taped it enough to scare fear back into it. Cruz's shoulder clicked every Wednesday and he clicked it back with a grimace and a prayer that sounded like "finish."

Ms. Rivera watched the boys the way a lighthouse watches a coast—steady, without melodrama. She added a second cooler next to the white line and labeled it **October**. The paper cups tasted like salt and bad memories. "Hydrate," she said, like a bedtime story. She instituted Friday morning check-ins that included one physical number and one sentence that wasn't about football. ("Chem test okay." "Mom got the job." "Haven't slept right.") The sentences mattered. She wrote none of them down, but she didn't forget.

Emily wrote a column called "Midseason is Made of Tuesdays" and made Coach laugh out loud for the first time in weeks.

"Homecoming crowns and highlight reels lie. This part of the story is drills and footwork and the small mercies of a trainer's water cooler. The courage that wins in November is mostly made in October, in classrooms and on film and in the quiet moments no one's filming."

She kept the index cards going, but more often she kept them in her pocket. Sometimes you don't hand courage out like candy; you just stand where a boy can see you and know he isn't doing this alone.

The scholarship lived in quieter rooms. Leah—the first recipient—helped Ms. Rivera run a middle school clinic in the auxiliary gym on a Saturday when the rain made the main floor sound like applause. She taped numbers to cones and turned **No Free Doubt** into a relay where sixth graders had to choose the right step before a teammate clapped. Eli demonstrated a three-step drop to a group of kids who thought quarterbacks were born and not taught. He tripped the first time because a sneaker squeaked wrong and then laughed at himself and started over. The kids laughed too and then tried harder.

"Grass first," Leah told a little girl who wanted to throw deep on her first attempt. The girl rolled her eyes and threw the checkdown to a friend anyway and discovered joy didn't need distance.

At school, Mr. Tanner returned midterm algebra tests with the severity of a hanging judge. Eli's was an 82 circled in red. It should have been relief. He stared at it like it was a blitz he'd recognized too late.

"You don't have to be a statistic," Mr. Tanner said, softer than usual. "You can be a student who made a plan and stuck to it. Office hours— Tuesday, Thursday. Show up."

Eli did. He put "Tanner" on Ms. Rivera's Friday list, and she circled it with a smile that said she liked when boys used sentences that started outside the hash marks.

Homecoming arrived with mums and a parade that ran two blocks long and still took an hour because the town insisted on waving at each other between floats. The team walked behind the marching band, helmets in one hand, the other hand grabbing stray toddlers who tried to eat Tootsie Rolls with wrappers still on. Emily perched on the back of a jeep with the yearbook staff, hair braided against the wind, pencil tucked behind her ear because it felt like a promise now.

The game itself was less coronation than grind. The opponent, East Hollow, ran a 3–3 stack and dared linemen to guess wrong. Will refused. Duo for three. Stick for five. Slant for eight when a backer blinked. By the third quarter, the student section had stopped booing the lack of fireworks and started chanting "First down!" with a rhythm that made the band jealous. Final: 23–13. The coronation happened anyway when the homecoming queen handed Eli a Gatorade and said "nice patience" like it was a compliment you could frame.

The week after, reality bit back. The bus to Clear Creek broke down a mile from the stadium and the replacement arrived with seatbelts that locked and wouldn't unlock without a ritual no one remembered. Eli took a helmet to the thumb in warmups and flubbed his first snap. Cruz missed a tackle on a counter he had called out before the ball moved. Coach's headset died in the second quarter and he borrowed one from the frosh coach that smelled like peppermint and despair. Somehow it was 10–9 with four minutes left and Lincoln trailing.

Eli huddled them on the nineteen. His thumb throbbed a drumbeat. He looked at Marcus, then at the line, then at the tape on his wrist. The word was there; the world didn't need to hear it.

"Grass," he said. "Then sky."

Duo for four. Stick for five. Sneak, knees churning, Will pushing politely impolite. On second and seven at the forty, the corner finally took the bait he'd refused since August. Marcus didn't even signal. Eli did. The ball left his hand on a line that made the away stands gasp. Marcus stacked, separated, and caught it with the indifference of a man retrieving a newspaper. Ten yards later he stepped out because the clock mattered more than style. Three plays after that, Micah made pragmatism look pretty. 12–10. The two-point conversion failed and Coach didn't bother yelling. "Win first down," he told the defense. They did, and then they won the last down, and the last, and the horn sounded like relief.

Losses still lived in other towns. Millbrook beat someone by forty. Ironwood, a name that could still make a few stomachs flip, stayed perfect and cocky on local sports radio. Coach muted highlight shows in the film room and drew brackets on a whiteboard in October with a marker that owed nobody prophecy. "Focus on our half of the yard," he said. "The rest is for people with microphones."

Marcus learned how to be a captain without pretension. He stopped giving speeches and started saying small things to the right people at the right time. To a freshman, quietly: "You don't have to be noticed to be useful." To a senior who wanted to freelance: "Your story's good without improvising." To Eli, once, between a curl and a dig: "You can miss and still be ours."

Will found the sophomore who would be his replacement in a year and taught him how to tape his wrists in a way that saved thumbs and didn't look ridiculous. Cruz started a Sunday morning text thread titled **Angles** where he sent a grainy clip of a college linebacker fitting split zone and wrote *be boring like this*. Half the replies were memes. Half were questions. All were a sign that boys were letting the right habits write on them.

Karen came to more practices than games now. The noise of Friday skinned her nerves, but the sight of boys running ladders in the late afternoon calmed something ancient. She and Ms. Rivera spoke on the track sometimes about nothing—recipes, a book neither had finished, how the new principal didn't understand the copy machine—and Ms. Rivera would slip, once in a while, and check Karen's pulse without meaning to. Karen let her. You don't argue with hands that have steadied your boy and are trying a new shape of mercy on your behalf.

John joined the chain gang for one home game and found the simple rhythm of moving sticks strangely consoling. Between quarters he would glance at the end zone corner where a small numeral had been painted fresh in August—**4**, no bigger than a hand. He never touched it. He didn't need to.

On a Wednesday, Ms. Rivera caught Eli at the cooler a beat longer than casual. "Thumb?" she asked.

"Ugly in the morning," he said. "Honest by practice."

"Write with a pen instead of a pencil for a few days," she said. "Less pressure on the joint."

He squinted. "That's a thing?"

"It is now," she said. "Truth?"

He laughed once. "Not yet."

"Good," she said. "Blue two if I call it."

He nodded. Rules were comfort in a world that kept trying to be poetry.

They did lose again—by one—on a night with fog that sliced the field into slices of breath. A tipped ball became a pick and a pick became a three they could never claw back. The locker room was quiet without being hopeless, the kind of quiet you start to trust because it means boys are letting disappointment dry into resolve instead of perform into drama. Coach wrote **NEXT** on the whiteboard and circled it once.

Emily wrote shorter, cleaner. *Lincoln is seven and two. The wins look like patience. The losses look like human. Both look like a team learning to carry a name without breaking under it.* She tucked the card that read **Ordinary is holy** into the back of her spiral so it wouldn't flutter out when the band truck hit potholes on away trips.

The last week of October the town did what towns do when they want to be decent: raked leaves for the people who couldn't. Leah organized sign-ups and handed out paper bags that curled in on themselves at the edges. Linemen discovered the peculiar joy of making neat piles. Eli learned the weight of wet leaves and the satisfaction of a clean curb. Karen watched from her porch as boys she loved and boys she didn't know dragged color into an orderly heap and felt her chest loosen against the season.

On Thursday, Coach taped the bracket outline to the corkboard by the door without filling any names. "Empty on purpose," he said when a freshman asked. "The paper doesn't give you a future. Your feet do."

Friday night arrived cold and still. Senior Night scattered flowers and awkward smiles along the track. Will hugged his mother in a way that embarrassed both of them. Cruz stood at attention for pictures like a man volunteering for service. Marcus tucked his jersey just so, then untucked it, then retucked it because hands don't know what to do when people are looking. Eli's parents stood quietly and clapped in the right places; his mother mouthed *breathe* and he did.

They beat South Ridge without theater. 17–6. Micah kicked like a metronome. Jamal ran angry at edges. Eli threw one pretty ball and seven correct ones. Coach shook a single referee's hand and thanked the chain gang, which made John snort behind his breath.

In the locker room after, the steam and laughter felt earned and not extravagant. Coach held up the marker like a stipend and drew a rectangle around **Playoffs** on the whiteboard because sometimes you're allowed to name the thing you've been walking toward.

"We are not last year," he said. "We are this year. We don't owe the town fireworks; we owe each other first downs. Tuesday, film. Wednesday, hurt. Thursday, sharp. Friday, true."

On the bench in the third row, second stack, the shadow box caught a scuff of light from a bare bulb and gave nothing back. It didn't need to. Across the room, Eli peeled the tape from his wrist, folded it once, and pressed his thumb to the faint ridges on his skin the way he'd seen a boy do last fall when October was louder.

"Truth," he said under his breath, not because he needed to sit, not because he needed to prove anything, but because the word still made the next breath honest.

Outside, the wind pushed a handful of leaves across the end zone where the small **4** had been painted. The leaves spun and settled. The field made space. November waited the way it always waits in towns like this—like a test you've already learned the language for.

Chapter Thirty-Seven – November

November in Lincoln arrived with frost on windshields and breath hanging above mouths like speech balloons. The field stiffened under cleats, each step crunching instead of sinking. Practice began in the dusky half-light after school, and boys wore sleeves not to look tough but because cold hurt.

The bracket was official now, taped fresh to the corkboard in the field house. Lincoln's name was penciled in against **Valley Heights**, a team no one loved to play—big, old-fashioned, the kind that lined up double tights and dared you to quit. They didn't beat you with speed; they beat you with the calendar, one yard at a time, until you ran out of patience.

Coach circled the name once. "We can match big. We can't match bored. Stay awake."

Film showed Valley Heights' tailback lowering his pads into linebackers with the mercy of a bulldozer. Cruz grinned at the clip. "That's mine," he said. "He wants collisions? He found one."

Will leaned back in his chair and cracked his knuckles. "Their nose is heavy-footed. I can move him."

Eli scribbled notes on a legal pad Karen had slipped into his backpack, each page marked with neat, motherly lines: *Homework first. Eat something. Truth.* He underlined *play-action* twice.

Marcus sat beside him, flipping a pencil. "They'll bite," he said. "They always do. Sell grass, sky will come."

Practice that week was bare-bones, the way November football demands. Cold air cut lungs; sweat froze into salt lines on jerseys. Coach kept the script tight. Duo, stick, hitch. Duo, stick, hitch. Over and over until it looked like muscle memory teaching itself.

Cruz's defense crashed gaps, shouting cadence louder than Eli. The scout team groaned, but Coach only said, "Good. If you hate practice, you'll love Friday."

Ms. Rivera wore two coats and still looked frozen, but her hands stayed quick with tape and salt. "Thumb?" she asked Eli after Wednesday's practice, nodding at the bandage he'd wrapped himself.

"Ugly in the morning," he said. "Honest by the fourth quarter."

She smirked. "You're learning how to answer."

Friday night. Quarterfinals. The air smelled of woodsmoke drifting from backyards. The crowd packed in, coats zipped to the throat, hands buried in pockets. Karen sat with John, scarf pulled high, eyes locked on the field. Emily perched on the press row bench, notebook balanced, pencil tapping against her teeth. Leah worked the concession stand again, ladling cocoa, her scholarship hoodie zipped tight.

Valley Heights opened exactly as promised: run, run, run. Four yards, five, three. First down. The drives felt like sermons—long, heavy, inescapable. By the end of the first quarter, they had kicked a field goal. 3–0.

Lincoln's answer was patience cloaked in boredom. Duo for three. Stick for five. Sneak. First down. Eli's passes stayed short, Marcus running sharp cuts into shadows. Jamal slipped one sweep outside for twelve, then was caught by the ankles on the next. They chewed the clock back, marched to the twenty, and let Micah tie it with his foot. 3–3.

The second quarter was trench war. Cruz smashed the tailback once, helmet ringing, both men grinning after. Will shoved their nose into the turf and whispered something that wasn't printable. The scoreboard refused to move until, with two minutes before halftime, Eli sold play-action so well the safeties bit like fish. Marcus streaked behind them, arms open. The throw spun perfect, caught in stride. Touchdown. 10–3.

The crowd roared. Emily scribbled fast: *Patience cashes in big.*

Halftime in the locker room was breath clouds and red ears. Coach didn't draw new plays. He pointed at the board. "Keep them bored. Keep them small. One yard is enough. First down is a feast."

Second half. Valley Heights doubled down. Twelve plays, fifty-eight yards, touchdown. 10–10. The stands groaned, the band missed a note.

Eli huddled the offense. "They want us to hurry. We won't. Grass first. Trust it."

The next drive lasted nearly the whole quarter. Duo, stick, hitch. Out for four. Jamal in motion. Marcus on a curl. First down, first down, first down. At the eight, Eli pulled on zone read and fell forward into the end zone. 17–10.

The crowd roared again. Cruz lifted his helmet toward the sky and screamed.

Fourth quarter. Valley Heights at midfield, two minutes left, desperate. Fourth and one. Everyone in the stadium knew the play. Hand off, tailback lowers pads.

Cruz shot the gap. Helmet met shoulder. The pile stalled, legs churned, whistles blew. The chain crew sprinted in. Short.

The crowd erupted. Karen clutched John's sleeve, sobbing. Emily dropped her pencil, then laughed at herself for it. Leah pumped a fist from behind the cocoa stand.

Lincoln took a knee, and the horn sounded like salvation. Final: 17–10.

In the locker room, steam clouded the air, laughter echoing. Coach didn't shout. He stood by the shadow box in the corner, touched the glass with one knuckle, then faced the team.

"Next week's bigger. But tonight? You learned patience wins more than games. It wins futures."

Eli sat with tape frayed, Marcus beside him, Will and Cruz across the aisle. He pressed his thumb to the word on his wrist. "Truth," he whispered, and for the first time it felt less like a plea and more like a promise.

Chapter Thirty-Eight – The Semifinal Rematch

The forecast had lied politely all week—"brisk," "seasonal"—and then Friday arrived with a wind that cut through jackets and made metal sing. Breath plumed over the track in steady ghosts. When the buses turned under the old stone arch of the college stadium, the lights were already on and humming, pooling on a field that remembered last year like a scar.

The bracket had put Lincoln against **St. Mary's** again. Same sideline for Coach. Same band with crisp uniforms for them. Same coach across the way who looked like he ironed his play sheet. The rematch tasted like unfinished business, but not revenge. Lincoln's boys carried different weight now.

In the tunnel, Coach Dempsey's voice stayed low. "They pattern-match and wait for you to blink. Don't blink. They'll offer you panic. Decline. Feet, hips, hands. No free doubt." He glanced at Eli. "If I say blue two, you love me later."

"Yes, sir," Eli said. He tugged the red jersey straight and checked his wrist tape by feel rather than sight.

They went out to warmups under a sky the color of a pencil eraser. The band's drumline ricocheted off the concrete. Ms. Rivera stood at the white line with a cooler labeled **NOVEMBER** and a knit hat pulled low, eyes doing math as boys jogged past. Karen and John found their seats above the fifty, gloves wrapped around a thermos.

Emily wedged herself between two band parents on the press row bench, notebook open, pencil sharp, a spare tucked behind her ear.

Captains at midfield. The handshake wasn't unfriendly. St. Mary's kids looked like they had walked out of a brochure again. The coin spun, flashed, landed. Lincoln received.

The first series was exactly what Coach had wanted. Duo for four. Stick for five. Sneak. First down. Eli's breath came in neat puffs. Marcus bent a curl at the right depth and made the catch with hands that were only briefly louder than the cold. Jamal motioned through the backfield to steal a safety's eyes. The drive crawled into the red zone and bogged when a linebacker knifed through a double team. Micah jogged out, tapped the ground twice like a ritual, and banged it true. 3–0.

St. Mary's answered with their catechism: RPO glance, zone read keep, a pivot route that made a linebacker step the wrong way by half an inch. Their quarterback slid like mercury and slid out of bounds when Cruz arrived with intentions. The drive died on the twenty-nine when Jamal undercut a hitch with greedy hands. The pick didn't return far, but it returned breath.

Second quarter, the cold settled into sleeves. Lincoln leaned on the boring beautiful. Out, hitch, draw. Will's feet whispered under a heavy nose. Marcus sold grass on a vertical, forced the corner to turn, then stopped dead on a comeback like a magician revealing the card you swore you hadn't picked. First down. At the twenty-one, St. Mary's spun late to one-high. Eli wasn't tempted. He hit the back in the flat and begged Jamal to break a tackle. He did not. Micah: 6–0.

"Win first down," Coach said into the headset as defense trotted. "Don't let them breathe."

St. Mary's refused to be suffocated. They strung a drive across five minutes and four conversions, each born from a quarterback who saw angles before they existed. On second-and-goal from the six, they ran a sprint-out flood that asked Jamal to cover two men and gave him neither. Touchdown. 7–6. Their band discovered warmth in volume.

Two minutes and a mood before halftime. Eli gathered the huddle by the twenty-five. "We've got time," he said. "Grass until they cheat. Then sky."

Out for seven. Stick for six. Draw for four. First down at the forty-six with forty-two seconds. St. Mary's stayed honest enough to be annoying. Marcus looked at Eli once: *now?* Eli shook his head: *later.*

With nineteen seconds, the safety cheated the half-step you wait a month to see. Eli didn't grin. He hit the top of his drop, hitched, and threw the hole shot to the sideline where Marcus' toes kissed paint like he was saying hello. Out of bounds, the clock polite enough to keep three seconds. Micah from forty-two, ball low but true. 9–7 at half.

Inside, the locker room collected breath and steam. Coach drew nothing new. "Top stays on. Offense, be the metronome. If you get bored, think about someone you love and keep doing it anyway." He looked at Eli. "Truth is still a tool."

Ms. Rivera pressed a salt cap into Eli's hand and another into Will's before he could say he didn't need it. "Thumb?" she asked Eli.

"Honest," he said.

"Keep it that way." She made eye contact long enough to say *I'm here* without words.

The third quarter arrived with wind. St. Mary's took the kick and assembled a drive that would have made a clock proud. Third-and-four at the Lincoln thirty-one, they ran orbit motion into a fake that corrupted good eyes. The quarterback threw back across the grain— dangerous and beautiful—and found a tight end rumbling into daylight. 14–9.

The home side crowd grew teeth. Karen's hand found John's sleeve and stayed. Emily wrote *poise is a temperature* and underlined it, annoyed with herself for getting fancy.

Lincoln's next drive started cold and warmed itself. Eli took a shot on second-and-six and missed Marcus by a hand length. Third-and-six, St. Mary's showed pressure and bailed, the kind of petty trick that ruins teenagers. Eli didn't ruin. He checked to a curl, took five, and sent for Micah because the yard line dictated honesty. 14–12.

Cruz's defense made a stand born of stubbornness. On first down, he stoned the tailback so clean the kid thanked him with a look. On second, Jamal came screaming off the edge like he'd been getting narrower since August just for this moment. Third and eleven, St. Mary's tried a tunnel screen. Will—on punt shield, sneaking a peek—called it from the sideline. The defense closed like a book. Punt.

Field position traded like baseball cards. The quarter bled into the fourth with the scoreboard taut as a drum: 14–12 and the ball at Lincoln's twenty.

"Four-minute drill if we can," Coach said. "If we can't, we'll pretend."

Eli nodded. The huddle leaned in, sound blocked by cold. "Grass," he said, and it sounded like a vow.

Duo for three. Stick for five. Sneak through a crease Will created by convincing a defender to visit another zip code. First down. Out for four. Draw for two. Third-and-four at the forty-one. The safety looked at Marcus too long. Eli didn't punish—yet. He hit Jamal on an angle route that stole five because arithmetic is legal in November.

Two minutes. St. Mary's tightened. First down at midfield became second-and-nine at the St. Mary's forty-nine when a corner shot a gap like a rumor. Eli felt the urge for sky rise in his chest like a second heart. He pressed his thumb to the tape and named the urge. "Truth," he murmured, not to sit, just to keep the room level.

He checked to stick. Marcus sat in the soft space because he'd built it with two months of film. Catch. Turn. Two more. Third-and-one. St. Mary's stacked the box with righteousness. Coach tapped his wrist: sneak. Will got low enough to worry gravity. First down.

St. Mary's burned a timeout to argue with the elements. One-oh-eight on the clock. Ball at the thirty-eight. The corner's hips finally told a story he couldn't untell. Marcus didn't signal. Eli did. Play-action, shoulders honest, eyes lying. He reset his feet into the teeth of a wind gust and threw the hole shot like it had been waiting since August to be admitted into evidence. Marcus stacked, separated, caught, and fell on the twenty-two, looking like a man who had just taken the world's most solemn slide.

St. Mary's used their second timeout to beg a god of details. Coach's voice crackled into Eli's helmet. "Win first down. Kick if we must. No free drama."

Duo for two. Forty-three seconds. Second-and-eight. Eli rolled left to change the picture and took the free four with his legs, sliding like an adult in a world that thinks bravery is louder. Thirty-two seconds. Third-and-four at the sixteen.

Micah warmed up his leg in tiny hops. Coach put a hand on his shoulder. "You good?"

Micah nodded, teeth clenched as if warmth could be generated by molars.

St. Mary's bracketed Marcus so tight it looked like a dare. Eli didn't mind being dared. He checked the tight end's delay—*Leak Storm* from a year ago, with a wrinkle that made Will smile in a very specific way. Snap. Eli sold Smash. The tight end chipped, waited, leaked into the flat exactly when the linebacker decided he had seen enough film to cheat. Catch at the nine. Down at the seven. First-and-goal. St. Mary's called their last timeout to try to make the night longer.

Coach looked at the clock, then at the men in front of him, then at Micah. "Three plays," he said. "One right. Two left. If they gift you six, take it. If not, we trust the man with the foot."

First down: duo right for one, bodies in a pile that groaned like a ship. Second down: duo left for two, the pile angling mercifully. Eleven seconds. The wind lifted, then dropped. Coach made the sign for field goal, and Micah jogged like he was walking into a test he'd studied for.

Eli clapped the huddle out, patted Micah's helmet, and put his hands under center with the curiosity of a boy who could so easily have demanded heroism. The snap came clean. The hold was good enough. The kick started left and remembered manners. 15–14.

Five seconds. Squib, shins, a lateral that looked like democracy under pressure, and Cruz ended it with the gentlest tackle of the year, easing a boy to ground because grace is also technique.

The horn cut crisp air. The stadium exhaled heat. Lincoln did not dogpile. They hugged like men who knew there was still another bus ride in them.

At the rail, Karen pressed gloved hands to her mouth and laughed without making sound. John pounded the fence post once, then looked embarrassed and patted it like apology. Emily forgot to write for five whole minutes and then scribbled a single line: *We are not last year—and that is the point.*

In the handshake line, St. Mary's quarterback said it with a smile that wasn't bitter. "You make boring look like art."

Eli grinned back. "We had a good teacher."

The locker room shook from the inside—a muffled drum of cleats and celebration. Coach walked to the shadow box, touched the glass, then turned. "State final," he said simply. "You earned a bus to December."

Ms. Rivera leaned against the doorframe, cheeks red, eyes bright without being wet. She held up the cooler. "Drink," she ordered. "And bring your math homework tomorrow like you said you would, Quarterback."

"Yes, ma'am," Eli said, and it felt good to be told to do something small.

Will set a big hand on Micah's shoulder and squeezed until the kicker made a sound. Cruz texted the **Angles** thread a photo of the scoreboard with no caption. Marcus sat and unlaced his cleats slowly, like a man making a ritual out of nothing special, and pressed his thumb to the faint ridges on his wrist because old habits had learned new reasons.

On the bus, the windows fogged and boys wrote triangles and plays and dumb faces with fingers that thawed slower than joy. Eli slid into his seat, leaned his head against cold glass, and let the quiet inside him expand. He took the tape off his wrist, folded it twice, and couldn't quite throw it away. He tucked it into the pocket of his hoodie instead. Some tools you keep even when the job is different.

Out past the stadium, snow threatened without committing. December waited with its own vocabulary. The boys were ready to learn it.

Chapter Thirty-Nine –
The Week Before State

The Monday after the semifinal felt like waking up in someone else's story. Posters bloomed in the halls—**STATE BOUND** scrawled in marker, the number **4** painted on banners alongside lions and helmets. The diner added a chalkboard special: "Truth Burger—plain, no free toppings." Even the principal, who had never understood football beyond the parking logistics, wore a Lincoln hoodie over his shirt and tie.

Coach hated it.

"Block it out," he growled in the first film session. "They want fireworks and drama. We want feet, hips, hands. State isn't magic. It's football with louder speakers."

He clicked play. The opponent—**Ironwood**, undefeated, all swagger—looked fast and mean even on a projector. Their defense shifted pre-snap like cats. Their quarterback had a cannon and a smile that made highlight reels.

Cruz leaned forward. "Finally," he muttered.

Practices were cold enough to sting. Frost painted the grass by the time the team finished warmups. Eli wore long sleeves under his red jersey, thumb still taped, breath coming out in white bursts. Marcus's gloves stiffened between reps, but his routes stayed sharp as math. Will's linemen shoved sleds through frozen ground until their cleats squealed.

Coach cut practice time, but not intensity. "Better one clean hour than three sloppy," he told them. "Trust your muscle memory. Don't go looking for miracles."

At the end of each session, the boys jogged to the end zone where the chalked **4** had been refreshed. One by one, they tapped it with gloved hands. No words. Just breath fog and the sound of cleats.

Ms. Rivera doubled her vigilance. "No heroics this week," she warned, glaring at Cruz's shoulder wrap. "If you feel something tweak, you tell me. Truth applies to trainers too."

Eli smirked. "You're scarier than Coach."

"Good," she shot back. "Means you're listening."

She handed him a fresh roll of tape. "Not for Friday. For your desk. Reminder that truth is boring and boring is holy."

Emily prepared differently. She filled three notebooks with scraps of quotes, sketches of plays, fragments of lines. She knew she wouldn't be allowed in the locker room, but she wanted the story ready. In the margins she wrote sentences she might never print: *They are carrying a boy's absence like extra pads. They are making patience into poetry.*

Karen and John found themselves visited daily—neighbors dropping off pies, casseroles, blue ribbons. John accepted with polite nods; Karen wept at every doorway. In quiet moments she sat at Aidan's desk, fingers tracing his old homework doodles, whispering: "They're still carrying you."

Friday before state, Coach gathered the team in the auditorium, lights dim, projector off. He didn't pace. He didn't lecture.

"You earned this," he said. "Nobody gave it to you. Nobody will give you Friday either. Ironwood's fast. They're mean. They don't care about your story. Good. Make them care about your feet and your patience."

He looked at Eli. "Don't chase sky. Let it come. If you need truth, say it. If you need blue two, I'll hear it."

He looked at Marcus. "Run the grass into art."

At Will. "Keep Eli clean. No free rushers."

At Cruz. "Make their quarterback hate you politely."

The room chuckled.

Coach finally set his cap down. "You'll hear noise. Tune it out. You'll feel weight. Carry it together. At kickoff, it's not about state or history or banners. It's about first down. First down is always the dream."

The boys clapped once, hard.

That night, Eli lay awake staring at the ceiling. His wrist was bare—no tape, just skin—but he swore he still felt the letters pressed there. He whispered them into the dark anyway.

"Truth."

Across town, Marcus dreamt of grass that turned into sky. Will rolled over with his fists clenched. Cruz muttered cadence in his sleep. Emily wrote one last card and tucked it in her coat pocket: *Boring Beautiful Wins.*

The town slept like a stadium before lights. Tomorrow, December would write its verdict.

Chapter Forty –
The State Championship

The buses rolled out of Lincoln before sunrise, headlights cutting through mist. The boys rode in silence, hoods up, earbuds in, windows fogged. No one spoke louder than a whisper. The closer they came to the capital stadium, the bigger the silence felt, like even words would use too much oxygen.

Eli sat by the window, thumb working the tape around his wrist. He hadn't written the word yet. He wanted to wait until the locker room, like a ritual worth saving. Marcus leaned his head against the glass, eyes half closed, hands folded over gloves he'd warmed in his hoodie pocket. Will chewed gum like it had wronged him. Cruz muttered scouting notes under his breath, body rocking to a rhythm only he heard.

When the buses pulled into the lot, the stadium loomed—huge, sharp under December sky, its scoreboard dark and waiting. Fans already crowded the gates, blue scarves and banners everywhere. Half the town had come. The other half would be listening on radios, TVs turned up too loud in living rooms.

In the locker room, the boys dressed like armorers. Jerseys snapped into place, tape wound tight, chinstraps buckled, undone again, buckled once more. The air smelled of liniment and nerves.

Coach stood at the front, cap tucked under his arm. "This is still football. Don't let the lights trick you. Don't let the size lie to you.

The field is one hundred yards, same as home. The rules haven't changed."

He paused. "Patience. No free doubt. One first down at a time."

Then he looked at Eli. "You made a bargain. We kept it honest. Finish it honest."

Eli nodded, then pulled a black strip of tape from the roll Ms. Rivera had handed him. With sharp strokes of marker, he wrote one word in block letters: **TRUTH.** He pressed it tight against his skin and felt the weight of it.

Kickoff was thunder. Ironwood's band blasted like cannons, their fans filling half the stadium in crimson and white. Their opening drive was efficient, a quarterback rifling passes into tight windows, a running back who didn't fall backward once. Eight plays, seventy yards, touchdown. 7–0.

Lincoln answered with patience. Duo for four, stick for five, sneak for one. First down. Out route to Marcus for seven, Jamal on a sweep for six. By the time they reached the red zone, the crowd had found its voice again. Third and goal at the five, Eli rolled right, saw Marcus break late inside, and zipped it. Touchdown. Tie game, 7–7.

The first half went back and forth. Ironwood scored again on a seam route; Lincoln answered with a long drive capped by Micah's field goal. Halftime: 14–10, Ironwood.

The locker room buzzed with adrenaline and cold sweat. Boys slumped against lockers, sipping water, chewing orange slices, helmets balanced on their knees.

Coach didn't change much. "They're strong. Good. So are we. Keep your patience. Keep your truth. They'll crack if you don't."

Ms. Rivera re-taped Eli's ribs. Her hands were quick, her voice quiet. "How's the pain?"

"Like halftime," Eli said, smiling despite himself.

She pressed the tape down firmly, then handed him the marker. "Write it again if you have to."

Third quarter. Ironwood leaned on their size, pounding inside runs, wearing the clock. Their kicker added three. 17–10.

Lincoln clawed back. Eli hit Marcus on a curl, Jamal turned a checkdown into twelve, Will flattened a linebacker to spring a draw. At the five-yard line, Eli kept on zone read, dove across the line, and the score was tied again. 17–17.

The crowd thundered. Karen clutched John's hand. Emily scribbled fast, her pencil scratching the page: *Patience fights giants.*

Fourth quarter. Five minutes left. The scoreboard: 24–24. Every breath in the stadium came heavy.

Ironwood drove deep into Lincoln territory. Third and two at the twenty. Cruz shot the gap, slammed into the running back, and the pile stopped dead. Fourth and one. Ironwood's coach hesitated, then sent the kicker. The ball sailed through. 27–24.

Two minutes left. Lincoln's ball, eighty yards from glory.

The huddle was tight, faces pale but steady. Eli's breath fogged between them. "Grass," he said. "Trust it. We've got time."

First down: stick for six. Second down: duo for three. Third and one: sneak. First down.

The crowd roared. The clock ticked.

At midfield, Eli faked a draw, rolled right, and fired to Marcus on the sideline. Catch. First down at the thirty.

Thirty seconds left.

Coach's voice buzzed in Eli's helmet: "Patience. No free doubt."

First down: out route, incomplete. Second: curl for eight. Third and two, ball at the twenty-two, twenty seconds left.

The play call came: zone read. Eli took the snap, read the end, pulled. He sprinted left, ribs screaming, defenders chasing. Ten yards. Five. He dove, stretched, ball across the line—touchdown.

Lincoln 30, Ironwood 27.

The stadium exploded—fans screaming, Karen sobbing, Emily standing on her seat with an index card in her hand: *BORING BEAUTIFUL.*

But the hit came late. Ironwood's linebacker barreled through, helmet slamming into Eli's ribs as he lay in the end zone. The sound was ugly, final.

Eli didn't get up.

The roar broke into silence. Ms. Rivera sprinted from the sideline, Coach on her heels. Marcus tore his helmet off, screaming Eli's name. Will dropped to his knees beside him.

On the turf, under the lights, with the scoreboard frozen at **Lincoln 30, Ironwood 27**, Eli lay motionless, the word on his wrist smudged but still legible: **TRUTH.**

The state championship was theirs, but the cost lay quiet in the end zone.

Chapter Forty-One –
The Aftermath in the Hospital

The ambulance's siren carved a line through the night. Fans had been screaming minutes earlier, stomping bleachers as Lincoln hoisted the trophy, but now a hush had followed the flashing lights. People parted at the gate, blue scarves and banners lowered, children lifted into arms as the stretcher rolled past.

Karen clutched John's sleeve so tightly her knuckles whitened. She whispered, "Not again," over and over, voice raw with memory. John kept his arm around her, jaw locked. Emily, still holding her notebook, stood at the rail, staring, too shocked to write.

In the locker room, the state championship trophy sat alone on a table, confetti still clinging to its base. No one touched it. Boys slumped in silence, helmets on the floor, tape still wrapped around wrists. Marcus sat with his hands in his hair. Will paced, muttering curses under his breath. Cruz punched a locker once, then pressed his forehead against it as if willing the world to make sense.

Coach Dempsey walked in, cap in his hand. His voice was rough. "We'll know more soon. Right now—sit. Breathe. Pray if that's your thing. We don't leave until we hear."

At the hospital, the fluorescent lights were cruelly bright. Ms. Rivera stayed at Eli's side, her voice low and steady as doctors moved around him. "Stay with us," she murmured. "You did your job. Let us do ours."

His ribs were broken, lungs bruised, but the monitors beeped a rhythm that gave hope. He was alive.

Karen and John rushed in, hearts in their throats. Karen froze at the doorway, the sight of tubes and tape pulling her backward into a year she hadn't escaped. John guided her forward, whispering, "Different boy. Different story."

Emily arrived minutes later, pale and trembling, notebook still in her hand. She didn't ask permission—she slipped to the corner of the room, tears streaking her cheeks. When Eli stirred faintly, eyes flickering open, she gasped.

He looked at Ms. Rivera first. His voice was a rasp, but the word was clear. "Truth."

Ms. Rivera pressed his hand down gently. "That's enough for tonight."

Word spread through Lincoln by dawn: Eli was hurt, but alive. The scoreboard photo had already made headlines—Lincoln 30, Ironwood 27—but the real story was unfolding under hospital lights.

The town gathered again—outside the hospital this time. Teachers, classmates, old men from the diner, band kids with instruments slung over shoulders. They prayed, sang, waited. Not in silence this time, but with a steady hum of presence.

Inside, Marcus, Will, and Cruz slipped into the waiting room, still in their jerseys, numbers faded with grass and sweat. They sat together without speaking until Emily walked over, clutching an index card. She set it on the coffee table in front of them. In block letters:

We finish together.

Marcus swallowed hard, then nodded. Will put a hand over the card. Cruz whispered, "Amen."

By afternoon, the doctor emerged. He pulled off his gloves, his face softening. "He'll need time. Weeks, maybe months. But he's strong. He's going to be okay."

Karen collapsed into John's chest, sobbing relief. Emily wept into her hands. Ms. Rivera leaned against the wall, eyes closing as if she'd been holding her breath all night.

Back in his room, Eli blinked awake fully this time. Marcus stood at his bedside, voice shaky but steady. "We won, Four," he said, using the nickname without meaning to. "Scoreboard says so."

Eli managed a weak smile. "State champs." He lifted his wrist, tape frayed but intact, and whispered the word one more time.

"Truth."

That evening, when the team returned to the stadium to collect their gear, the field was empty except for confetti blown into corners. The trophy gleamed under the lights. They gathered around it, not cheering, not lifting it high, but standing in a circle, quiet.

Coach placed a hand on the metal and spoke softly. "This doesn't belong to one night. It belongs to every Tuesday, every tired rep, every choice to do the small things right. It belongs to him"—he glanced toward the hospital—"and to the boy who taught us all to say truth first."

The players touched the trophy one by one, not for glory but for gratitude.

Lincoln was state champion, but more than that—they were alive, together, and still learning how to carry the word that had outlasted pain, loss, and even victory.

Chapter Forty-Two – The Celebration

The Monday after state, the town of Lincoln looked like a festival had spilled across every block. Blue ribbons fluttered from lampposts, storefronts hung posters with **STATE CHAMPIONS** in bold letters, and the high school gymnasium filled so fast the fire marshal gave up counting.

It wasn't just a pep rally. It was a reckoning—of grief, of joy, of everything in between.

The team walked in first, jerseys over hoodies, medals clinking softly. Will and Cruz led the way, Marcus beside Eli's empty spot. The cheerleaders flanked the entrance, pom-poms subdued into ribbons. The band struck up the fight song, loud enough to rattle the rafters, but softer than usual at the end, like even brass knew how to bow.

Then the gym rose to its feet when Eli appeared.

He wasn't in pads. He wasn't even in blue. He wore sweats, ribs still wrapped tight, moving carefully between Ms. Rivera and Marcus. His steps were slow, but his smile was steady. The ovation was thunder, long and unbroken, echoing into every corner of the gym. Karen pressed a hand to her mouth. John clapped until his palms hurt. Emily wrote nothing—she just wept, her pencil useless in her lap.

The mayor stood at the podium first. He read the proclamation with his voice cracking: "December 12th, 20XX, will forever be known as

Lincoln Lions Day. A team that carried more than pads, a town that carried more than cheers."

The state trophy sat center stage on a table, ribbons draped around its base. Tucked next to it was the shadow box from the locker room: tape, towel, confetti, a lion sticker. Two legacies, side by side.

Coach Dempsey stepped up, hat in hand. "Champions are remembered by numbers," he said. "But legends are remembered by habits. This team learned patience is louder than panic. They learned boring beautiful. They learned truth." He turned, gesturing toward Eli. "And he taught us that bargains can be honored without breaking."

The applause rose again, not just cheers but stomps on the bleachers, the whole gym moving like a drum.

Then Emily climbed the stage, notebook in hand. She wasn't on the program, but the crowd quieted anyway.

"This town has carried two stories in one year," she said. "One of loss, one of survival. They aren't separate. They belong to each other. Aidan showed us truth can outlast fear. Eli showed us truth can outlast pain. Together, they remind us that first downs are love languages and small choices become victories. The scoreboard reads 30–27, but the real score is a town that learned how to carry each other."

She stepped back, trembling, the gym hushed and then exploding with applause.

Finally, Eli took the mic. His voice was rough, his ribs protesting each word, but he spoke anyway.

"I can't explain how it felt in that end zone. Pain and joy all at once. But I can say this: I didn't win that game. We did. Will kept me clean. Cruz made them fear us. Marcus gave me routes when I had nothing else. Every freshman who ran scout, every parent in the stands, every teacher who made us pass our classes—you won that game. And

Aidan…" He paused, pressing a hand to the tape still on his wrist. "Aidan showed us how to live truth. We just followed."

The gym erupted, half the town chanting: "Truth! Truth! Truth!"

Eli raised his hand, asking for quiet. "The trophy will sit in the case. But the word—" He tapped his wrist. "—this word belongs everywhere. Don't let it fade."

That night, the trophy was placed in the high school lobby, beside the retired number four jersey. Kids pressed their hands against the glass, parents took pictures, and Ms. Rivera taped a small note to the case: **Ordinary is holy.**

Karen lingered long after others had left. She touched the jersey, then the glass over the trophy. For the first time, she smiled without tears. "Both of you," she whispered. "You finished together."

Outside, the December wind cut cold, but the town walked home warm—champions in record books, and more importantly, in habits that would outlast even memory.

Chapter Forty-Three –
The Winter That Follows

December slid into January with the kind of cold that made the field look like a promise sealed in glass. Snow settled in the seams of the yard lines; the small **4** in the corner of the end zone lay under a white sheet that did not erase it. The trophy case in the school lobby took on a second life—fingerprints smudged the glass every morning, small handprints from elementary kids who visited with their older siblings and believed metal could tell stories.

By the first week back, the banners were down from the gym and the pep-rally echo had drained from the rafters. Lincoln returned to the business of winter: algebra, lunches that steamed in their trays, band rehearsals in the parking lot where breath turned instruments into chimneys. The football boys moved through it like everyone else— hats low, backpacks heavy—state champions who still had to remember locker combinations and cafeteria PINs.

Eli's world shrank in a useful way. Physical therapy in the morning. Classes. Check-ins with Ms. Rivera at the white line that now lived in the hallway. "Pain?" she asked without ceremony, hands ready, eyes reading posture. "Less," he'd say, which most days meant honest, and on bad days meant stubborn. She never punished the days it meant stubborn. She adjusted tape and expectations and wrote **rest** on a sticky note she tucked into the edge of his math notebook.

He went to Mr. Tanner's office hours twice a week, the clock on the wall ticking like a metronome for a different kind of patience. On the first Thursday back, Mr. Tanner slid a practice test across the desk with a pencil—not a pen. "Show your work," he said.

Eli smirked. "Story of my life."

After a week of not throwing anything heavier than a stress ball, he stood in the gym one afternoon with a foam football from the elementary closet. Marcus tossed him routes on air, half-speed, the ball floating like a joke that was also a prayer. The first throw sailed. The second wobbled. The third hummed in the right way and they both exhaled. "We've got time," Marcus said, as if he'd been put in charge of time. "Grass first."

Will lived in the weight room like he paid rent. His ankle had forgiven him by New Year's; his shoulders never would. He took a freshman guard by the wrist and showed him how to wrap tape without cutting off circulation. "Thumbs are citizens," he said. "Treat 'em right." He put names on the whiteboard under **Chairs to Move / Things to Carry / People to Help**, and then, because he loved lists that made sense, added **Homework to Finish**.

Cruz looked smaller without pads and somehow more dangerous with a clipboard. He took over Wednesday **Angles** meetings in the film room, switching the projector on to show a college linebacker fitting split zone like a thesis statement. "Eyes," he'd say, tapping the screen. "Eyes before violence." Half the boys nodded. Half texted memes to the thread and showed up anyway.

The scholarship committee swapped ribbon-cutting for ledger-balancing. Leah ran point on a winter service day that had middle schoolers packaging toiletry kits for the hospital where panic had once lived. She printed labels that read **No Free Doubt** and made sixth graders say it out loud before they sealed a bag. The white-haired custodian with grammar opinions found her in the hallway and whispered, "Adverbs sparingly," and Leah rolled her eyes respectfully and kept going.

The diner changed the chalkboard special from **Truth Burger** to **Ordinary Omelet** on Tuesdays. It came with toast and a Post-it stuck to the check: *Thank you, #4* in someone's grandma handwriting. Ms. Rivera found herself drinking coffee there more than at the hospital some mornings, which felt like growth and also like cheating. She took her clipboard anyway, out of superstition and muscle memory, and answered two questions an hour from townsfolk who had never asked about lactic acid before.

Karen and John learned the new shape of evenings. The house was still too quiet in the way houses are when someone is not in them on purpose. But the silence softened at the edges. Karen found herself laughing at a sitcom without punishing the laugh afterward. John started keeping a small notebook by the door where he wrote the names of boys to pray for on Thursdays because Thursdays had been travel days, and rituals ask to be fed. He added **Eli** to the top of the page one week, then underlined **Leah** when she called to ask if they'd speak at the spring scholarship night. They said yes. They practiced saying yes to small things.

They went to therapy once a week in an office that smelled like eucalyptus and sounded like a fish tank. The therapist asked Karen to name three places where she could breathe in town. She said "the field when no one is there," "the grocery store at eight a.m.," and, after a long pause, "the stands, if I sit near the stairs." They practiced sitting near the stairs in January. It felt like cardio and homework. They passed.

Emily wrote. She wrote at her desk and in the band hallway and on the bleachers when the sun was a rumor. Her long piece for the school paper started as notes and grew into something with a spine. She called it "Winter Practice," and it wasn't about football, not really. It was about the way a town could learn to keep moving the chains when there were no chains, about how January teaches you August if you let it. The journalism advisor tried to cut a paragraph she loved. Emily moved three sentences and saved it anyway, then won a small statewide award and pretended she didn't care. She told no one about the scholarship essay on her laptop titled **Patience as a Dialect**. She told Eli to do his practice test and stop looking out the window when it snowed.

One Saturday, the team shoveled driveways block by block with the kind of competence that makes good pictures and better neighbors. Jamal discovered ice under powder the hard way and then salted like a man who believed in the gospel of traction. Eli took his time, ribs complaining in small, honest ways, and a grandfather on Birch Street stood on his porch in slippers and said, "I saw the game on television," and then, after a beat, "Glad you're here now." Eli nodded like that was the whole point.

Coach Dempsey tried retirement for exactly three days in early January—retirement from speeches, not from coaching. On day four he wrote a one-page note and taped it to the inside of the field house door with blue painter's tape.

Tuesday Letters:

- **To players:** You are students. Prove it in classes first.

- **To parents:** Thank you for the rides and the food and the patience.

- **To January:** We hear you. We will not be dramatic.

- **To the town:** We will serve on Saturdays. We will lift on weekdays. We will hydrate.

He signed it, —**Dempsey**, and someone wrote **Amen** underneath in Sharpie that looked exactly like Aidan's handwriting and wasn't. He left it there. He added a new letter every week until February, when he let the space breathe again.

On a Tuesday evening, coach called a short meeting in the auditorium without lights or slides. "We retire number four at Spring Night," he said. "We do it with gratitude, not theater." He looked at Will and

Cruz and Marcus and then at the juniors who would be seniors. "You'll carry it without wearing it. That's a better bargain anyway."

In late January, Karen invited the team to her house for spaghetti because feeding boys is a way to rename grief. John stirred sauce with a concentration that would have made the chain gang proud. The boys took off shoes in a pile that turned the foyer into a museum of mud. Will fixed a wobbly chair without being asked. Cruz dried dishes like he was competing with the dishwasher. Marcus wandered into Aidan's room and stopped at the threshold without entering; there was no shrine, just a neat bed and a desk with scuffs and a dried-out Sharpie in a mug.

Karen found Eli in the doorway and pressed the marker into his hand. "It doesn't work," she said, smiling like a person learning a second language. "But I like how it looks in someone's hand."

He held it carefully, like it could still write something that mattered. "Thank you," he said, which covered too many things.

On the way out, Emily stood on the porch in a hat with a pom, steam rising out of the casserole dish she refused to take back. "The piece runs next week," she told Karen. "It's clean. Honest."

"I like honest," Karen said. "Even when I don't."

February thawed enough to reveal the field in strips—green like intention, brown like truth. The first day the sod didn't bite back, Eli walked the sideline with a foam ball and threw to Marcus from the numbers to the hash. Ten yards. Then twelve. Then a brave fifteen that he regretted for twenty seconds and forgave after a stretch. Ms. Rivera watched from the track with a stopwatch she didn't click and a smirk she didn't hide. "Boredom before bravado," she called. "It's my love language."

Leah stuck a bulletin board by the cafeteria doors titled **Small Right Things** and pinned index cards with student handwriting: *Walked my neighbor's dog. Asked for help in chem. Texted my grandma.* The board filled in two days. She moved it to the main hall and stapled butcher paper to the wall when they ran out of space. "Scale the virtue," she said to anyone who'd listen. "Scale is how you win."

The state sent medals for the boys who hadn't been at the official ceremony in December. The principal handed them out on a Tuesday in the library like overdue books being returned. Eli's was heavy and cold in his palm. He slid it into the side pocket of his backpack behind a pencil, a folder, and a roll of black tape he no longer wore every day but kept because some anchors don't sink you; they keep you from drifting.

On Valentine's Day, the band played a medley at lunch that included the fight song by accident or design. Cruz danced in the line to make a freshman laugh and knocked over a stack of milk cartons. He cleaned the mess before Ms. Rivera could glare. Marcus taped a heart on the receivers' room door that read **Route tree > roses** and nobody disagreed enough to take it down.

On the last night of February, more sky than month, Coach stood at the fifty in a coat that looked like it had coached other men decades ago. He stared at the corner of the end zone where the small **4** would be repainted in spring. He put his hands in his pockets and took them out again. He didn't say anything lofty or long. He said, to no one and to the bleachers and to the weather, "We're still here."

He was right. Winter had not been a pause so much as a new tense— present continuous. The boys still texted at odd hours about film and algebra. The town still brought casseroles for no good reason. Ms. Rivera still carried tape even to non-sporting events. Karen still walked the track on Wednesdays once around, twice when the wind permitted. John still pressed his thumb into the ridge of a pocketed coin when a siren passed, and his hand came away calm.

On the first Saturday in March warm enough to lie, the field hosted a youth clinic. Six-year-olds in oversized Lions shirts sprinted in crooked lines. A girl in pigtails stiff-armed a boy twice her size and learned the word **leverage** the fun way. Eli demonstrated a three-step drop and let a child sack him with theatrical despair. Marcus tossed perfect spirals to kids who would remember the arc longer than they remembered his name. Will held a blocking pad and didn't move, because you can't teach success by pretending to fail. Cruz took a knee to tie a kid's shoe, then taught him to tie it himself. Leah ran registration and wrote down two names upside down without thinking about it.

At the edges, Emily scribbled in a notebook while pretending not to. She wrote: *Winter doesn't end the story. It changes the lighting. Ordinary becomes visible. That's where the truth lives when confetti is busy.* She crossed out *confetti* twice and kept it anyway.

As the clinic wound down, Eli stood by the rail with the foam ball tucked in his elbow and looked at the trophy case through the open lobby doors. The glass caught afternoon sun and threw it back as a quiet glare. He didn't go in. He didn't need to. He pressed his thumb to the faint groove where the tape had lived all fall and said the word out of habit, out of gratitude, out of a plan that hadn't changed just because the month had.

"Truth."

A kid at his knee looked up. "What'd you say?"

Eli smiled. "First down," he said. "Want to learn how to get one?"

The boy nodded solemnly, the way small people nod when big ideas are translated for them. The field took new footprints. The snow receded another inch in the shade. And winter, which had been the part of the story where everything slows down and gets heavy, revealed itself as a season where heaviness can be carried by more hands than one.

Chapter Forty-Four – Spring Awakening

Spring arrived in pieces. First the snow retreated from the shady margins. Then the track showed through like an old scar. By the second week of March the field stopped crunching underfoot and started giving back a little. Boys tested it with easy strides and decided it was safe to run again.

In the weight room, metal clanged like a metronome. Will wrote a fresh list on the whiteboard—**Chairs to Move / Things to Carry / People to Help / Homework to Finish**—then taped a Sharpie to the frame so no one could claim they "couldn't find a pen." Cruz stretched bands around a squat rack and lectured a sophomore on the angle of shoulders into contact: "Eyes first. Hands next. Violence last." The sophomore nodded like he understood. He didn't yet. He would.

Eli shuffled in with a foam ball tucked into his elbow and the careful gait of a person negotiating with his own ribs. Ms. Rivera met him at the door with a look that managed fond and unsparing at the same time. "Honest pain?" she asked.

"Honest enough," he said.

She wrapped a light bandage anyway, even though they both knew it was more ritual than medicine. "You get twenty throws," she said. "Not a theological twenty. A counted twenty."

Marcus grinned from the doorway. "She means nineteen and a half."

"Don't make me deputize him," Rivera said, nodding at Marcus.

"Too late," Marcus said. "I already took the job."

They went out to the numbers, early sun on their backs. The first throw sailed like a nervous promise. The second thumped into Marcus's chest with too much air. The third hummed right, air and lace and wrist snapping into something that felt like memory. Eli swallowed and let himself smile. "We've got time."

"Grass first," Marcus answered, settling into the rhythm. "Sky will return your calls."

By the third set of five, Eli's breath edged thin. He stopped before Rivera had to call it, which earned him a quiet, "Thank you," and a paper cup of water with a salt packet balanced on top like a ticket you get punched for doing the ordinary right.

Spring brought meetings, too. The scholarship committee moved from casseroles to spreadsheets. Leah ran the agenda like a foreman. "Applications close April tenth," she said. "I want three letters for every nominee. Not from coaches. From teachers and neighbors. If you babysat for someone all year, I want to hear about it."

Karen and John sat in the second row, hands laced, not hiding their pride when Leah spoke like a person grown. When it was their turn, Karen read the line she'd underlined on her note card twice: "Show us the small, right things." She looked up at the auditorium, at the boys on the back row and the girls in the middle and the history teacher grading papers during civic virtue. "You don't have to win anything to be worthy of help. You do have to keep showing up."

Afterward, a shy freshman approached her with an envelope he'd addressed in block letters. "I'm not good at football," he said. "But I walk my little sister to school."

Karen took the envelope like it was heavy. "That's the language," she said. "Thank you for speaking it."

Coach announced Spring Night with zero fanfare and a photocopied flyer that said simply:

SPRING NIGHT

- Community scrimmage (touch)

- Youth clinic

- Scholarship awards

- **RETIREMENT OF #4**

He taped it to the field house door with blue painter's tape and walked away like he hadn't set a bolt of lightning on the wall.

The days leading up to it tasted like cut grass and Sharpie. The band trekked a pep medley without the fight song, at Emily's suggestion— "We play the quiet parts this time." The cheer team practiced a tunnel made of ribbons instead of pom-poms. The white-haired custodian with grammar opinions painted a small **4** in the end zone by hand, steady brush, steady eye. He didn't trust stencils for important things.

Emily drafted the Spring Night program. She laid out names, times, a paragraph on the scholarship's purpose, and a page titled **Why Retire a Number?** She wrote: *Because sometimes a communal promise needs a shape. Because young men need a visible reminder that courage can be quiet. Because we are grateful for what this town learned from one boy's patience and another boy's survival.* She showed it to Coach, who pretended to grumble and then folded it into his pocket like a letter.

On Thursday, Ms. Rivera swept the training room and lined up coolers: water, water, and, on the end, a small one labeled **April** in tape. "It's just water," she told Cruz, who squinted suspiciously. "But it's April water. Different vintage."

"Notes of hose," Cruz said, sniffing theatrically.

"Hints of responsibility," she replied.

Spring Night arrived with blue dusk holding the edges of the field. The bleachers filled with grown-ups in windbreakers and kids in jerseys that hung like dresses. Little Lions sprinted down the track and tripped over their own feet; eighth graders carried themselves like they'd been born on varsity. The scoreboard was on but blank, numbers waiting for a story. The trophy case in the lobby caught the last sunlight and threw it back as a quiet flare.

The youth clinic went first. Eli tossed foam spirals that made six-year-olds shriek. Marcus taught toe taps to a semicircle of children who insisted on tiptoeing everywhere for the next thirty minutes. Will held a blocking pad and let kids hit him, then didn't move, then told their parents, "See? We coach patience." Cruz got mobbed by a pack of boys who wanted to learn how to tackle and left learning how to bend their knees and look where they were going.

Then a short touch scrimmage, seniors and faculty mixing in, which produced a series of glorious disasters: a physics teacher catching a slant and weaving like he'd been waiting twenty years to do it; the principal running out of bounds to avoid being tagged by Cruz, who still slowed down and apologized while grinning. Jamal cut once for show and remembered he was supposed to be gentle. He tried again and succeeded in being charming instead of terrifying.

When the sun settled and the lights took over, Coach walked to the far sideline and gestured to the lift. The banner lay rolled on the turf— a simple blue rectangle with a white **4** and a name in block print: **McALLISTER**. He looked at Karen, then at John. "You ready?" he asked. Not for permission—for consent to a ritual none of them had asked for, all of them had earned.

Karen nodded. "Grateful," she said, the word round in her mouth like bread.

The lift rose slowly. The banner climbed toward the rafters of the home stands, toward the place where championship photos and principal portraits never felt right. The band held a single soft note and let it bloom into something like breath. People stood without being told, hats off without instruction.

Coach didn't take the microphone. He lifted his cap and kept his mouth shut. The announcer read three sentences, each short, each true: "Lincoln retires the jersey of number four. We honor patience, courage, and ordinary work. We thank the McAllister family for letting us love your son in public."

The banner reached its bracket. Two bolts turned. It hung still.

Karen stepped to the track mic because someone had to say something and because silence is a great teacher but not the only one. "We don't stop saying his name," she said, voice steady over the PA. "And we don't stop saying the word he loved. We will keep asking for the small, right things. Thank you for helping us carry him."

John put a hand on her back and didn't try to speak. When he sat, he found Emily's hand briefly on his shoulder—a small pressure, enough to count.

Leah came next with an envelope stack and a grin that made administrative tasks look like joy. "This year's scholarship recipients," she said, "taught us patience in hallways and kitchens and on porches." She read names. A sophomore who walked his sister to school. A senior who worked nights and still turned homework in with crisp edges. A junior who taught clarinet to a fifth grader for free and wrote **Practice is a kind of love** in a margin. The gym clapped like a heartbeat.

Emily stepped to the mic with the program in her hands and folded it closed without reading. "Some numbers become stories," she said. "Some stories become habits. Tonight is for both." She looked up at the banner, then at the corner of the end zone where the small **4** glowed in paint. "We'll keep moving the chains."

She stepped back. The cheers came low and warm.

Coach turned to the team. "Touch the paint," he said, pointing to the end zone. "Not because it's magic. Because we practice remembering."

They jogged—players, coaches, managers, boys who'd be seniors in August and boys who would only ever be alumni with a whistle. They brushed fingers over the **4** and kept moving. Eli went last. He knelt without drama, pressed his palm to the number, and felt the grit of paint under his skin. He didn't say the word out loud. He had already said it all year. He let his breath carry it and stood.

After the crowd thinned, after pictures and hugs and folding chairs, the field turned back into a place where people could think. Karen and John lingered by the rail. The banner hung quiet. The night smelled like cut grass and cold electricity.

"Feels different," John said.

"Feasible," Karen answered, surprised by her own word.

They walked the track once, and Karen didn't need to count the exits.

Ms. Rivera locked the cooler that said **April** and tucked the key into her pocket with the reflex of a person who knows rituals are cheaper than miracles. Coach clicked the field lights in pairs until the place exhaled into dark.

At the gate, Emily slid the last folded programs into a cardboard box and wrote **Keep** on the top in big letters, then smaller under it, **for the freshmen who will ask**.

Eli and Marcus stood at the numbers with a real ball now, a quiet toss-this, catch-that in the dark hum. Twenty yards felt like flirtation. Fifteen felt like respect. Eli paused, pressed his thumb to the faint ridge on his wrist where tape had lived, and exhaled.

"Summer's coming," Marcus said.

"Yeah," Eli said. "But first—April. Tuesdays. Algebra."

"Boring beautiful," Marcus said, and jogged to the sideline to retrieve a ball that had decided grass could be a pillow.

They walked in together, cleats clicking softly on concrete. Behind them, the banner hung where it should, not shouting, not whispering—just present. The little **4** in the end zone waited for July paint crews and August cleat marks. The trophy in the lobby caught the last person out and held his face for a second as he passed.

Spring had awakened the field but, more than that, the town: into a season where memory wasn't a weight so much as a shared tool. The boys would lift with it, run with it, carry it into classrooms and kitchens and the small errands of being decent humans. They would practice the language they'd been given until it sounded like their own.

Grass first. Sky later. Truth always.

Chapter Forty-Five – Summer Work

By June the air in Lincoln felt thick enough to drink. The field grass grew fast and shaggy, the paint lines faded into suggestion, and the weight room became the town's loudest furnace. Fans hummed but barely helped. Sweat pooled in shoes, shirts clung, and the boys discovered that truth in summer was mostly about persistence.

Coach called it **the ninety days nobody sees.**

Every morning at seven, the field house filled. Will led linemen through sled pushes until the rubber mats squealed. Cruz barked sprints across the width of the gym, timing with a whistle he'd claimed as his own. Marcus taped a cone to the floor and taught freshmen how to sell a route with their hips.

Eli worked in increments. Ms. Rivera gave him a laminated sheet labeled **June: 30 Throws Max.** He counted them honestly. First week, the ball wobbled, ribs still stiff, breath uneven. By the third week, he had rhythm again. Ten-yard outs turned into fifteen-yard digs. On a Wednesday, he zipped a seam ball to Marcus that thudded against his gloves, clean and certain. Marcus grinned, tossed it back. "That's July, not June."

"Don't tell Rivera," Eli said, but she was already watching from the track.

"Truth," she called, smiling despite herself.

The town found its own rhythm. The diner's chalkboard menu switched to **Ordinary Lemonade, Half Price**. The scholarship committee ran a rummage sale that turned the gym parking lot into a flea market. Karen worked the table with John, selling Aidan's old stack of comic books for ten dollars to a boy with wide eyes. She hesitated before sliding the box across. John's hand found hers under the table. She let go, and the boy carried the stories like treasure.

Emily spent afternoons in the library, drafting an essay she called *The Grammar of Patience*. She quoted Coach ("first down is a feast"), Ms. Rivera ("boredom before bravado"), and herself ("ordinary is holy"). She didn't know if she'd submit it for college or tuck it away for herself, but the words kept insisting.

July heat arrived with no apologies. Practices shifted to evenings, lights buzzing over mosquitoes. Eli's throws stretched to thirty, then forty. He wrote **Truth** on his wrist only once a week now, saving it for scrimmages. Most days he carried the word in his breath instead.

Leah organized a service day at the hospital. Players painted benches, scrubbed windows, and wheeled books into the children's wing. Will read picture books with a voice too low for the kids to hear, but his patience won them over. Cruz turned hallway races into lessons about form. Eli sat with a boy who had taped a number four to his IV pole and tossed a foam ball back and forth until the nurse scolded them.

That night, he lay awake in bed, ribs healed but mind restless. He whispered the word anyway. "Truth."

In August, the state sent out preseason rankings. Lincoln landed third, behind Ironwood and Millbrook. The town buzzed, proud but uneasy. Coach tore the clipping off the bulletin board before the team could see.

"Rankings don't block, tackle, or study film," he said. "We will."

On the first official day of camp, the heat index topped ninety-five. The boys ran anyway. Helmets clattered, water coolers emptied, whistles shrieked. Eli's arm felt whole again, crisp balls slicing through sweat-heavy air. Marcus danced through routes. Will anchored the line like an oak. Cruz barked at the defense until his voice gave out.

At the end, Coach gathered them at midfield. He pointed to the empty sky above the lights.

"Season's almost here," he said. "The field remembers everything, but it demands fresh work. We don't owe last year trophies. We owe this year Tuesdays. We owe each other truth."

The boys clapped once, sharp. Eli pressed his thumb to the ridge of his wrist, no tape, just skin. He exhaled, steady, certain.

Summer had done its work. The team was ready to be ordinary again—ordinary enough to be beautiful.

Chapter Forty-Six – A New Season

The banner hung where it should, quiet and sure in the rafters. The small **4** was repainted in the end zone—just a hand's width tall, as if the field itself were signing the corner. The trophy case in the lobby had been Windexed to a ruthless shine. On the glass, a cluster of kid fingerprints already smudged the morning's best intentions.

Coach refused to say **defending**.

"We're not defending anything," he told the team the week of the opener. "Trophies live in cases. We play ball. New year. New ledger. Feet, hips, hands."

The town ignored him with affection and strung **STATE CHAMPS** across Main Street anyway. The diner chalked **Ordinary Omelet** into block letters and then added **Truth Burger** below because habit is a kind of love.

The schedule maker had a gift for theater: **Millbrook** in Week One, under lights, ranked two in the state and loud about it. Their coach did interviews in a golf polo; their quarterback had a social media account that produced arrogance like a confetti cannon. Their student section traveled with coordinated hand signs. Last year's loss sat in Lincoln's ledger like a thumbprint.

New captains led warmups—Marcus, a senior now, band on the bicep; Eli in the red jersey, ribs healed and breath even; Jamal, promoted from gadget to grown-up; and Trey, the lineman Will had taken under his wide hand for two years, his stance finally a sentence with punctuation. Will and Cruz stood at the rail as volunteer helpers, alumni in T-shirts and pride.

Ms. Rivera rolled a cooler to the white line and slapped a new strip of tape on it: **AUGUST**. She met Eli at the numbers, thumb on his radial pulse for a beat like a metronome. "Honest?"

"Honest," he said, and didn't need to joke about it anymore.

"If your breath lies to you," she said, "tell it the word and slow it down."

"I know the word," he said, and didn't need to show her the tape; he wore none. The letters lived in muscle now.

Karen and John took seats five rows up from the fifty. She could sit there again. She could look at the banner without squinting. John squeezed her hand when the band blared. Emily balanced her notebook on a knee and wrote a first line she trusted: *Every season is a debut, even for champions.*

The coin flipped; the noise tilted; the ball left the tee.

Millbrook came out hot and vertical, tempoing like they had somewhere better to be. First play: bubble for ten. Second: slant for sixteen against a sophomore corner who learned the phrase *eye discipline* in real time. Third: quarterback draw into a daylight that had been there a second, wasn't now, but he found it anyway. The drive died at the twenty-nine when a pressure package Eli would later call "Cruz's ghost" hurried a throw. Their kicker had a leg and a personality; three points, a point to the student section, a dance that would not age well on film.

Marcus clapped the huddle in at the twenty-five, voice steady. "Grass first. Don't let their drumline rush you."

"Grass," Eli echoed, smiling. The ball felt right. The lines looked familiar. He took the snap and married himself back to the language that had gotten them here.

Duo for four. Stick for five. Sneak. First down, the bleachers remembering how to chant it like punctuation. Out to Marcus, toes quiet on the paint. Jamal in motion, stealing a step from a linebacker who resented him for it. The drive reached midfield and hiccuped on a false start that annoyed no one more than Trey, who mouthed *my bad* and got a palm on the shoulder from the guard beside him. Third and eight. Millbrook spun late to one-high like a prank. Eli checked to curl; Marcus sat down between a flat-footed corner and a safety whose hips told a lie. Catch. Turn. Two gratuitous yards. First down.

Red zone arrived like a slow sunrise. First down: draw for two. Second: leak to the tight end who'd learned to hide until the defense forgot theater was part of his job. Jamal fell on the six like he'd been pulled by a magnet. On third-and-goal, Millbrook brought six and a rumor. Eli retreated one step too far, planted—too soon—and threw behind Marcus. Incomplete. Micah, steady as April water, chipped it in. Tie game.

The quarter turned messy. Millbrook's quarterback found a seam; Lincoln's freshman safety took a bad angle and paid tuition. Seven points later, the visitor side shook the rail. Eli took a sack on a green dog he should've seen. Marcus smacked his helmet with both hands and then moved on because he had promised himself to be a grown-up about mistakes this year.

Between quarters, Coach didn't bark. "Feet first," he said into the huddle, as if that could be the whole gospel. "Their highlight is not your job."

Second quarter, the defense tightened into a stubborn organism. Trey and the new nose pinched a zone so hard the back bounced and met an unamused linebacker. Jamal undercut a slant and nearly kept it. Three and out. The punt came off the foot like a slice of luck, wobbled, and died at the forty-eight.

"Short field," Marcus said, delight disguised as calm.

"Grass then sky," Eli said, like a home address.

They took the grass—hitch, draw, stick—until the sky finally gave permission. On second-and-four from the thirty, the boundary safety cheated a half-step toward Jamal's jet action, and the corner's hips wandered like a bad sentence. Marcus's stance said *now*. Eli didn't need the signal. He hitched once and loosed the hole shot like a boy who had practiced boredom until it sang. Marcus stacked, separated, and caught with a shrug that said he'd been there since June. Touchdown. 10–10.

Halftime came with popcorn steam and brass echoes. In the locker room, helmets hung off knees; August sweat polished forearms. Coach drew nothing new. "We are not in a rush," he said. "We will not audition for their cameras. We will write our story in six-yard sentences."

Ms. Rivera retaped a wrist just because someone asked. She slid a salt packet at Eli and didn't look when he palmed it. "If you need blue two," she murmured.

"I'll call it," he said, and meant it as collaboration, not surrender.

Third quarter belonged to defense and weather. A summer storm sneaked a breeze through the bowl; flags hiccuped. Millbrook completed an out for nineteen and then got greedy; the ball sailed into hands that had practiced arriving on time and not earlier. Eli took the turnover to the thirty-five and treated it like porcelain: duo, duo, stick. On third-and-three, Trey's feet became advice and a lane opened like a door into a kitchen. Jamal slipped through, slid down when the safety measured malice. Micah from forty-three, ball starting left, remembering manners. 13–10.

Millbrook answered with noise and speed and a busted coverage Lincoln's film room would hate tomorrow. 17–13. Coach put a hand on the headset like it had offended him. "We are not a meme," he told no one in particular. "We are a team."

Late in the third, Eli took a hit under the ribs that felt more like a conversation than a threat. He stayed down one extra second because August is honest. Marcus leaned over him. "I can carry two series if you need," he said, deadpan.

Eli blew a breath into the turf that came out as a laugh. "You can carry the whole county. I'll still want the ball."

"Truth?" Marcus prodded.

"Not yet," Eli answered, and he wasn't being brave. He was being accurate.

Fourth quarter arrived with a scoreboard that made the town's stomachs talk: 17–13, red side up, twelve minutes that would try to be a movie. The huddle shrank to a sweet small circle, helmets nearly touching. Eli tapped Trey's forearm. "Hat placement first," he said, a phrase stolen from Will and given back to a boy who nodded like it was permission to just do his job.

They marched. First and ten became second and six became third and one became first and ten again. Stick when the linebacker's eyes came nosy. Duo when the box got light. A bootleg for six when the end chased a rumor. At the twenty-eight, Marcus pointed his facemask at the boundary flag and then ran a dig so sharp the safety had to respect geometry. Catch. First down. The student section remembered to breathe.

At the twelve, the sequence the program had been built to love: duo for two, duo for two, duo for two. Fourth and four. The band hummed a note like prayer. Coach looked at Micah, at the clock, at the wind. He looked at Eli and lifted a single finger. "We will go up one," he said. "And then we will ask the defense to be old men."

Micah's kick held its line like a man holding a door in a storm. 17–16. Two minutes, ten seconds.

Millbrook's quarterback trotted out like a commercial and nearly made good on the ad buy. First down on a strike that fit past a fingernail. Second down, a curl turned cruel when a corner slipped. Third-and-one at the Lincoln forty-seven. They hurried to the line, set, snapped—a sneak that met a center who had rediscovered himself. The pile bunched into a question mark. Fourth and inches. Their coach, intoxicated by his own tempo, kept the offense out there.

The play was the same. The result wasn't. Trey's hat got under a jaw. The feet behind him dug into a month of mornings. The spot came with drama nobody wanted. The chain strolled in like a judge. Index card shy.

Lincoln's sideline didn't explode. It exhaled.

Eli took the ball on the forty-seven with one sixty-two left and two timeouts in his pocket. The temptation to hunt sky rose like a tide. He pressed his thumb to the place where tape had used to live and made the right sort of fist.

"Grass," he said. "We're not auditioning."

Duo. Stick. Sneak. They made Millbrook spend both timeouts on principle. With thirty-one seconds left and a third-and-three at the thirty-five, Coach said nothing in the headset because silence can be coaching.

Eli kept on zone read not to be heroic but to be exact. He slid at thirty-two, good manners to the clock. Fourth-and-inches. Millbrook's front loaded the A gap like a dare. Trey put his hand in the dirt and grinned like a memory of Will had borrowed his face.

Sneak. Push. A polite avalanche.

Eli took a knee twice and the horn was a warm noise. Handshakes; a band trying to decide whether it was allowed to be loud; the home side chanting *First down!* as if it were a blessing.

At the rail, Will slapped Trey's helmet so hard the boy saw adjectives. "That's it," Will said. "Hat under hands. Feet first. Welcome to the language."

Cruz hugged the sophomore corner who had gotten baptized on the second play and recovered into competence by the fourth quarter. "Angry eyes," he advised. "Nosy in the right way."

Ms. Rivera didn't ask Eli for a number. She looked at his face and nodded. "Truth?" she asked out of habit.

He shook his head, smiling. "Not tonight. Just water."

Karen stood and clapped until she realized she didn't have to anymore and then kept clapping for herself. John leaned on the rail and let the late-summer light put a soft edge on the banner in the rafters. Emily wrote one line and put her pencil down: *They didn't defend a title; they defended an identity.*

In the locker room, the music was less roar than hum. Coach set the marker down and didn't touch the board. "One and oh," he said. "A feast of first downs. No free drama. Next week is hungry."

He looked up at the ceiling so his eyes would pass by the banner on the way. "We will keep being ordinary until it becomes beautiful without surprise."

Marcus bumped Eli's shoulder with his own, then sat and unlaced with deliberate slowness. "You ever miss the tape?" he asked.

"Sometimes," Eli said. "I still feel it when I say it."

"What?"

He didn't need to whisper, but he did. "Truth."

Marcus nodded, satisfied, the way men nod when a tool is in the right drawer. He held up the game ball to Trey and tossed it underhand. "Protection," he said, echoing a year that had trained him to speak like a captain.

Trey caught it against his chest like a secret he'd earned.

Outside, the small **4** in the end zone glowed dim in the rinse of stadium lights cooling to dark. The banner didn't move. The town walked home under a sky that had nothing to prove. Lincoln was one and oh, but more importantly, it was itself—again, on purpose. Grass first. Then whatever the sky wanted to be.

Chapter Forty-Seven – Lessons in September

The win over Millbrook hung in the air like humidity, but Coach refused to let it harden into identity. On Monday morning the film room smelled of stale sweat and pencil shavings. The screen showed missed tackles, overthrown hitches, a false start that had cost rhythm.

"Don't get sentimental," Coach said, laser pointer tapping the pause screen. "One and oh is not a personality. It's a line in a ledger. Erase it if you stop learning."

The boys groaned at the drills that followed. Tackling circuits doubled. Receivers ran out-routes until their cuts looked mechanical. The line repeated combo blocks against sleds that squealed like angry cattle. Will, standing on the sideline as an alum-helper, clapped with grim delight. "Make your steps honest," he barked. "Liars don't win fourth quarter."

The next opponent was **Clearwater**, a middling program with more pride than speed. Their coach preached ball control, their fans brought cowbells, their quarterback looked like a mathlete who'd grown into pads late. But Friday night games don't care about paper.

The first half proved it. Clearwater strung a drive of thirteen plays, eating clock and courage. They went up 7–0 while Lincoln sputtered. Eli threw behind Marcus once, Jamal lost his footing on damp grass, Trey misheard a cadence and earned a five-yard flag that turned a manageable third into a punt.

The bleachers muttered. Karen wrung her hands. Emily scribbled a line she didn't like: *Champions look bored when they forget boredom is the point.*

At halftime, Coach said little. "Reset your eyes," he told Cruz. "Run through grass, not through ghosts," he told Marcus. "One first down at a time," he told Eli. Then he walked out and left the silence behind him like a dare.

The third quarter opened with patience rediscovered. Duo, stick, sneak. First down. Hitch, draw, slant. First down. Jamal on motion, stealing steps. Marcus on a curl that looked like a sigh. At the ten, Eli faked draw, rolled left, and lofted a ball Marcus high-pointed with grace. Touchdown. Tie game, 7–7.

Clearwater answered with a field goal. 10–7. The cowbells rattled.

Lincoln's next drive was ugly but honest—two drops, one holding call, then a miracle. Fourth-and-four at midfield, Coach considered punting. Eli shook his head. "Grass," he said. The line leaned forward. Marcus winked. The snap came clean. Stick route, catch, fall across the stripe. First down.

Two plays later, Jamal slipped outside and sprinted thirty yards, dragging hope behind him. Cruz howled on the sideline, the defense feeding off it. Clearwater's mathlete quarterback threw one too high; the ball tipped and fell into hands that had learned patience in summer heat. Short return, enough.

Eli managed the clock, Micah managed the leg, and with forty-three seconds left, Lincoln pulled ahead 13–10.

The defense closed it. Cruz stuffed the draw, Trey swallowed the sneak, and the final heave sailed harmlessly into the dark.

The locker room after wasn't jubilant. It was quiet relief. Helmets sat heavy, tape frayed, breath still short. Marcus leaned back against the wall. "Not pretty."

"Not supposed to be," Eli said. He pulled the tape from his wrist and studied the faint ridges on his skin. "Truth isn't."

Ms. Rivera poked her head in. "Nobody pulled anything stupid?"

"No free stupid," Cruz called back, earning laughter that drained the tension.

Emily's article ran Monday under the headline: **Lincoln Wins the Ugly Way, Which Is Still a Win.** Her closing line stuck in every hallway: *State champions aren't made in December. They're made in September, when the grass is wet, the games are ugly, and ordinary feels harder than heroics.*

By the end of September, Lincoln stood 3–0. The scores weren't gaudy. The margins weren't kind. But each game left the boys with dirt in their mouths and proof that patience travels.

Coach taped the month's ledger to the corkboard: three small checkmarks, each the size of a fingernail. Nothing else. He left room for many more.

And in the corner of the end zone, the little **4** endured rain and cleat marks, still visible, still waiting.

Chapter Forty-Eight – The Midseason Storm

The weather app lied politely all week—chance of showers, scattered at most—and then Friday arrived with a sky the color of a bruise. Wind came first, shouldering through the light poles. Then rain, hard and vindictive, hissing on aluminum bleachers and turning the field into a green sponge.

Coach stood under the eave of the field house, hands in his jacket pockets like he was holding a small animal still. "Storm doesn't care about you," he said to the boys as they laced. "The grass still wants the same things. Feet first. Hips second. Hands last. No free doubt."

Ms. Rivera double-checked every roll of tape, then checked them again because water makes liars out of good wraps. She scribbled **RAIN** on a strip and stuck it on the cooler like labeling weather might domesticate it.

Karen and John found their seats with ponchos that tried and failed to be boats. Karen's hands were steady—another small mercy that would have surprised her last winter. Emily tucked her notebook under her jacket and tested pens like a magician testing cards.

The opponent was **Westfield**, a team that had figured out who they were—big backs, heavy sets, a kicker who looked like he'd been born wearing cleats. The coin toss fluttered in the wind like a moth and landed unconvincing. Westfield deferred, the rain nodded, and everything began.

From the first snap the ball felt disloyal. Eli's fingers, usually fluent, spoke with an accent. The first out route slid off his hand and into the dark. Marcus caught it anyway with fingertips that burned. Duo for two became duo for minus-one when a tackle skated on mud. Jamal's feet found water where grass had signed a lease. Punt.

Westfield answered with certainty: iso, iso, iso, then a bootleg that died in Cruz's hands because some angles travel even in weather. Their kicker squinted into the rain and struck a 38-yarder through the heart of wind. 3–0.

Lincoln huddled at the twenty-five, rain marching off facemasks. "Grass first," Eli said, more reminder than rhetoric. "Stay small."

They tried. Stick for five. Sneak. First down. Trey and the guard double-teamed a nose who had enjoyed breakfast; the double held until it didn't, and Eli slid in the soup like a kid discovering physics. Another punt, this one angling out near midfield, the ball skidding and sulking.

Lightning forked over the visitor stands on second-and-eight. Whistles, waves, frantic pointing. The officials chopped both arms and the stadium groaned the way a building does when you take the heat away in January. **Delay.** Thirty minutes, minimum. The band filed to the tunnel, trumpets dripping. The student section booed the sky and then laughed at themselves because booing the sky is a good way to learn you're small.

Inside, the locker room steamed. Helmets clattered onto cement, water pooling under benches. Coach didn't draw anything. He handed out towels like wisdom. "Reset your breath," he said. "We don't beat weather; we outlast it. Be boring on purpose."

Ms. Rivera moved from body to body with a towel around her shoulders like a cape. She pressed thumbs into forearms and asked numbers—pain, breath, honesty. Marcus rolled his hamstring on a beat-up foam roller, face steady until it wasn't. She crouched. "Talk."

"Tight," he said. "Not a string. A stubborn."

"Two series off if you feel that bite," she said. "Truth?"

He hesitated, then nodded. "Truth."

Out near the doorway, Eli peeled wet tape from his wrist and wrapped fresh with hands that didn't shake. He didn't write the word. He didn't need the ink tonight; he needed grip. He caught Coach watching and lifted his chin. Coach raised one finger—*first down*—and Eli smiled because some languages survive weather.

The all-clear came with a cheer you could almost see. They went back out into rain that had negotiated itself down to relentless.

The rest of the half was trench math. Westfield inched, Lincoln refused. Micah's punt caught a gust and died on the seven like a wounded bird. Westfield's back ran through two shoes and anger into a third-and-goal from the five. Cruz filled like a rumor. Field goal again. 6–0.

Halftime was five minutes shorter by decree and felt longer. Coach chewed once on nothing. "No hero ball," he said. "Their kicker's feeling himself. Make him kick too much."

Third quarter, the storm mixed literal with figurative. On second-and-six, Trey's ankle did what ankles do on a field that has decided to become a memory of a lake. He hopped, swore politely, and sat hard. Ms. Rivera slid in and palpated like a piano tuner. "Mild inversion," she announced to him and no one else. "We can brace and try. You tell me if you lie."

Trey's face said *no lies* even as his pride said *I'm fine*. He taped into a boot and stood like a stubborn fencepost.

Two plays later, Marcus's hamstring sang the wrong note. He shut it down without theater, the sign of a senior who'd made a promise to December while standing in August. "Two series," he told Eli, handing the job to a sophomore wideout named Cole who had good hands and a cowardly relationship with weather.

Eli looked at Cole. "Grass is small tonight," he said. "Find five yards. I'll find you."

Cole nodded like he'd been given a life raft. On third-and-four, Eli found him at three and Cole turned to five because turning is a teachable courage. First down. The bleachers remembered how to shout into rain without wasting breath.

Westfield's kicker didn't miss. 9–0.

Lincoln finally made the kind of drive that makes statistics blush. Duo, stick, duo, stick, out to Cole, draw because the box begged, sneak because Trey's taped ankle was still smarter than physics. At the eight, Eli kept on zone read because the end ate Jamal like a rumor. He slid at the three because ego has no traction in weather. Micah trotted and kicked a ball that sounded like a drum when it left his foot. 9–3.

Fourth quarter. The storm brought doubt like a cousin. Westfield bled the clock the way teams do when they prefer calendars to choreography. Their back fell forward with conviction and his line fell forward with him. On third-and-seven at the Lincoln twenty-nine, their quarterback faked boot, reset his feet, and tried to throw through rain instead of around it. The ball fluttered and found Jamal's chest like a gift. He slid twenty yards in mud before anyone remembered to tackle him. The stadium turned its volume back on.

Eli huddled them at the forty. Marcus rolled his hamstring with his heel on his helmet, eyes saying *one more*. Ms. Rivera shook her head once at him from the white line, a no that cared. Eli saw the exchange and didn't ask. "Cole, you're still now," he said. "Jamal, eyes straight until I lie to you."

Duo for three. Stick for five. Sneak, Trey's taped ankle negotiating with science and winning by inches. First down. It came down to fourth-and-two at the Westfield twenty-four with the clock behaving like a debt collector.

Coach could have kicked. He didn't. He looked at Eli and touched his wrist—a sign older than this storm. "Your feet," he said.

Eli nodded. He checked the end, pulled on zone read, and stepped into a wall that moved like a drip of concrete. He churned and slid and reached. The spot felt like a negotiation with a tired god. The chain came out, the index card came in. Short, by the thickness of the rain.

The groan from the home side sounded like a bridge shifting in winter.

Two plays later, Westfield's back broke contain for twelve honest yards, the kind that murder hope and teach tenacity. Lincoln burned timeouts because that's what you do when you need time to remember who you are. The final snap was a punt that died in the corner like a letter you forgot to mail. The horn cracked the weather open. Final: Westfield 12, Lincoln 3.

No boos. No announcements. Just rain clapping for itself.

In the handshake line, Westfield's coach said, "See you in November," which is the kind of thing grown men say to each other because they are trying not to apologize for luck and weather and linemen with good feet.

The locker room was a maritime museum. Everything dripped. No one talked loud because the room had done enough listening tonight.

Coach set his cap on the bench and leaned both hands on the back of a chair. "We lost a weather game," he said. "We lost it the right way. We didn't panic. We didn't freelance. We didn't give up explosive stupidity. We will fix the feet that slid. We will stretch the hamstring that argued. We will ice the ankle that tried. We will study the film that looks like it was shot through a shower curtain and take from it what matters. We are not the scoreboard. We are the next Tuesday."

He pointed with his chin toward Ms. Rivera, who was already bracing Trey tighter and eyeing Marcus like she was negotiating a treaty. "Truth," he said. "If she calls blue two on you this week, you will love her for it in October."

Marcus nodded first. "Truth," he said without being asked.

Trey swallowed pride like a pill. "Truth."

Eli peeled the wet tape off his wrist and didn't replace it. He pressed his thumb into the faint ridges of skin that had learned the word by heart and exhaled. "Truth," he said, not as surrender, as orientation.

Out under the eave, Emily stood with her hood up and scribbled one clean sentence before the paper gave up: *Weather is a liar; the field still tells the truth.* She would remember it by feel later. She would write a second line at her desk: *Lincoln learned that boring beautiful bends but doesn't break—even in rain.*

Karen wrung out the bottom of her poncho by the gate and realized she wasn't shaking. John watched her realize it and put the knowledge in his pocket like a coin.

By Sunday the storm had moved east and left behind a field pocked with cleat marks and pride. Trey showed up in a brace and a bad mood—both honest. Marcus jogged straights and walked the turns. Ms. Rivera raised an eyebrow and got a hand wave. She let him have it because men who keep promises deserve five minutes of pretending.

Coach wrote **3–1** on the corkboard and didn't underline it. He drew a small square under it and wrote **Tuesday** inside the square, then capped the marker and walked away.

Eli found Cole after lifts and put a ball in his hands. "Five yards," he said. "Any weather."

Cole nodded. "I know the language now."

"Good," Eli said. "We'll make you teach it to a freshman next year."

The banner in the rafters didn't care. The little **4** in the end zone had lost an edge to the rain and would get repainted by a custodian with grammar opinions on Monday afternoon. The town would go back to jobs and bills and casseroles and the work of being decent. Lincoln would go back to first downs.

The storm had come and gone. The season stayed. Grass first. Even when it's mud. Truth anyway.

Chapter Forty-Nine –
October Resolve

The Westfield loss lingered like a bruise. Not sharp pain, but a dull reminder every time someone stretched. On Monday morning, the hallways buzzed quieter. A sophomore whispered, "We're not perfect anymore," and Marcus stopped him with a glance that wasn't angry but final. "Nobody's perfect in October," he said, and the kid shut his locker softer than usual.

Coach used no metaphors at film. He just rewound plays until the whine of the projector became the week's soundtrack. "Feet," he said. "Read it again. Feet. Now hips. Now hands. Truth is boring. Learn boring."

Practice grew sharper. Trey in a brace refused pity, anchoring his side with stubborn pride. Marcus stretched long, walked straights, jogged cuts, whispered *truth* each time his hamstring held. Eli threw short all week, refusing sky even when tempted, reminding himself grass is how you breathe.

Ms. Rivera added a new cooler label: **OCTOBER**. She shook her head when Cruz asked what was inside. "Same as September. Different month. You'll thank me." She taped Trey's brace like she was signing a contract. "Truth?" she asked. He nodded, less pride, more patience.

Friday night, the stands filled despite a chill that pinched cheeks. The opponent was **Northwood**, a team built on misdirection—wing-T plays that turned games into mazes. Their quarterback was small but fast, their backs slippery, their line undersized but mean.

The first quarter proved the scouts right. Trap, sweep, reverse. Lincoln defenders looked left, the ball went right. Cruz barked himself hoarse, but Northwood finished a 75-yard drive with a sweep into the corner. 7–0.

Eli gathered the huddle on the twenty. "Stay boring," he said, the word sounding heavier after last week's storm. Duo, stick, sneak. First down. Marcus on a shallow cross for seven. Jamal bouncing outside for eleven. By the red zone, the drive had taken ten minutes and stolen the crowd's anxiety. At the six, Eli faked draw and hit Cole—his sophomore understudy—for a touchdown. Tie game, 7–7.

Second quarter, Lincoln's defense adjusted. Cruz shadowed the wing, Jamal stayed home, the linemen pinched tighter. Northwood's trickery hit a wall. Punt.

Lincoln answered with another patient march: hitch, curl, slant. Micah from 36. 10–7.

The half ended with Lincoln up, but unsatisfied. Coach in the locker room didn't shout. He held the marker but didn't use it. "Ordinary wins October. Don't try to be pretty. Try to be exact."

Third quarter. Northwood broke one—a counter that found daylight and gashed forty yards. The bleachers groaned, ponchos rustled. At the ten, Cruz stepped into a pulling guard like a man settling an argument. Fourth and goal, sweep right, Jamal knifed under the block and dragged the back down at the line. Turnover. The sideline exploded, the town exhaling in one voice.

Lincoln's offense responded with the longest drive of the year: sixteen plays, seventy-four yards, ending in a sneak that Trey braced open with fury. 17–7.

Fourth quarter. Northwood struck fast on a broken coverage— touchdown. 17–14. The game teetered.

With four minutes left, Eli huddled the team at the twenty. "No drama. Grass until they cheat."

Duo. Stick. Sneak. First down. Out to Marcus for five. Jamal inside for three. Third-and-two. Eli faked draw, rolled left, found Cole in the flat for four. First down again. The clock bled.

With thirty seconds left, Micah lined up for a 41-yarder to ice it. The snap clean, hold steady, kick true. 20–14.

The horn sounded with Northwood's final desperation pass falling into Cruz's arms. The bleachers thundered, the banner in the rafters swayed with the vibration.

In the locker room, helmets clattered to the floor. Coach finally smiled. "Four and one," he said. "We don't love the storm, but we love how we answer it."

Marcus leaned back against his locker, hamstring tight but holding. "Ordinary is holy," he muttered.

Eli pulled the tape from his wrist, the word faint on his skin without ink. "Truth," he whispered, more steady than last week.

Emily, in the press row above, wrote her headline before leaving: **Lincoln Finds Its Balance in the Rain's Aftermath.**

October had asked for resolve, and Lincoln had delivered—not with highlight reels, but with drives that looked like prayers said in small syllables. The town walked home with wet shoes and warm hearts, learning again that boring beautiful was not a slogan. It was survival.

Chapter Fifty –
The Stretch Run

By late October the air in Lincoln smelled like woodsmoke and frost. The trees along Main Street burned orange, and every lamppost wore blue ribbons that had survived rain and wind. The season's ledger read **4–1**, but the real story was the weeks ahead—two rivals back-to-back, playoff seeding at stake, and a town buzzing with equal parts pride and worry.

Coach kept his tone flat. "Records don't win November. Tuesdays do."

Still, he let the boys see the bracket scenarios. Beat both rivals, and Lincoln could host the first round. Split them, and they'd travel. Lose both… no one wanted to say it out loud.

Rival One – Fairview

Fairview was cocky by birthright. Their band traveled with cannons, their fans wore shirts with slogans like *October is ours*, and their quarterback had a grin that played well on local TV.

The first quarter went ugly fast. Fairview intercepted Eli on the second drive, turning it into seven points. 7–0. Their sideline barked, their cheer block sang songs too clever for high school.

Eli settled. "Grass first," he said in the huddle. The drive that followed was a sermon: duo, stick, hitch, curl. At the five, Jamal slipped inside untouched. Tie game.

The rest of the half was a trade of patience. Fairview struck with big plays, Lincoln answered with long drives. Halftime: 14–14.

In the locker room, Coach tapped the board. "They want sky. We'll keep grass."

Third quarter, Marcus sold grass vertical, then cut sharp on a dig. Eli hit him in stride. Touchdown, 21–14. The home bleachers thundered.

Fairview answered immediately—seam route, broken tackle, tie game again. 21–21.

Fourth quarter, two minutes left. Score tied. Eli huddled the offense at midfield. "No panic. Boring beautiful."

They marched. Out for four. Duo for three. Third-and-three, Cole found the flat again for five. First down. The clock bled. At the twenty, Micah lined up. Forty yards, wind at his back. The ball sailed true. 24–21.

The defense held. Cruz slammed the quarterback on the last play, polite enough to help him up. Lincoln 24, Fairview 21.

Rival Two – Westgate

Westgate was meaner. Less flash, more fists. Their line outweighed Lincoln's by thirty pounds a man. Their linebackers snarled. The game felt like a bar fight.

First quarter: 0–0. Second quarter: 3–0, Westgate. Third quarter: a punt returned to the house, 10–0.

The bleachers went quiet. Karen pressed John's arm so hard his sleeve wrinkled. Emily scribbled furiously, heart pounding.

Then Eli found Marcus on a slant, Jamal sprung a draw for twenty, and Cole slipped into the corner for a touchdown. 10–7.

The fourth quarter was survival. Westgate hammered inside runs, bleeding time. With ninety seconds left, they lined up for a field goal to ice it. Snap. Hold. Kick—blocked. Cruz's hand, pure violence. The ball skittered.

Lincoln recovered at midfield. No timeouts. Eighty seconds.

Eli breathed once, pressed his thumb to his wrist. "Truth."

Stick for seven. Out for nine. Duo for three. Forty seconds. At the twenty-eight, Eli lofted one toward Marcus. He caught it, two toes in. At the ten.

Twenty seconds. First down. Eli faked draw, rolled left, threw across his body. Jamal toe-tapped in the end zone. Touchdown. 14–10.

The bleachers shook, the band screaming. Westgate's last gasp fell incomplete.

Lincoln finished the stretch 6–1. First seed in their bracket. November at home.

Coach wrote it on the corkboard in blunt strokes: **HOSTING.**

He didn't underline it. He just capped the marker and said, "Now the season begins."

Chapter Fifty-One – The Closing Chapter

November sharpened the air into glass. The field crew repainted every line, the end zones glowing fresh under the lights. In the corner, the small **4** was redrawn carefully by the white-haired custodian who grumbled about grammar and paintbrush width but hummed while he worked. "Details matter," he muttered, steady hand, steady heart.

The playoff bracket pinned Lincoln against **Harborview**, a team with a bruising fullback and a reputation for ruining dreams in the first round. The town buzzed all week—casseroles delivered, blue ribbons tied tighter, the diner chalkboard declaring: *Ordinary Omelet – Playoff Edition.*

Coach kept it simple. "We don't carry December yet," he said in Tuesday film. "We carry first downs. One at a time. Grass, then sky if it arrives polite."

Ms. Rivera handed out fresh tape on Friday, labeling the cooler **NOVEMBER** with a marker that bled in her gloves. She wrapped Trey's ankle, double-checked Marcus's hamstring, and eyed Eli's wrist. "You need the word tonight?" she asked.

Eli shook his head. "It's already here."

Kickoff cracked the cold. Harborview smashed forward, iso after iso, a fullback who looked like he'd been forged in a blacksmith's shop. Cruz met him every snap, grin feral. "Not free," he hissed.

First quarter bled 0–0. Second quarter, Harborview struck on play-action, tight end slipping behind coverage. 7–0. Their sideline roared.

Lincoln answered. Duo for four, stick for five, sneak for one. Jamal cut outside, Marcus snagged a curl, Cole caught a flat with soft hands. At the twelve, Eli faked draw and rolled right. Marcus cut once, twice, opened by an inch. Ball, catch, touchdown. Tie game, 7–7.

Halftime in the locker room: helmets steaming, breath clouds rising. Coach tapped the board once. "Keep boring. They'll panic first."

Third quarter turned into trench math. Harborview kicked a field goal: 10–7. Lincoln answered with Micah's 38-yarder: 10–10.

Fourth quarter. Five minutes. Score tied. The stadium's breath visible, Karen clutching John's hand, Emily scribbling too fast to read.

Harborview drove to the twenty. Fourth-and-two. They lined up heavy. Snap—Cruz shot the gap, Trey braced, the fullback met a wall. The pile stopped. Turnover. The home stands thundered like salvation.

Two minutes left. Ball at the thirty. Eli huddled them close. "Grass first," he said. "Sky if it begs."

Duo for three. Stick for five. Third-and-two. Jamal churned into the pile, emerged with three. First down.

Forty seconds. At midfield. Marcus lined up wide, eyes steady. Eli looked once, then checked down. Out route, Cole. Catch. Timeout, twenty seconds.

Second down, the safety cheated half a step. Marcus didn't signal. He didn't need to. Eli hitched, threw the hole shot, ball humming. Marcus toe-tapped at the twenty, the bleachers erupting.

Ten seconds. First down. Micah trotted on, nerves hidden behind routine. Snap clean, hold steady, kick rising into cold air. True.

Lincoln 13, Harborview 10.

The horn split the night. The sideline exploded. Boys hugged, helmets high, coaches clapping shoulders. The town roared.

In the handshake line, Harborview's coach muttered, "Patience beat us." Coach Dempsey only tipped his cap.

The locker room was chaos—music, laughter, tears. Coach let it ride before raising a hand. "One game at a time. Tonight, you honored patience. Tonight, you honored the word."

He pointed at the shadow box in the corner: tape, towel, confetti, a lion sticker. "You carried him. You carried each other."

Eli sat on the bench, tape frayed, sweat freezing on his neck. Marcus dropped beside him, helmet under his arm. "Truth," Marcus said.

Eli smiled, thumb pressing the faint ridge of skin where the word had once been written. "Always."

That night, long after the crowd had left, Karen and John walked the quiet track. The banner with **4** hung still, the field lights humming. She touched John's hand, steady. "It feels like closure," she whispered.

"Closure," John agreed. "And beginning."

Emily lingered too, notebook shut for once. She whispered her last line to the empty field: *They didn't just win a game. They finished a story Aidan started, and began one that belongs to them.*

The little **4** in the corner end zone glowed faint under the lights, waiting for tomorrow's footsteps. The trophy case in the lobby would catch the morning sun. The boys would wake sore, the town would wake proud, and truth would keep its place—boring, beautiful, holy.

Lincoln had won. More than football.

Epilogue –
Fourth and Forever

Winter came back to Lincoln, as it always did—snow softening the bleachers, frost tracing the edges of the banner where **4** hung quiet in the rafters. The field went still, stripped bare of lines and noise, waiting for spring crews and cleat marks. But the quiet didn't erase what had been carried there.

Aidan's name was still spoken in kitchens, in hallways, in the diner where the chalkboard specials never lost their sense of humor. His legacy lived not in the scoreboard, not even in the trophy case, but in habits—small right things done over and over until they became a language the town could speak together.

Eli healed, then grew. Marcus graduated with scar tissue and poise, Cruz with shoulders built for more than football, Will with hands that could lift more than weight. Leah led the scholarship committee into its second year, adding names to a ledger that felt like scripture in blue ink. Emily mailed off essays that carried truth between the lines, her words reaching beyond the county but always pointing back here.

Karen and John learned to live inside memory without drowning. Some days still pinched, but more days offered laughter without guilt. They found that grief could be companion instead of warden, and that sharing their son's story aloud kept him present without reopening wounds.

Coach stayed the same and not the same—still sharp on footwork, still short on patience for excuses, but slower now when practice ended, walking the field in silence, sometimes touching the painted **4** before leaving. Ms. Rivera never put away her coolers, not even in winter; she just relabeled them by months, as if hydration could mark the calendar as well as any clock.

And the town itself—students, parents, alumni, neighbors—carried on. Driveways got shoveled, casseroles delivered, exams taken, instruments practiced, babies held. First downs weren't just on the field anymore. They were in every ordinary thing that made patience a way of living.

Because that was the story all along: football as the language, truth as the word. Grass first, sky later. Ordinary as holy.

And so Lincoln kept moving the chains, even in winter, even in silence, even when the field was buried under snow. Fourth and forever wasn't just a down and distance. It was the way a small town carried its boys, carried its losses, carried its victories, and found a way to keep going—together.

www.ingramcontent.com/pod-product-compliance
Lightning Source LLC
Chambersburg PA
CBHW051530260626
47170CB00003B/862